MW00658634

HE'S WALKED INTO A DEADLY TRAP.
HE'S ABOUT TO WALK AWAY . . .

"Tell us, Thompson." The Arab leaned forward. "We are insulted that someone would send an incompetent such as you after us. It's like a bad joke. So tell us everything. If your memory slips"—he smiled—"we have a marvelous mnemonic device invented by the French in Algeria. It's similar to your cattle prod. Only much more powerful."

I picked up the coffee canister, thumbed up the flip top on the plastic cylinder, and threw the boiling contents in his face, following the motion of my arm, going over the coffee table, slamming him back in his chair. I went for his throat, and jerked the Ruger free from his belt. The woman in the room had dropped to the floor, yanking loose the cord of the lamp, plunging the room in darkness. I started for the door, as an automatic pistol stitched holes in the wall above my head . . .

THE HERACLES COMMANDO

EDWARD McGHEE

POCKET BOOKS
New York London Toronto Sydney Tokyo

This book is a work of fiction. Names, characters, places and incidents are either the product of the author's imagination or are used fictitiously. Any resemblance to actual events or locales or persons, living or dead, is entirely coincidental.

An *Original* Publication of POCKET BOOKS

POCKET BOOKS, a division of Simon & Schuster Inc.
1230 Avenue of the Americas, New York, NY 10020

ISBN: 0-671-66419-0

First Pocket Books printing June 1989

10 9 8 7 6 5 4 3 2 1

Printed in the U.S.A.

THE HERACLES COMMANDO

chapter 1

They won't kill us. It's ridiculous to be afraid. They almost never kill anybody. Trevor's right. Do what they say. Don't provoke them. All they want is two million dollars and publicity. My grandfather would give it to them if he knew. That man they killed. He was a fool. I'm glad they threw his body out the door. The stench was awful. Don't think about it. Got to keep my nerve. It'll be over soon. I might even get an article out of it. *Time* would love it. First person account of hijacking by Dolores Sindona. God, Trevor is a weakling. His voice was shaking. I'm going to break with him when this is over. But he's right. I've got to keep my cool. That Arab keeps looking at me. He wants me. I can almost feel his hands on my body. Why did they bring us up here? How many? Twenty maybe? Jews and Americans. What is he doing? She must be six months pregnant. Oh, my God. No. No. No. What's he saying? If their demands aren't met they will kill one of us every hour? Why doesn't somebody do something? There are three hundred of us and only five of them. Why don't some of the men jump him? Trevor? Don't look at me with those cow's eyes. Do something. What does he want now? He's looking at me. It hasn't been an hour. I can't be next. That was stupid. Don't resist. He caught me by surprise. If he wants to fondle your breast, let him. Don't be a little fool. Play along with him. If he thinks you like him, he'll leave you alone. What does he want now? Where are we going? But I don't want to go to the john. What? Oh, God, no. Don't fight. Let him do it. Oh, Jesus, it hurts so much. Okay. It's over. He'll leave you alone now. He got what he wanted. It's really all over. Try to forget it. Be calm. He won't kill you now. Why is he pushing me toward the door? What did he say? Mother of God, no. Please.

The office dominated the city, an eagles' nest in the highest tower on the hill. Huge picture windows gave off each end. To the right the Chouteau River twisted through the city like a dirty brown snake. On the left, lush green suburbs, striated by bands of shopping malls, supermarkets, junk-food shops, and used-car lots spread to the horizon. Facing the door an immense Miró, a confusion of lines and triangles in spare red and black on a stark white background, stood all alone on an expanse of black stone.

The big man rose from behind a massive glass-and-chrome desk and came around to greet me. "Wilbur Purvis, Jr., Dr. Thompson. Mighty pleased you could come." The southern accent was slight but there. The big meaty hand enclosed mine with controlled strength, letting you know he had it, but not pushing it. He was big. Six-three, around two forty, mid-fifties, paunch sucked in but pouching over his belt, an athlete going to seed, fighting it and losing.

"This is not the first time you've been to our city?"

"No. I wrestled here a couple of times in college."

"Yeah. I read it in your file. USC, wasn't it? Almost made it to the Olympics before you got hurt."

I waited. Southerners take their time. You can't rush it. It was his nickel. He'd paid my way from Santa Cruz and put me up at the Fitlin Hotel, understated elegance decorated in

French bordello modern with superb plumbing and a good chef.

"How come a jock like you went into academe?"

"Short hours. And, as my Ozark cousins say, 'hits inside.'"

Purvis laughed, showing his teeth. "Well, you're not exactly a good ole boy, Thompson, but we might be able to do some business. It says here"—he tapped a green plastic folder lying closed on his desk—"you killed some folks out in Vietnam. Not too particular how you did it either. Real mean mother. At least that's what the file says." He looked me over. "You don't live up to the billing. In fact, you come on kind of wimpy, Thompson. You lose something in 'Nam?" His voice had changed, the greasy courtesy turning hard.

I met his eyes. I don't look people in the eye normally. Where I grew up, if you looked somebody in the eye too long, you'd wind up fighting him. It was sort of childish, but I played along with him. He'd spent a fair amount of money getting me here, and there was obviously a lot more where that came from. I had fifteen dollars in my bank account and a small château in France with a roof about to cave in. I looked away finally, letting him have it. I didn't want to fight him. I wanted his money.

"'Course, what we want you to do won't take being tough."

"What do you have in mind?"

"This file says you're not only hard but discreet. It also says you're not to be trusted. That right?"

I shrugged.

"Says here you'll sell out to the highest bidder."

"Who's writing the opinion?"

"Fella named Xerxes. Frank Xerxes. You know him?"

"Yeah." Xerxes was a CIA covert-operations specialist. An enforcer. I'd crossed him in Berlin a couple of years earlier.

"He don't like you much."

I leaned back in the chair, not answering, remembering the cold terror I'd felt sinking into the Berlin canal, the German's fingers clawing for my throat.

"Only thing is, we tried just about everybody else. Francis and Childress, Ltd., in London. Charlot Frères in France. Even some German outfit whose name I can't pronounce. Got nowhere. Bribed a few cops here and there. Worked through these goddamn useless international lawyers. CIA ain't worth a shit since they can't kill and torture anymore. So Xerxes came up with you."

"You want to tell me what it's all about?"

He reached in the breast pocket of his blazer, four initialed gold buttons flashing on the sleeve, and tossed me a bundle of hundreds. "There's five thousand there. You can walk out of here when I finish talking and keep it. No obligations. Except you keep your mouth shut about what I'm about to tell you, hear? Otherwise I'll have your fucking legs broke."

I riffled through the money. It wasn't enough for a roof, but it was a nice start. "Who do you want me to kill?"

This time he really laughed, throwing back his head and showing the gold-crowned rear teeth. "Shit, boy. If I want somebody killed I can get it done for a tenth of that. You gotta do something difficult. And delicate."

"What?"

He leaned forward. "Remember that British Airways hijacking six months ago?"

"The one the Egyptians blew up on the tarmac in Malta?"

"Yeah. You recall anything about it?"

"They put a bullet in the head of one hostage every hour for six hours. Americans and Israelis. Then the Egyptians went in and killed about sixty people trying to rescue them."

"Yeah. Killed almost everybody but the terrorists. Four of them slipped out of the plane just as the attack began. Somebody in the airport warned them. The Egyptians got one, a girl. She was too scared to jump."

"What's your interest?"

"Remember the names of the ones they shot?"

"No."

"Dolores Sindona. My niece. She was one of them. Belongs to my sister who is married, to or was, José Maria Sindona y Suarez."

"The Mexican oil man?"

"Yeah. My old man sent her off to Radcliffe to keep her away from the riffraff, and she up and marries this goddamn spic."

"The gunmen killed your niece?"

"Put a 9mm in the back of her skull. Just about blew her head off." He scratched his belly and suppressed a belch. I had the feeling he wanted a drink. It was ten o'clock in the morning. "The Egyptians worked on the lady terrorist. She was in pretty bad shape, but she could still talk. They hurt her some more and she gave us a name before she died. Head fella in the group. Call themselves the Brigade of the Fifteenth of January."

"The date Rosa Luxemburg and Karl Liebknecht were killed."

Purvis grinned. "You're like all schoolteachers, Thompson. Got a head full of useless bullshit. Yeah. Anyway, we been trying to nail this asshole for six months, and we've come up empty."

"You want me to kill him?"

"Look, professor. We don't want you to kill anybody. First, I ain't persuaded you could do the job, and second, because we got a team of professionals set up to do that. All we want you to do is finger him. Nail him down for us. Him and the rest of that bunch. We'll handle it from there. Xerxes says you're some sort of genius at research. Locating people."

I'd discovered some submerged Nazi war criminals a couple of years before, more or less by accident, creating a serious international incident which, given the mutual interests of East and West, had been shoved under the rug. Xerxes had done the shoving.

"Well, what about it? Can you do the job?"

"What name did the girl give you?"

"Dieter Wohlgemuth. We've got a file on him."

"Can I see it?"

"If you agree to take the job, and if we agree to hire you." He glanced at his watch. He had an actor's face. A little like Curt Jurgens in his prime. Or a television preacher. Once-lean jawline running to fat, handsome fleshy face topped by a mop of graying hair. "My father's waiting for us next door. The spic is with him. They will give final approval if I think you're okay. You want the job?"

"What does it pay?"

"Twenty-five thousand if you nail all four of them for us. And expenses."

I shook my head. "No way."

He looked incredulous. "Why, you little shit. You ain't got a pot to piss in. You're flat broke. I checked you out. You bought some broken-down old château in France and it ate everything you made on the Berlin deal. You take our offer or leave it, sonny."

I got up and turned toward the door.

"Wait a minute. I didn't say you could leave."

I turned and met his eyes. "You want to try to stop me?"

He stared at me for a few seconds and started to grin. "Naw, I don't want to stop you, Thompson. Just trying you out. How much do you think the job is worth?"

"Twenty-five thousand up front. Seventy-five more if and when I deliver. All expenses paid. And they'll run high."

"How come you think we're willing to pay that kind of money?"

"You want them bad. Nobody else has come through. Also, you know as well as I do I'm risking my life. Once I start after these crazies, they'll know it. If I get close, they'll waste me."

Purvis shook his head. "It's too expensive. You ain't worth it." As he finished, a disembodied voice came from a concealed speaker.

"Junior. Bring him in."

Purvis looked over his shoulder, body stiffening. "Right away, Pop." He stood up and motioned toward a massive carved wooden door in the rock wall. It opened onto a room identical to Purvis's but dominated by a massive mahogany boardroom table inlaid with tropical woods. At one end, with his back to the river view, an old man sat hunched over a delicate Chippendale desk. He stood up then, tall and emaciated, almost a skeleton, and came around to shake my hand.

"Wilbur Purvis, Dr. Thompson. This is my son-in-law, José Sindona."

"Happy to meet you, Mr. Thompson." Sindona was a slim man with straight black Indian hair, dark skin, and startling hazel eyes. He had a faint British accent. The old man slumped into a chair at the head of the conference table and motioned us to seats.

"Your price is stiff, Dr. Thompson, but we'll accept it," Purvis said. "On one condition."

"Which is?"

"You deliver all four of them to the hit team. Otherwise you don't get paid."

"All right."

"How long do you think it will take you to locate them?"

"I've got four months. The term at Santa Cruz ends May fifth. I have to be back a day after Labor Day. If I haven't found them by then, you're out expenses. I'll return your twenty-five-thousand-dollar advance if I haven't delivered."

"Fair enough."

"I'll need all the leads you can give me. Especially somebody who was on the plane."

"Trevor Myles," Sindona said, his mouth curling with contempt.

"Myles?"

"My daughter's young English lover. Reuters correspondent in Berlin. He was with her on the flight. He watched them kill her and did nothing."

"What would you have done, Spic? Taken them on with

your manicured little hands?" The younger Purvis was staring at his brother-in-law with hatred.

"Don't call me that, Junior," Sindona said.

"Why not, Spic? I've beat the shit out of you before, and I can do it again."

"Shut up, Junior," the old man said. "We'll give you all the information we've got. Myles lives in Berlin. His address is in the file along with the confidential Egyptian interrogations of the surviving terrorist and various police reports including a CIA assessment and a report from MI6, the French Service de Documentation Extérieure et de Contre-Espionnage and the Bundesnachrichtendienst."

"What if I find him?"

"You let Junior know when you're getting close, and he'll mobilize the hit team. All you've got to do is point him out to them. Then you're through."

"Who have you got?"

Junior Purvis intervened. "None of your fucking business."

The old man ignored him. "There are seven of them. Four ex-Special Forces non-coms, a former French paratrooper, a Brit who was once with the SAS, and the leader, a former Special Forces captain. I'll take you up to where they're training tomorrow morning, so you'll know who you're dealing with."

"I'll start on May fifth."

The old man nodded and got up to shake my hand. Junior Purvis and I started toward the door when Sindona spoke to the big man's back. "Still having trouble getting it up, Junior?"

The younger Purvis turned, handsome face distorted with rage. He took a couple of steps, and one big hand flicked out with surprising quickness and caught the Mexican across the cheek in a backhanded slap, spinning him up against the wall beside me. Sindona's hand moved in a blur, the little automatic appearing in his hand as he swiveled toward Purvis in a classic two-handed shooter's crouch, arming the gun as he moved. I caught his wrist as he squeezed off the first shot and twisted it behind his back, keeping the muzzle pointed upward as it coughed again, and increased the pressure until it slipped from his fingers. I pushed him away and picked up the little gun, a superb 7.5mm Steyr, one of the best handguns made. It was the plastic version, similar to the Glock 17, guaranteed not to set off airport control mechanisms. I removed the magazine and ejected the shell in the chamber, reinserting it in the clip, and slipping it back in the gun. Sindona stood facing me, massaging his shoulder.

"Thank you, Dr. Thompson. It would have been unfortunate if I'd killed the oaf." I offered him the gun, butt first.

"Please accept it as a gift. It would bring me bad luck to carry it now." He bowed slightly and held out his hand to the old man. "Good-bye, Wilbur. I hope we find the son-of-a-bitch and kill him. Slowly. If it is convenient, I really think you should consider delivering them to me in Mexico."

"I will if I can, José. But I reckon we'll be lucky just to kill the bastards clean."

Sindona turned to leave. As he reached the door the old man called out. "José."

"Yes?"

"You put a bullet through my Picasso lithograph. Cost me ten thousand dollars. Shot the satyr in the ass. I'll expect a check to cover restoration."

A smile twitched at the corners of the Mexican's mouth. "You'll have it, Wilbur."

"Junior, I want to talk to you," the old man said, voice a whiplash. He must have been eighty, big-boned body shrunk within his skin, massive workman's hands veined and corded with muscle and age. He had the same eyes as his son, only his were embedded in the face of an ancient bird of prey. He was dying. "My secretary will show you out, Thompson. Be here at ten tomorrow morning. I'll take you in the chopper to meet the hit team."

I spent the rest of the day in the public library doing research on the Purvis family. The old man was eighty-two.

He'd been born near Dahlonega, Georgia, on a mountain farm, leaving at fourteen after a shootout over a whiskey still. His brother and two neighbors had been killed. Riding the rails west, he landed a job as a roustabout in the Oklahoma oil fields, already six feet tall, a big, rawboned kid who looked twenty. By 1922 he was chief driller on one of the primitive oil rigs of the time, and in 1925 he bought his first independent well, hitting it big in the years that followed, making money and raising hell. He'd brought in a Cajun girl from New Orleans and installed her in a mansion to the dismay of the society of the town, half puritan Baptists and half Ivy League–educated Pennsylvania oil millionaires who had followed the gushers west. He played poker all night at the Petroleum Club, shot big game in Africa, and brought in one wildcat well after another.

In the late twenties he plowed his money into the stock market, plunging on margin in 1929 fascinated by the new game. By the end of 1930 he was broke and back on the rigs, starting over. He paid his debts in three years, scorning bankruptcy, and in 1934 he banked his first million from the legendary Owasso field, which was to make Purvis Oil the biggest independent producer in the country. And he'd settled down, married Etta Mae Cameron, daughter of another millionaire redneck driller, and, in quick succession, bred six children on her before she died of breast cancer. When the Second World War started he joined the Marines as a private in January 1942, already forty years old, and wound up a colonel with the Silver Star and three Purple Hearts, having fought from Guadalcanal to Okinawa.

After the war, Purvis Oil had expanded exponentially into the Middle East, Southeast Asia, and Latin America. The aging Purvis, a loner obsessed with his business, maintained apartments in London, Beirut, New York, Hong Kong, and Caracas, keeping, or so rumor had it, a mistress on tap in each one. He had scattered his millions far and wide, establishing the Museum of Western Art in his headquarters city and endowing the local university beyond its means to absorb the money. His purchase of Catlins and Remingtons had driven prices for these two modest genre painters into the stratosphere. Now, at eighty-two, he was slowly dying of cancer of the prostate, refusing treatment, gutting it out.

His oldest son, Wilbur Junior, had followed him into the business, training as a geologist, playing fullback at the state university and building a reputation as a stud that still echoed among the ladies of his generation. Over the years he'd moved up inside the family business. Beginning as a roughneck on a remote drilling platform, he had become manager of the Middle Eastern Division, vice-president for exploration, senior vice-president, and finally president and chief executive officer as his father moved up to chairman. Along the way he'd scattered three wives and six children across the landscape.

The other three daughters and two sons of the founder, raised by tutors and schooled in the best academies of the eastern establishment, had escaped the old man's orbit. The men were lawyers, one a partner in New York's Burling, Stone and McAdam, attorneys for Purvis Oil, the other an assistant secretary of commerce responsible for trade with the Middle East. The two younger daughters had married well and divorced early, folding into the restless jet set that wintered in Davos and the Costa Smaralda and summered at secluded estates in Maine, swathed in a cocoon of money which bought them lovers, friends, and discontent.

The oldest, and her father's favorite, was something else. She'd taken a degree in art history at Radcliffe and there met the dashing José Maria Sindona y Suarez, then at Harvard settling down after a decade as one of the world's top race car drivers and international Don Juans. Dolores Sindona was the only issue of a long and tempestuous marriage which, against the odds, had lasted twenty-five years. Claire Sindona, mother of the murdered girl, was now editor of *Chic,* a women's magazine catering to the upper middle class hoping to lose the middle. The older Sindonas had maintained a weekend marriage for a decade, Sindona commuting to New York or she to Mexico City before finally separating a year before.

Their daughter had inherited it all. Her father's spectacular good looks, her mother's brains, and her grandfather's willpower. At twenty she had a master's degree from Yale in political science and had caught on as a stringer for *Time* magazine in Berlin while working on her doctorate on the origins of the East German uprising of June 1953. She and Trevor Myles, the Reuters correspondent with whom she was having an affair, had been on the way back to Berlin from a vacation in Athens when their plane was hijacked.

I was still fitting the pieces together the next morning when the old man joined me aboard a civilian version of the AH-64 Apache attack helicopter. When we had settled into the bird on the rooftop helipad of the Purvis Oil Company building, he plugged in his helmet, shutting out the noise, and asked over the intercom, "Ever ride in one of these things before?"

"Yeah."

"Vietnam," he said. "Of course. I'd forgotten."

"If they take a hit in the right place they've got the same flying characteristics as a falling safe."

"Don't like the damned things myself. But it's the only way to move quick. We're going to Roman Springs, a resort town up in the Ozarks. The team is training on a tract of hunting land I own up there. Ten thousand acres way back in the hills. Been up there for a month. I've got them under contract for six. The leader is a former Special Forces captain." The old man grinned. "Like you, he left under a cloud. Been working as a mercenary ever since. I believe you know him. Michael Halloran."

"Mad Mike? He's a psychopath."

"Yes," the old man said. "He admires you, too."

"Who are the others?"

"Faceless killers, the four Americans. People Halloran worked with here and there. The Frenchman, or whatever he is, is a former Foreign Legion paratrooper. Older than the others. Steadier. I think he was a Polack originally. Speaks about six languages. Kind of an intellectual thug. And the Brit." The old man stopped and stared out the window.

"What about him?"

"He's the killer. I mean the specialist in taking people out in a crowd without leaving a trace. Spent fifteen years in the SAS, that British special operations outfit. Some sort of broken-down aristocrat, I think. Mean bugger. Mike says he's good at getting information out of people."

The chopper made too much noise to talk, despite the earphones. We flew in silence across the green landscape. The flat Oklahoma prairie gradually changed to low foothills, then to the worn, rounded ridges of the Central Ozarks, split by gullies and creeks swollen with the spring rains. Here and there a deep blue lake backed up by a government dam seeped up into the hollows.

"Looks deserted," the old man said. "It's not, though. Used to be they grew corn and made whiskey. Now it's dope. Biggest cash crop in Arkansas is marijuana."

I'd spent a lot of my youth in the hills below us. My half-Irish, half-Creek father would park me and my Polish emigré mother with his brothers while he went to war as a union organizer for the teamsters. When I was fifteen the news came that he'd been shot in the parking lot of a Kansas City bar. They found his killer two blocks away, dead with a knife in his gut.

The chopper lifted over a ridge and the town of Roman Springs, its houses hanging from the hills like Victorian toys, spread out before us. We circled an immense stone pile of a hotel, and the pilot drifted onto its rooftop landing pad, setting the chopper down in a gentle rocking motion. The old man led me down a short flight of stairs into a massive timbered living room furnished in dark natural leather and decorated with Indian-and-cowboy artifacts. Linked picture windows overlooked the narrow winding streets of the nineteenth-century spa. Over the massive stone fireplace a Remington showed a Cheyenne brave about to drive a lance into a buffalo running flat out, tongue hanging loose, eyes staring wildly. The hit team was scattered about the room, drinking coffee out of earthenware mugs. The old man introduced me. The Americans were of a piece, except for Halloran. Former rednecks honed by the military into a semblance of disciplined conformity. Underneath, a wild, mean streak which had attracted them to war and, finally, to killing as a way of life. Permanent outsiders with the hooded paranoia of their kind.

"Well, as I live and breathe, if it ain't the Indian. How's your hammer hangin', hoss? It's been a while." Mike Halloran unfolded himself from one of the rough leather chairs and enveloped me in the long sinewy arms, deceptively unmuscled, which, in a Special Forces karate class, had almost broken his Korean instructor in two when he had dared his students to punch his belly. A graduate of Tulane, scion of an old Delta planter family, Halloran affected the manner and accent of a Louisiana swamp rat. "Indian here saved my ass in the Triangle. Remember that bucket of shit?" he asked as we made the rounds.

I shook hands with the ex-Berets and Mike stopped me in front of the former French legionnaire.

"This here's Eric Malhe." He was a slim dark man of medium height with pale gray eyes and a long scar on his cheek. "That ain't his name, and he ain't really French. Polack. Speaks frog, Polack, and anything else you can name. He don't look old enough but he's put in his time. Dien Bien Phu. Algeria. Deserted the Legion and worked for ARVN freelance after de Gaulle gave up Algeria. Oh, yeah. And he's a graduate burglar and thief."

"Dzien dobre panu. Jak sie pan ma?" The Polish greeting my mother had taught me as a child came out strangely, distorted by an American accent.

"I'm well," Malhe said in elegant upper-class accents. "How is it that you speak Polish?"

"My mother is Polish."

"You don't say!"

The Brit stood up as we came to rest in front of him. "This is Graham De Crecy. Known by the boys, behind his back anyway, as 'The Creep.' SAS. Got throwed out for screwing a twelve-year-old boy in the ass. Right, Graham?"

"Chacun à son goût," the Brit murmured in impeccable French. He was another of the deceptive ones, looking frail and unmuscled, a dancer, always on the balls of his feet, eyes flickering like a snake.

"Good with a knife?"

"One of the best. Cut your throat and your head will fall off before you feel it. He's the butcher. The rest of us will back him up and do it dirty if he can't do it clean."

"Can we talk?"

"Sure." He turned to the others. "You've got until tomorrow morning. You know the rules. Stay out of trouble or you're out. The chopper leaves for the lodge at eight." They filed out, leaving the old man, Halloran, and me alone in the big room, immaculate, smelling of leather, furniture polish, and disuse.

"They're kind of noticeable."

"It will be summer, Dr. Thompson," the old man said. "Europe is full of American tourists. We'll costume them appropriately. Nobody will look twice."

"What about hardware?"

Halloran frowned and looked at the old man. "It's none of your business, Alec. You're supposed to finger the target. We'll handle the rest."

"Bullshit."

The old man intervened. "We don't figure on fighting the Second World War. One of my tankers will deliver identical weapons packages to Cherbourg, Hamburg, Barcelona, and Genoa, where they will be stored until the team needs them. If necessary I can arrange to get them across European borders in one of my tank trucks. Purvis owns a piece of a big European wholesale company, Eucom Oil."

"What if they're in the East? Czechoslovakia?"

The two men exchanged glances. "Eric has contacts," Halloran said. "They can handle getting us in and out. It's not impossible to work there. Once in, it's easy. They're not used to crimes of violence. A couple of Ecuadorean hit men just took out their ambassador in Budapest and walked away clean."

"A former cop."

"Yeah. They tucked him away in Hungary figuring he'd be safe there. Couple of hard greasers took him like a liquored-up virgin."

"How do I contact you?"

"Eric and De Crecy are going to set up an advance post in Paris. We'll give you the address. The boys and me will be in Scotland in about a week. Out in the middle of a shoot Mr. Purvis owns. We can get anywhere in Europe in three to six hours by private plane. You find 'em and we'll waste 'em. Just like the old days, huh?"

"Suppose I need help? Can I use Malhe and the Brit?"

Halloran hesitated. "Compromise the command structure. You know how these slopes are. You gotta dominate to keep them in line. If we split their loyalty, we lose control."

The old man intervened once again. "Halloran doesn't altogether trust you, Dr. Thompson." He smiled faintly, showing his false teeth. "Called you a chilly, amoral, duplicitous son-of-a-bitch devoid of loyalty to the unit. He also says if somebody offers you a higher price, you're more than likely to sell us out."

"Your admiration is touching, Mike."

"Try not to crack up. Mr. Purvis is right, though. I figure we'll tell you only what you need to know. If these villains are as good as their reputation, you're going to be walking into their hive. When they start tickling your balls with a cattle prod, I'd just as soon you didn't know my number."

"Who are they?"

"You've got the file," the old man said. "When you read it you'll know as much as we do. Main structure seems to be

German but with some French and Lebanese input. Shiites, we think, but we're not sure."

"Two of them trained at that terrorist camp in Czechoslovakia. Karlovy Vary."

"Yeah," Halloran said, "and the other three, including the girl, at the East German camp in the Bekaa Valley."

"So they're getting Soviet support."

Halloran shrugged and the old man looked doubtful. "We're not sure. The Bundesnachtrichtendienst, the German CIA, thinks the Soviets have distanced themselves from groups like this. Too hard to control. No real willingness to submit to the party's dictates. They're mavericks these days. Likely to fuck everything up just at the wrong time. But they were trained initially by the KGB. And when they need to run, the Soviets give them a safe haven. Usually East Germany or Czechoslovakia."

"Qadaffi involved?"

"Maybe. At least with logistical help. Guns through the diplomatic pouch, some money. He's reduced his support for the IRA and the French groups lately. With the price of oil so low he's having trouble coming up with the scratch. We're just not sure who's behind them. Could be Khomeni, Assad or, shit, Carlos for all we know."

"Is he still active?"

Carlos was a Venezuelan who had led the kidnapping and murder of eleven Israeli athletes at the 1972 Olympic games in Munich. He was a legendary terrorist figure reputedly now retired in East Berlin.

"Look, amigo. It don't matter who they work for or who's financing them. Just find the bastards. We'll handle the rest."

"How do you plan to begin?" Purvis asked.

"Check Wohlgemuth's background, dig into his family, probe for recent contacts. Build a psychological profile. Find his interests. Check out his old lovers, friends. Nobody cuts himself off completely. Presumably he's human. Do the same thing with the girl. She's dead. People might be more willing to talk about her. Find a thread leading to the group. Reel it in. I'd like to check out Malta, then see this guy Myles in Berlin."

Purvis nodded. "I'll give you the name of the policeman in Malta who sat in when the Egyptians interrogated the girl."

"He'll cooperate?"

"He'd better. He's been bought and paid for. After Malta and Berlin, what will you do?"

I shrugged. "There isn't much time. If I can get close enough, I'll try to provoke them into coming after me."

The old man looked at both of us. "I don't follow you."

"You know how they catch tigers in 'Nam?" Halloran asked. "They stake out a goat in a clearing, cut one hamstring to make him scream, and wait for the tiger. We used to do the same thing with the Cong. Put some green clowns just over from the States on patrol, let 'em blunder around in the jungle for a while until it drew Charley. He'd set up his ambush. When he was ready to jump, we'd be there ready to waste him."

"Sounds dangerous for the goat," the old man said.

"Yeah," Halloran said, lighting a hand-rolled cigarette. "He don't usually make it."

chapter 2

Purvis stood up and shook my hand. "I'm going to turn in, Thompson. The chopper will drop you at the airport tomorrow. My son will be your contact if you need any special assistance. Your briefing folder contains addresses in Paris, London, and Rome where you can get through to him. You'll also be issued a scrambler which you can attach to any telephone mouthpiece. And, as a final precaution, we'll use a code name for the hit team." He turned to Halloran, frowning. "What was it that slimy Brit suggested?"

"The Heracles Commando."

"What the hell is Heracles?"

"Sort of an ancient Greek superman. Romans called him Hercules."

"Sounds a little hifalutin' for a bunch of hired guns."

"That's pretty much what Heracles was."

Halloran watched him leave, ancient body bent with pain. "There goes two billion dollars on the hoof, give or take a hundred million, and it ain't gonna do nothing for that cancer that's eatin' at his guts."

"How'd you get the contract, Mike?"

"After they threw me out of the army, I sort of drifted into the mercenary business. Angola, Ethiopia, Rhodesia. I was down in Honduras with the Contras when one of Purvis's men contacted me. The old man had been helping finance them. Nothing big. Million or two here and there. Fellow said he needed a little muscle. I could make a quick hundred thousand."

"What about the Pole and the Brit?"

"I knew Eric in Rhodesia. The Brit is a specialist. He hires out to kill people real quiet. The old man's right. He's slime. But you ought to see him with a knife or a silenced .22. Hit a fucking bug's-eye at twenty paces." He stood up. "Come on, hoss. I'll buy you dinner. There's a rib place down by the creek sells real good old-style barbecue."

The hotel had been designed in the late nineteenth century for the state's newly rich to take the waters. They built a single-gauge railway line through the hills from the state capital. The building's ornate Victorian elegance had fallen on hard times with the advent of the automobile in the nineteen thirties when Purvis bought it from a friend on the verge of bankruptcy. He had maintained it in seedy grandeur over the years.

"Looks like a high-class English whorehouse," Halloran said as we stood in the teak-paneled lobby with its crystal chandelier, heavy maroon drapes, cracked leather furniture dominated by an original Degas ballet scene over the massive stone fireplace. We walked out of the air conditioning into a darkness enveloped in humid warmth.

"Sort of reminds you of 'Nam, huh? Remember that last fucking sweep in the Triangle?"

I'd been in a replacement camp, under informal arrest, awaiting a decision on a court-martial, when the Viet Cong decimated a newly arrived cavalry regiment running a sweep through the Iron Triangle outside Saigon. The area, honeycombed with tunnels, was supposedly secure. The regiment, under a gung-ho colonel on his first Vietnam tour, had started a classic search-and-destroy operation through an area which had been fought over for thirty years, a tangle of new-grown jungle rising to cover the battlefield after each operation. As they moved forward, tanks leading the way, the spider holes had opened behind them and black-clad figures would pop up and pick them off in quick bursts before disappearing like smoke into the underground maze of tunnels.

The depot commander, an aging mustang lieutenant colonel on the verge of retirement, had called in Halloran and me. "Siddown, gentlemen," he said, offering us cheap Indonesian cheroots, the kind with the little bamboo straw sticking out one end. "You two have got heavy problems with the JAG from what I see here in your files." He glanced at me. "Looks like you and a couple of your sergeants might have let go of a Cong prisoner up in a helicopter. Pore devil fell out. Course that's understandable if you wuz holding him out the door by the heels." He grinned. "They gonna hang yore ass, Thompson. High on the flagpole at high noon."

He rolled the little cigar in his mouth and stared at Halloran, pale, slim, almost albino, with light blue eyes and a scar down his left cheek. "As for you, Halloran"—he sucked in a lungful of the foul-smelling smoke—"you blew away a whole fucking village when one of your men got sniped. Course, they might have overlooked that, but letting your men scalp the bodies and hang them upside down from trees"—he shook his head—"that got your ass in deep shit."

"Koreans do it all the time. Fuckin' Cong won't come within ten miles of a Korean bivouac."

"Yeah. Well, they're allies, see? You're an American. Not some fucking slant-eyed barbarian. Can't be doing stuff like that. Anyway, both yore asses are in a sling."

"What's the fuckin' deal, Colonel? You got a load of smack you want delivered? Couple of competitors wasted?" Halloran asked. Rumor had it that the camp commander was big in the drug trade.

"You got a big mouth, boy. Had you back in the bayous, we'd teach you some manners. However"—he eyed the coal on the tip of the cigar—"you two just might be able to get off the hook if you feel like volunteering for a little special duty."

"What?"

"That cavalry outfit up in the Triangle, the 110th. It's taking a lot of bad hits from the tunnels. Now, the general here asked me to scrounge up some tunnel rats. Turns out both you fellas punched yore tunnel ticket."

"They got teams all over the place. How come us?"

"General got headquarters pissed off at him. Sumbitch thinks he's Patton. They told him to find his own team."

"We'll need some backup."

"Couple of yore boys are in the stockade, Thompson." He glanced down at a slip of dirty paper. "Morgan and Wilson. In that chopper with you, wasn't they? When the slope fell out, I mean."

I nodded. The ARVN had come up with intelligence on the location of a Viet Cong divisional headquarters in the Parrot's Beak. We'd lost half a dozen men trying to locate it when Morgan, Wilson, and I had captured the two Cong couriers. They wouldn't talk, even after the ARVN interrogator had worked them over, pouring water down their nostrils, attaching electrodes to their balls. So we'd taken them up in the chopper and dropped one into the jungle from 2,000 feet. The other had babbled like a baby all the way back to the airfield.

"They'll be here in a couple of hours. I sent 'em down to the special weapons armory in Saigon to pick up the gear. You boys do a good job up there, and the word is they'll lose your files, hear?"

It was midnight before the two sergeants showed up. Morgan reeked of cheap Japanese bourbon, and Wilson was so spaced out on dope he could hardly keep his eyes open.

"What did you get?"

"Fuckin' gunsmiths didn't have nothin' we could use. We

finally found King Kong, remember him? That little spic midget. Lost an eye in the tunnels up to Hue. He's still got a stash of shit. Gave us a couple of twenty-twos with silencers. Some flashlights. Knives. We picked up a couple of forty-fives. Gas masks. Wilson here got hisself a Uzi from an MP. Cost him a hundred bucks."

"All right. Now, listen, assholes. We're facing a couple of hundred years in Leavenworth unless we can slide out from under. So it's yessir and nosir and no fucking trouble. Get rid of that goddamn weed, Morgan. This regiment is fresh out of the States. They'll bust yore ass for smoking rabbit tobacco."

"Where we going, Captain?"

"Up into the Triangle. We're going to bring out a few gook bodies, try not to get dead, and come out heroes."

"Why don't we just go out on patrol and get us some slopes, stick 'em down in the holes when nobody's looking, and go in after them the next day? Make us look real good."

Wilson was looking at Halloran. "He going with us, Captain?"

"Captain Halloran is part of the team."

It took most of the night to get to the combat zone. The tanks were already moving, lifting clouds of dust over everything. The green troops were dug in, tense as cats.

"Goddamn, we'll get wasted by these pussies before we get close to the fuckin' Cong," Morgan said as three young troopers armed their rifles when we approached the perimeter.

"Where's Major Jackson?" Morgan asked one of them, watching his finger trembling on the trigger of the M-16. "And quit pointing that fucking thing at me."

"Yes, sir. In the command tent, sir." He nodded toward a clearing surrounded by tanks.

"Looks like a western movie, wagons all circled," Halloran said, suppressing a laugh as we came into the headquarters area.

"Major Jackson?" It had to be him. He stood in a huddle

of officers barking orders, clean shaven, pressed, with the jawline of a Hollywood actor, West Point tattooed on his forehead.

"Sir!" The roar came out of the gut. "Goddamn you, Captain, in this regiment we maintain good order."

"Major Jackson, sir," I said. "Tunnel detail reporting for duty, sir."

"About fucking time," Jackson said, turning to his assembled officers and growling his remaining orders before motioning for us to follow him. We moved outside the perimeter about fifty yards.

"You can start here," he said, pointing to a six-foot crater.

Morgan sank to his haunches and contemplated the hole, chewing on a kitchen match. "Ain't no opening, Captain," he said, looking up at me, pale blue eyes wide with innocence.

"We dynamited the fucking thing, wise-ass. I want you to excavate an opening and bring out the bodies."

"Might be more useful to find a new hole and kill a few fresh ones, Major," Halloran said. "Take less time."

The West Pointer stared at us. "And how the fuck do you propose to find the damn things? We spent four days up here and found six holes. Fell into them is more like it." The sun was coming up, an orange ball rising suddenly, bathing the decimated landscape of broken trees and artillery craters in a soft glow before the heat came.

"We'll go out ahead of the tanks, Major. See what we find. Give us a patrol, maybe thirty men, for a couple of hours."

He nodded. "An hour. After that we move out." He turned on his heel, almost a parade ground maneuver, and disappeared. Ten minutes later a second lieutenant and twenty or so troopers showed up, faces tense.

"Okay, Lieutenant. Here's what we're going to do. The four of us are going to spread out and look for tunnels. The

Cong are out there watching us. They'll let us go past, then open up from the rear. Now, you form a skirmish line about twenty yards behind us with half your men. Then another twenty yards behind that form up the other half. If we're lucky, when we move out some gooks will pop up and let off a burst, then drop back in the spider holes. I want your guys to spot the holes. Never mind the gooks. Just spot the holes. We'll do the rest. Oh, and, Lieutenant."

"Yes, sir?"

"Try to keep from shooting us in the back."

We moved out cautiously, punching the cementlike laterite with sharpened sticks, watching for the mine tripwires sure to connect the holes. We'd gone a slow forty paces when Morgan's low whistle stopped us. I moved over to him. He pointed to the mine concealed under straw camouflage. We followed the wire to the second mine, a vicious Soviet version of the claymore antipersonnel device that cuts like a scythe through anything within twenty yards. It took ten minutes to follow the wire to the spider hole with its tight-fitting bamboo lid.

I motioned Halloran and Wilson forward another twenty-five yards to cover escape holes and ventilation tunnels. Morgan inserted a machete into the edge of the hole and flipped up the cover, revealing an empty space about four feet deep. Off to one side, at a forty-five-degree slant, an access tunnel disappeared. I nodded to Morgan and moved off to cover the area to the right. The smoke grenade went off with a muffled cough as it hit the bottom of the hole. Ten seconds later puffs appeared at four points in front and behind the spider hole. Two were narrow ventilation tunnels, too small to enter. Another was a spider hole and the third, an escape tunnel. I motioned the lieutenant forward.

"We're going down. Tell your men to look before they shoot anything coming out of the holes. It might be one of us." I handed him a ball of cord and tied one end to my ankle. "Have one of your men pay it out as I go. I'll jerk it periodically. Once means I'm okay. Two means trouble and three means I'm hit and somebody is going to have to come in to get me. If it quits jerking, forget the body. They'll have it booby-trapped. Okay?"

"Who's going to come in to get you, Captain? I mean, if we have to."

I nodded toward his platoon. "Appoint a hero. If he won't do it, shoot him for disobeying orders. That way next time you'll get a lot of volunteers."

The Cong often dug indentations in the sides of the tunnels big enough for a man to lay in wait ready to knife anybody coming by. At intervals crude crossbows fixed to tripwires fired razor-sharp bamboo spears, and once in a while a pit viper was tied inside a hollow bamboo stick ready to slip out and strike if the stick was jiggled.

Morgan and Halloran took the other two holes, and I squeezed through the tunnel next to the first one. The technique was simple. A concussion grenade down the hole, then in behind it quick, flashlight tied to the end of a three-foot stick probing ahead. I hit the main connecting tunnel about five yards down and turned left toward the entrance Halloran had entered, feeling my way along the floor with a knife point, looking for the hatch to the second level of the complex. It came fifteen yards along the tunnel, an intricately woven bamboo circle covered with dirt.

Ahead a light flickered. I gave the agreed signal of two short and one long flashes and got an answer. Halloran met me five yards farther along.

"Got an opening," he said.

"Yeah. There's another one behind me. Let's drive them."

The technique was for one man to descend to the second level, again following a concussion grenade, and try to spook the Cong into escaping through the upper level connecting tunnels. There they would be ambushed as they came out.

I slid back past the hatch and dug into the tunnel wall,

widening it enough to give myself some leverage. The sudden muffled roar of the grenade reverberating through the compacted air of the tunnel was answered almost immediately by the low-pitched chatter of a Kalashnikov. Then silence. The hatch popped up suddenly, flipping back, and a figure in black pajamas came out in a blur of agility, moving toward me dragging a rifle. I cut his throat as he came opposite my niche, pulling his head back, hearing the blood and air gush into the dirt. I pushed the body down the tunnel as the next slender figure squeezed out of the hatch. The knife entered his throat just back of the chin, a death spasm lifting him out of the hole. I flung the body down the tunnel as Halloran's voice drifted up.

"I'm hit. Got a slope corpse in front of me. There's one, maybe two more down here. Drop a grenade and come in after it. I'll light up and cover you."

I dropped the grenade and went down the hole headfirst, landing in a widened underground room. Halloran's flashlight was flickering over the walls. On the right, in a sleeping niche, a black-clad figure was curled in a fetal crouch. I put three shots from the silenced .22 into him as Halloran's .45 spat behind me, answering a Kalashnikov.

"You okay, hoss?"

"Yeah. You?"

"Got creased a little. Gonna have to drag me outta here."

"Captain?" Morgan's voice came down from the hole above.

"Yeah. Come on down, Lester. We've got to get Halloran out of here."

Suddenly, on the left, part of the wall fell away and a slender figure with a Soviet grease gun wiggled into the tunnel, opening up on Halloran, blowing his light. I put three shots from the Ruger into the muzzle flash and the weapon fell silent.

I slipped the flashlight stick forward full stretch and pulled the cord to light it. A girl who looked about fifteen lay facedown, one of my .22 slugs in her temple. Ahead Halloran had flipped half over on his back. I moved to him and slapped a bandage on the chest wound, taping it to him. Behind me Morgan had dropped into the main room, methodically exploring the tunnels leading off it.

"You cleaned 'em out, Captain. Ain't nobody left." We moved the bodies into a side niche and pulled Halloran to the entry tunnel, attaching a rope under his arms, pulling him up to the second level, then out into the air. An hour later five Viet Cong bodies were lined up neatly on the ground as the West Point major paced back and forth, hitting his palm with his fist.

"Goddamn well done, Thompson. Good fucking job. I wouldn't have believed you and your scumbags could have done it. I'll get you and Halloran Silver Stars for this. Bronze for him"—he pointed to Morgan—"of course."

"Just keep me out of the slammer, Major. I already got a Bronze Star," Morgan said.

The officer stared at him, started to say something, then turned to me. "Let's get on to the next tunnel. The lieutenant says you've discovered a way to find them."

"Yeah. But going down each one will take too long. You need a couple of guys in each platoon out ahead trying to locate the openings." I explained the tactics. "Once you've smoked out a series of holes, you cave them in with dynamite charges. It'll take the slopes a while to dig out. When they realize you're killing anybody who pops out of the spider holes and shutting off escape routes, they'll begin to lay low. We'll mark the holes and clean them out later."

"Wonder whatever happened to that fucking gung-ho major? What was his name? Jackson? Goddamn football-playing asshole."

"He made brigadier a year or so ago. Don't knock him. He kept us out of Leavenworth."

We had emerged onto the main street of Roman Springs, a double row of late nineteenth-century two-story stone buildings now housing an endless array of shops selling mountain handicrafts and Taiwanese gewgaws.

"De Crecy says this joint has good ribs," Halloran said, stopping at a low shingled building next to the gingerbread railway station which had been converted into the town museum. We walked under a faded wooden sign advertising Li'l Abner's Barbecue into a long room with a bar along one wall and ancient scarred wooden booths along the other. Neon signs advertised Ozark Beer and Good Ole Boy chewing tobacco. A nineteen thirties jukebox and pinball machine stood like modern art statuary in one corner. A pool table occupied the other end.

Four rednecks in jeans and denim work shirts glanced over from the bar as we came in, and an overweight blonde in a punk hairdo and purple lipstick sauntered over to take our order.

"What'll it be?"

"Pitcher of Coors. Two orders of ribs."

"What do your tigers do for amusement up here, Halloran?"

"Place is full of aging hippies. They dropped out and landed in backwaters like this when the sixties and seventies party was over. Women in their late thirties with a couple of kids, no man, and no prospects. Men are burnt-out cases. Chemically brain damaged. It's hard not to score."

"So you run your boys up and down hills, shoot a little, do some hand-to-hand combat, and scratch your balls."

Halloran took a sip of beer. "What else? De Crecy will make the hit. Eric will back him. We'll cover them. It's not something you can train for. We're just collecting pay and humoring the old man. He's seen too many movies."

The barbecue was greasy and the beer cold. Halloran filled his stein again and tipped it back, drinking greedily. "I've been thirsty ever since Angola. Fuckin' near died of heatstroke at Cangamba in '81."

"What happened?"

"In Angola?"

"No. After 'Nam."

Halloran stared into the beer. Over at the bar one of the rednecks started to laugh. "You ever try coke?"

Thompson nodded.

"You know the high? Hard to describe to somebody who's never sniffed it. Well, combat got to be like that for me. When they threw my ass out, I couldn't take the chickenshit of civilian life anymore. I was selling cars in L.A. when some guy came through recruiting for Angola, so I signed on. Went from there to Ethiopia and Rhodesia. Wound up in Honduras with the contras." He stopped talking, pale eyes suddenly still, staring at something over my left shoulder.

The big redneck leaned on the table, muscles in his forearms bulging, a heart-shaped purple tattoo with "Esther" in the middle rippling as his weight pressed down.

"The faggot bar is down the street, girls." He had a shaved head, red-rimmed blue eyes set close together, a nose flattened by too many breaks, lips thickened with scar tissue. "You hear me, faggots?"

Halloran moved the heavy beer stein to the right, gripping it by the handle, staring at the big man, body coiling.

"How much is Purvis paying you?"

Halloran shifted his eyes, meeting mine, body relaxing. "Yeah. Sure," he said, getting up slowly. "We're not looking for trouble, mister." He threw a twenty on the table and moved around the big man, never turning his back. The redneck reached out and grabbed his shirt in a big paw.

"Aw, let the pansy alone, Luke. Come on over and drink your damn beer," the bartender said. "You fuckin' near cost me my license last month. I don't want no more trouble." His hand came out from under the bar with a sawed-off baseball bat.

The big man relaxed his grip. "Sure, Lem. Only I just don't like these fuckin' faggots drinking on my turf."

On the street Halloran turned and stared at the bar door.

"Think of the money, Mike."

"Yeah. But it won't buy everything."

"I told my old man that once, when I was a kid. Know what he said?"

"What?"

"'You're right kid. But what it won't buy, ain't worth havin'.'"

Halloran laughed. "See you in Paris, hoss. I got a date with an aging, horny ex-hippie."

chapter 3

I left Santa Cruz to catch an early Washington flight, riding in a van with a skinny halfwit in running shoes and a torn T-shirt advertising the Marijuana Marathon. He flew blind most of the way, rubbing a small hole in the befogged windshield, changing lanes without looking and talking uninterruptedly.

"You from Santa Cruz? Me, too. Great little town. I used to live in Mississippi, but I couldn't take the religious horseshit. Everybody talking in tongues and screwing his sister. Went up to Alaska for a while, but it's cold as a whore's heart, man. Went east. Couldn't take it, man. Everybody walking around in suits and ties talking through their noses. Dope at twenty bucks a bag. Then I heard about Santa Cruz."

"Lots of aging hippies hanging out."

"Yeah. They kind of washed up against the ocean. Guys in their forties with long hair, freaked out on speed and LSD. Talking to themselves. But it's warm and the fuzz leave you alone if you don't bother the natives. What do you do, mister? For a living, I mean?"

"Teach at the university."

"No shit? I drive a lot of the girls to and from the airport." He swerved into the fast lane without signaling, setting off a cacophony of horn blowing behind us. All the windows except the windshield were totally fogged now. He licked his lips and glanced over at me. "I hear you guys get to screw the students."

"Against the rules."

"Yeah, but I mean for grades? They'll spring for you for a good grade, huh? I heard that." He was missing a couple of teeth on the right side of his mouth, and his skin was a matrix of pockmarks through the scraggly Ho Chi Minh beard.

"You want to look at the road?"

"Huh? Oh, yeah, sure. Nervous, huh? I know a lot of people get nervous in cars. Don't bother me none. You think drivin's dangerous, you ought to try going up into the hills."

"What's up there?"

"You kiddin', man? Dope fields coming up for harvest. First crop. Every mother and his brother is up there with Kalashnikovs and Heckler Kochs guarding his field, man. They blow you away for a nickel bag, man. It's just like 'Nam."

"Were you in Vietnam?"

"Naw. I had a hernia. Wouldn't let them operate. Got me a truss." He giggled. "I'm kind of sorry, now. Guys say they had a ball out there screwing themselves blind with Vietnamese chics. Throw a dollar on the ground and they'd give you a blow job."

He pulled into the airport fifteen minutes early, almost running into a bus. "That'll be seventy-five bucks, mister." I gave him a hundred and told him to keep the change. Purvis Oil could afford it.

It could afford first-class, too. I settled down in a reclining seat, accepted a glass of champagne mixed with fresh orange juice, and began to go over the file for the third time. There was a lot of paper and not much content.

Dieter Wohlgemuth, born July 15, 1950, in Regensburg, a

picture-postcard university town in southern Germany, famous for being an outpost of the Roman Empire and its ancient university. Father, a German state functionary, former member of the Waffen SS; mother, a nonpracticing medical doctor. Graduate, Goethe Gymnasium, 1968. Doctorate in political science, University of Berlin, 1974. Thesis: Lasalle and Marx: Romanticism and Realpolitik in Pre-Bismarckian Prussia. He had a police record beginning in his first year at the university. Nineteen sixty-eight. The year it all started. The year the French students almost chased de Gaulle from power and broke apart the postwar consensus in European society. Arrested for throwing a brick through the glass doors of the U.S. mission in Berlin, headquarters of our occupying army. The rest was a litany of arrests and releases for riots and demonstrations, gradually becoming more violent.

In 1972 he was picked up on suspicion of being a courier for the Baader-Meinhof terrorist gang. Refused a government job in 1974 for subversive activities. Submerged into clandestine terrorism. For a decade Wohlgemuth had belonged to a succession of small terrorist bands which formed, were betrayed, or split apart over minuscule ideological differences, reformed and continued to battle against authority, any authority. He was arrested a dozen times and released for lack of evidence. Their goal was the overthrow of society and the establishment of some sort of structureless commune, a utopian anarchy without constraints, deindustrialized, pacifist, and agrarian.

In 1978 Wohlgemuth began an affair with Gudrun Skorzeny, another terrorist, and, after almost two years of training in Karlovy Vary, Czechoslovakia, they founded the terrorist gang that was the nucleus for the Brigade of the Fifteenth of January. Police identified the group first as the perpetrators of a bank robbery at the Kiel Commerzbank in February 1981. They walked off with the equivalent of $250,000 and never looked back. Within months they had shucked off the discipline imposed by the Soviets, becoming a wild card out in the ideological ozone.

Following the murder of the mayor of Cologne in 1982, killed by a bomb thrown from a motorcycle in a traffic jam in the center of the city, the group hijacked Luftwaffe Flight 772 to Rome, killing a security guard and a steward. They forced the plane to land in Beirut, where they slipped away from the plane in the night with the aid of the PLO after demanding the freedom of four members of the band serving time in German prisons for murder and robbery.

Wohlgemuth's luck ran out in 1985. He was arrested in a Hamburg café on an anonymous tip to the police and brought to trial. His lawyer, a long-haired German leftist named Otto Skierka, had turned the trial into a circus, using it as a platform to condemn the German government and Western society. He'd gotten away with outrageous charges and courtroom theatrics because the Germans were unwilling to appear repressive during a trial being carried on television around the world.

Then, a day before the verdict was scheduled and just following a visit from Skierka, Wohlgemuth shot down two unarmed German prison guards and went over the wall in a burst of gunfire. Skierka was accused of smuggling him the weapon but was released for lack of evidence.

The police lost track of Wohlgemuth and his group for a while, and they were believed to have splintered in one of their periodic paroxyms of ideological disagreement before re-forming a year later. Two more bank robberies were attributed to Wohlgemuth and Skorzeny as they replenished their funds and made plans for attacks on nuclear installations. The group was believed to have diversified and recruited from terrorist organizations in France and the Middle East shortly before the British Airways hijacking in which Dolores Sindona was killed. Somewhere along the line it had begun calling itself the Brigade of the Fifteenth of January.

I turned to the files on Gudrun Skorzeny and Hildegarde Bohnerth, the young terrorist who died under interrogation after the Egyptians captured her in Malta. Skorzeny's file was a mirror of Wohlgemuth's. She was suspected of throwing the bomb that killed the Cologne mayor and positively identified during the Rome hijacking. Unlike Wohlgemuth, she had avoided being taken into custody by the police during the demonstrations and riots of the seventies. There were no good recent pictures of her and no fingerprints.

Hildegarde Bohnerth was of a new generation. Younger than the other two by a decade, she came out of the Greens movement, the idealistic young environmentalists who took Germany by storm in the eighties, preaching peace at any price, a clean environment at the expense of industrialization, an end to nuclear energy, and an antidemocratic sort of consensus government which some specialists in German history linked to the same romantic tradition that had produced the Nazis. Unstructured, intolerant idealism. My way or no way, as a weary cynic put it, watching the chanting masses defy a moderate Social Democratic government bewildered and finally frightened by the phenomenon. At some point during the past year Bohnerth had moved from activism and demonstrations into terrorism. She was captured on the plane in Malta clutching an Uzi submachine gun, bullets from which had killed two of the passengers.

The other members of the brigade were more shadowy. One, a Palestinian Arab named Ibrahim Assad, was believed to be the same Assad who had studied medicine at the University of Heidelberg. Virtually nothing more was known of him. The other, Edward Patrick O'Faolin, aka Paddy O'Grady and Sean Doolin, a member of the Marxist Provo faction of the Irish Republican Army, was a former priest who had studied medieval literature at the Sorbonne, specializing in François Villon, until he was defrocked for seducing Eliane de la Margerie, a fifteen-year-old convent student he was tutoring in Latin.

The police reports were straightforward descriptions of the assassinations and robberies committed by the gang along with a detailed analysis of its operational methods. They seldom bothered with disguises. And they unhesitatingly snuffed out any resistance with coldblooded ferocity. Witnesses were reluctant to identify them for fear of reprisals, and a network of sympathizers seeded throughout the German intellectual community enabled them to submerge instantly following an operation. They were suspected of crossing to the East, probably Czechoslovakia, between attacks to regroup, train recruits, and rest.

Their relations with the Soviets and their surrogates were complicated. Contemptuous of authority, regarding the Communist Party and the Soviet Union as antediluvian, they nonetheless accepted asylum when threatened. The East Bloc provided safe havens because, despite their lack of discipline, ideological impurity, and anarchic tendencies, Wohlgemuth and others like him were a destabilizing influence on German society that contributed to the atomization of the political consensus. In theory, anything that disrupted capitalist nations, particularly in a country as strategically important as West Germany, was good.

The reports were classic government documents, linear, full of facts, and devoid of insight. I needed somebody who could take me into the terrorist mind, dig into the subsconcious, winkle out the weaknesses they didn't suspect. Which was why I was stopping off in Washington for a session with Dr. Michael Duveen, author of *The Roots of Dissidence* and *The Terrorist Psyche*. He was also a leader of the neoconservative movement and a Senior Fellow at the Columbia Foundation, a think tank which espoused a U.S. campaign to destabilize hostile leftist regimes by using the same sorts of subversion and guerrilla warfare supported by the Soviet Union. He had agreed to meet with me for his usual consultant's fee of five hundred dollars an hour.

His office was in a converted late-nineteenth-century row house on Capitol Hill with a view of the Library of Congress through the window behind him. Underneath piles of newspapers, magazines, and books in Italian, French, and Russian was the office of an English gentleman, all maroon leather, Persian carpets, and a fake Empire-style oak desk. The walls were papered with brutal cartoonists' depictions of the slender, bearded Duveen, dominated by one showing him as Dracula drinking the blood of a helpless maiden labeled "liberalism."

He got up when I came in, flicking the ash from a seven- or eight-inch cigar with the circumference of an ax handle, and extending a surprisingly muscular hand. "Glad to meet you, Dr. Thompson. My secretary collected a check from you? Okay. You've got exactly one hour. Starting now. What can I do for you?"

"Dieter Wohlgemuth."

"What about him?"

"I need his address."

"Why?"

"To kill him."

"Hit me with that again."

I outlined the Purvis proposal, leaving out details of the killer squad.

"You're the Thompson who wrote the Sepp Dietrich biography?"

"Yes."

"And got your ass in a sling with the CIA in Berlin recently?"

"You could say that."

He sucked in a lungful of vile-smelling smoke and grinned. "I checked around on you. Xerxes sends his regards. Sounds like he's willing to let free enterprise do a little of his dirty work. Now, what do you want from me?"

"I need some background. What drives people like Wohlgemuth. Where they get their support. What the mechanisms are. How much assistance the Soviets still give them. Where they go under to hide and recuperate. How much cooperation there is between different groups. And most important, I need a psychological profile of him and the others in the cell."

Duveen inhaled and expelled a cloud of carcinogens toward the ceiling, slumping in his big leather executive chair and cocking a pair of almost new John Lobb handmade brogues on the desk, careful not to scratch the polished surface. "You're a historian, Thompson. So you know that nothing is without antecedents. To understand today's terrorists you have to look to their beginnings in nineteenth-century Russia."

"The conditions are different today. You haven't got a country full of serfs with barely enough to eat and a regime full of incompetent aristocrats unable to recognize that a massive explosion was brewing."

"True. Czarist Russia presented some special conditions. Nonetheless, the Baader-Meinhof gang is a direct descendant of Nechaev and Bakunin."

"The robber is the only true revolutionary."

Duveen nodded. "Bakunin is often acknowledged as the spiritual father of modern terrorism. But Necahev and his revolutionary catechism had an even greater influence. Stuff like: 'We recognize no other action save destruction though we admit the forms in which such action will show itself will be exceedingly varied—poison, knife, rope.' "

"He was a blowhard intellectual. Never killed anybody except a traitor in his own group. If he hadn't fascinated Dostoyevsky into writing *The Possessed,* nobody would ever have heard of him."

Duveen chewed on the cigar and slumped lower in the big leather chair. "Okay. But the bottom line is still that, though there are major differences between the different groups, they share crucial similarities. Take the Arab. If a genius is somebody who can hold two contradictory thoughts in his head at the same time, then you have to be a genius to grasp his psyche. Objectively, Wohlgemuth and this Palestinian accomplice, Ibrahim Assad, don't have much in common. Assad is a Middle Eastern mystic. Like all Arabs, when you scratch him you find a landscape almost as alien to Western rationalism as Mars. They're all poets. Reality is in the mind, not out there in the streets of Riyadh or Beirut. Thought processes are circular, not linear. Progress is not a concept readily available to the Arab culture. Their world is static, not in motion toward some goal. Man's fate is in large measure written on his forehead. The Koran is a long prose poem describing a dreamlike world to which all Arabs instinctively strive, even the grubbiest Lebanese old-clothes dealer in a back street in Lagos." He sucked in another lungful of smoke.

"Wohlgemuth on the other hand is a bundle of German neuroses dating back to Armenius. When that hairy barbarian came out of the mists of the northern forests and slaughtered a couple of Varus's legions, the Teutonic genie was out of the bottle. You can argue that since that battle in the Teutobergerwald in A.D. 9 the history of Europe has been a defensive struggle of civilized Latin cultures against the encroachments of the Goths."

"So he wants power?"

"Respect. Power, too, of course. All young men want power. But mostly respect. You're an expert on the Germans, Thompson. You know the pride, bordering on arrogance, they have in their *Kultur*. It's nothing beside the hubris they developed in their military prowess after 1871, even though all they've done for a hundred years is lose wars they should have won. A good comparison is the American South, living a romantic myth that guts, talent, and grace can defeat mediocrity and superior steel production. That's not the way the world works."

"So the krauts are suffering from a gap between the world's perception of their worth and their own. And Wohlgemuth is a symptom of their frustration."

"Yeah. If you want to put it that way. But it's not that complicated. Remember what Freud said about cigars."

"Sometimes a cigar is just a cigar."

He grinned. "Wohlgemuth and his generation see Germany as the key to the heartland of Europe, the bastion against invading Asiatic hordes."

"That's an echo of Hitler."

"And Hitler is an echo of every German statesman since Frederick the Great."

"Not Bismarck. He looked to the East as Germany's destiny."

"As a frontier to be conquered and ultimately Germanized. As a market for German industrial goods and a supplier of raw materials. Not as an equal partner. Today the older generation in Germany sees this magnificent cultural entity sundered and dominated by two clearly inferior intellectual and political competitors. The Soviet Union and the United States. Asiatics on one hand and the dregs of Europe gathered together in a messy mongrelized state with no soul on the other. Even worse, within Europe such worn-out degenerate peoples as the French and the British conspire to keep Germany hamstrung. With that cosmology is it any surprise that he's frustrated?"

"Why doesn't he get himself elected and work within the system?"

"Why did the Germans allow themselves to be sucked into the First World War by a bunch of musical-comedy idiots in Vienna? It was clearly insane to fight a two-front war against the combined military might of Europe and Czarist Russia even if they had had a good reason. Which they didn't. If the Prussians had not allowed themselves to be drawn into World War One, Germany would have dominated Europe by 1927. Same thing in 1939. If Hitler had stopped short of invading Poland and harnessed his Germanized and highly talented Jewish minority in the cause of German nationalism, everybody in Europe would have been driving a Volkswagen by 1950. Inevitable."

"If my aunt had balls she'd be my uncle."

Duveen glared at me and glanced at his watch. "You've got a half-hour left. You want to use it up trading insults or talk seriously?"

"Where can I find him?"

"He's extremely well organized. As Gertrude Stein said, 'The Germans are not efficient, they're methodical.' After I talked to Xerxes, I ran a computer pattern on all the known actions the group has conducted. They specialize in hijacking planes and political assassination. When they need money, they rob banks. Each operation is meticulously planned. You have to realize that while the police are usually as intelligent as most common criminals and a good bit more disciplined, we're dealing here with people with IQs in the hundred and sixties. They are extremely well-trained for up to two years in Soviet and satellite camps. They are better armed than the police. They vary their methods, never presenting a pattern."

"And they don't get caught."

"Not very often. And when they do they exhibit a ruthless brutality that criminals usually are incapable of. Witness Carlos the Jackal shooting down two policemen who came to arrest him."

"You've found a weakness in Wohlgemuth."

"Maybe not a weakness, but a preference. All other things being equal, he and Skorzeny prefer to hole up in Paris. Defectors from the group have confirmed this and so has the only objective evidence we have."

"Why?"

"Big cities are the safest places to go to ground. Paris has seven million people. It's always, winter and summer, full of foreigners. The French are xenophobic. They don't mix with strangers. They also mind their own business. Most important, however, is the attitude of the French government."

"I don't follow you."

"The French made a deal, maybe a decade ago. As long as terrorists leave their people alone and don't conduct terrorist acts on French soil, the French will look the other way. Why? Their economic interests in Arab countries such as Syria, Lebanon, Tunisia, Algeria, and Morocco are immense. Terrorism is centered in the Middle East. The

Brigade of the Fifteenth of January has especially close ties with the Arabs. Look for him in Paris."

"Your contacts with Mossad are well known, Dr. Duveen. Can you give me the name of a contact in Europe?"

He rolled the cigar between thumb and forefinger. "I have absolutely nothing to do with Mossad, Thompson. You're repeating vile and unproven rumors about me. But even if I did, I fail to see what self-interest the Israelis or I would have in helping you hunt down a German terrorist."

"He's wired to a Palestinian."

"True. But he has conducted no known operation against Israel. I see no point in arousing still another potential enemy."

"Like the French."

He shrugged. "You're a historian, Thompson. Nations, like people, if they are rational, conduct their affairs on the basis of self-interest, not emotions or moral imperatives. My main purpose in life is to assure the survival of the Israeli state. Your somewhat baroque assignment does not seem to further that goal at this time."

"What about your duty as an American?"

"America is rich and powerful. It will survive even its periodic bouts of moral madness. Underlying all this hypocrisy is a solid base of coldblooded Anglo-Saxon practicality. Israel is a fragile flower. It needs nurturing." He glanced at his watch. "Your hour is up, and I've told you all I can. I wish you luck."

I walked down Pennsylvania Avenue toward the White House, resisting an impulse to call my ex-wife, stopping off at the new Pei wing of the National Gallery to wander through an exhibit of the aging Picasso's erotic sketches. It was a mistake. I found a public telephone and made the call.

"International Computer Systems," the operator said.

"Mrs. Thompson." She'd kept my name after the divorce. Easier than changing it back to Clark.

"Research." The secretaries must have been clones. They all had the same clipped, no-nonsense voices.

"Mrs. Thompson."

"Who shall I say is calling?"

"Mr. Thompson."

She didn't gasp, but it was close. Marianne came on the line a couple of seconds later. "Alec? Where are you?"

"Around the corner. How about lunch?"

"Damn. I'm meeting a client. What about dinner?"

"I'm flying out late this afternoon."

"Hang on." She put me on hold for a couple of minutes and came back on. "Okay. Got out of it. Where shall we meet?"

"It's your town."

"What about the Hay Adams? There's a good French restaurant there."

"Sure."

She was fifteen minutes late, a tall young woman with shoulder-length blond hair and the grace of a natural athlete. As she stood in the dining-room doorway, I remembered her on a ski slope in Colorado, wind blowing her hair, going into a crouch, attacking the hill with fluid ferocity. Her arms were around my neck and her body glued to mine, wiggling against me a touch before she let me go and stepped back.

"God, men are disgusting. They never change." She ran a finger along my temple. "A touch of gray, couple of lines under the eyes. You still stay in shape?"

"More or less."

"What are you doing in Washington? Why didn't you warn me?"

"Spur of the moment. What's with you?"

She shrugged. "Nothing much new. They gave me the title, but I still do the same thing."

She was, at thirty, vice-president of one of the top opinion-polling institutes in the country, having started as a typist a decade before to help put me through graduate school. Five years later she was making fifty thousand dollars a year and the only job I could get was in Santa Cruz. We'd commuted for a couple of years, then split. Amicably. She'd been promoted to vice-president and transferred to Washington a couple of years later.

"What's with you? A new book?"

"Yeah. I'm researching the Charlemagne Division."

"The French SS?"

"Yeah." She had never been interested in my work, but she absorbed everything and forgot nothing. I described the offer Purvis had made me. She stared at me, light blue eyes searching my face.

"You didn't accept it?"

"Sure."

"They'll kill you, Alec."

"Not if I see them first."

"Jesus, you're still an incorrigible romantic."

"I seem to remember your working on some sort of a survey of the SDS when you first got started."

"The Students for a Democratic Society Project?" She nodded. "We were asked to contact a lot of ex-radicals, follow up on them, do a profile. You know, do a statistical dissection of them intellectually and politically."

"What did you come up with?"

"Privileged kids playing at revolution. Spoiled, bored, aggressive youth mouthing slogans from Marcuse, Gramsci, Lukacs, and Reich. Oh, and Regis DeBray."

"The Frenchman captured with Guevara in Bolivia?"

"Uh-huh. A fourteen-carat phony if ever there was one." Her father was a miner in the West Virginia coal fields. She'd worked her way through a community college. Her contempt for intellectual pretension was total.

"What conclusions did the study come up with?"

The waiter, an aging Italian, let his eyes run over Marianne with the sensual appreciation of a connoisseur before presenting us with the menus. Marianne ignored hers. "I'll have a salad and a broiled trout, no butter."

He turned to me. "Grilled steak with french fries. Wine?"

"No." She glanced at her watch. "That client I was

having lunch with is coming in this afternoon. He's a shark. I've got to be at the top of my game. Where were we?"

"The study."

"Oh. Sure. We profiled them, the whole bunch from Savio to Rubin. The bottom line was simple when you cut through the bullshit." Her eyes were on mine, softening now. "Do you still have nightmares?"

"No. What else did you get on the SDS?"

"Well, when you stripped away all the ideological garbage and posturing, you know what made them demonstrate?"

"What?"

"The draft. They didn't want to fight. The war was behind it all but not as some sort of idealistic paradigm of evil."

"They disagreed with it."

"Oh, sure. They disagreed with it. But you know what was interesting? The day conscription ended, so did the demonstrations. Nothing happened after that. Those taking advanced degrees to keep from being drafted quit school, and those hiding out and the deserters came out of their holes. The protests ended. All of a sudden nobody gave a damn about Vietnam, one way or another."

"It's got to be more complicated than that."

"Not really." The waiter brought a slab of pale fish and placed it in front of her. She began to devour it with single-minded intensity, talking between bites. "We talked to everybody, not just the SDS. You'd be amazed. Nobody believed in the war, but the sons and daughters of the workers went into ROTC because they needed scholarship money to get through college. And they went to war. So did the workers' kids right out of high school. The upper classes opted out. It was the first time in our history they refused to officer our armies. You know what that means?"

"First signal of degeneracy in a society is when people with the most to lose won't defend it. The decline of the West."

She grinned and reached across the table to lay a slender

hand on mine. "Funny, I remember the first time you said that at a party where everybody was giving you a lot of crap because you were a war hero. How are you, Alec?"

"I miss you."

"Me, too. Why don't you get a job here in Washington? With your credentials, it would be a cinch. The spooks would hire you tomorrow."

"Get back together?"

"Maybe. You're a stubborn, difficult man, but you're a man. It's a hard commodity to replace. Everybody else is a little bland." I pushed my plate away.

"You think this place would rent us a room?"

She leaned back in her chair, laughing. "A quickie?"

"My plane doesn't leave until six."

"I'd love to, Alec. But I can't. This client is worth a couple of million to us." She glanced at her watch. "And I can't afford to be late." She stood and leaned down to kiss me on the mouth, lips soft with promise. She walked away, trim, purposeful, arrogant, half the male eyes in the room following her hips.

On the flight to London I watched a movie about some guy turning into a fly for an hour or so, soaked up the free Piper Heidsieck, ate a plastic meal, and watched a tall, lean-jawed athletic type approaching middle age hustle the blond German stewardess. He'd said good-bye to his wife in the airport, a clone of the stewardess with a few more pounds and a few more years.

She shook my shoulder gently a few hours later. "We'll be in Heathrow shortly, sir. Please fasten your seat belt and put your seat in an upright position." I picked up my luggage and got in the taxi line behind the aging athlete and the stewardess.

"I'll pick you up at seven, then," he said. "We'll have a bite to eat and take in a show."

"Why don't you come over a little earlier?" the girl said, German accent barely noticeable. "We could get to know each other a little better. It always makes for a more relaxed evening.''

He went a little pale under his expensive tan. ''Uh, sure. If you like.''

I took a taxi to Gatwick and managed to get the last Air Malta Flight of the day for Valletta.

chapter 4

You don't hear much about Malta these days. It sits in the middle of the Mediterranean sixty miles south of Sicily, a blip on the radar screens. It's a living museum, encrusted with the remains of every civilization from the Carthaginian to the British Empire, which ruled it from 1800 to 1974. Valletta, the capital, was built by the Knights of St. John, who were made a present of the island by Charles V of Spain after being driven out of Rhodes by the Turks in 1522.

The knights were founded as a religious order to free the Holy Land from the infidels. Over time the order had degenerated into a clan of religious pirates recruited from the aristocratic families of Europe. It was too powerful to ignore, too influential to be allowed to perish, a convenient dumping ground for troublesome younger sons. The European powers arranged for the order to take over the barren island at a time when Turkish power was sweeping the inland sea.

In the spring of 1565, provoked by the continuing attacks of the knights on his shipping, the Turkish sultan, Suleiman the Magnificent, attacked the island with a force of forty thousand Mamelukes, the most feared troops of their time. It was defended by some seven hundred knights and nine thousand mostly local Maltese soldiers. The siege lasted more than six months before the Turks, unable to break the defenders' will, were forced by the onset of winter to take to their ships and sail home.

For the next three hundred years the knights ruled their little fiefdom and led a charmed existence. Their galleys prowled the Turkish sea lanes, exacting tribute from ships passing to the south on their way to Tunis and Algiers, investing the proceeds in opulent palaces and precious art works.

Napoleon captured the island in 1798, expelling the knights, only to lose it two years later to Great Britain. For a hundred and forty years the Maltese lived in peace and tranquillity as a British colony. The island was moderately prosperous as a result of the huge naval base used by the Royal Navy to dominate the Mediterranean and protect their trade routes to India. The Maltese had a brief moment of agony and glory in the Second World War when the Germans, intent on securing the lifeline to their troops in North Africa, bombed it uninterruptedly for two years. The populace, on the verge of starvation, held out, and British planes, using the island as a floating aircraft carrier, sank more than half the ships supplying the Axis forces in Libya.

In 1974 Malta became a republic and in the years that followed severed its last ties with Britain. The closing of the naval base and the departure of the last British sailor left the economy in ruins. Seeking aid from any source, the leftist regime of Premier Dom Mintoff established close ties with the Libyan regime of Muammar Qaddafi, receiving subsidies of up to forty million dollars a year. Mintoff used this support as leverage to gouge further contributions from Italy and other Western nations to assure that the strategic island did not fall into the Soviet orbit. Tourists, mostly British, and money from Maltese living overseas, remained its major sources of income.

I called the contact Junior Purvis had given me, Detective

Inspector Frank Rafalo. "Ah, yes, Dr. Thompson. Mr. Purvis telephoned me you would be coming." He spoke perfect English with a curious singsong intonation. "You are at the airport? I suggest that I meet you there. Shall we say in half an hour? In the restaurant?"

Rafalo was short and compact, like most Maltese, with olive skin and a western gunslinger's mustache. He bowed slightly and extended a square, muscular hand. "Happy to meet you, Dr. Thompson. Mr. Purvis said you were coming on his behalf to continue the investigation of the hijacking. I should tell you that my cooperation with the Purvis family is"—he hesitated—"shall we say in mild conflict with my official duties. It would be better if we were as discreet as possible."

"I don't want much. Just look around. Maybe have a talk with the Maltese who was allowed on board. What was his name? David Mifsud?" Mifsud, catering director of British Airways on the island, had been allowed at one point to bring food and drink onto the plane. He also was suspected of delivering a message from an intelligence officer in the Libyan embassy which allowed the terrorists to escape.

"Ah, yes. David. Unfortunately, he is not in Malta. He has accepted a position as manager of the Hotel Ta Xlendi on Gozo."

"Gozo?"

"Malta consists of two main islands, Malta itself and Gozo, which is much smaller. A charming place. Not hectic and full of tourists like the main island."

"How long would it take me to get there?"

Rafalo stared into his coffee cup. "He will not cooperate, Mr. Thompson," he said in his soft voice. "Also, it could be dangerous."

"Tell me about it."

"Mifsud is a truant." He used the archaic word naturally as if it were part of his day-to-day vocabulary. "He went to London as a youth and spent his early years as a petty criminal, becoming connected with the Mafia. As you know, we are quite near Italy here. Our contacts are close. He came back several years ago as catering manager for British Airways and used his position to smuggle contraband, mostly drugs, into England. We were unable to obtain proof, however, and until the hijacking British Airways refused to dismiss him."

"You know he helped the hijackers?"

"We are certain."

"Why don't you prosecute?"

He shrugged. "Libya is our nearest neighbor, Mr. Thompson. We receive a large subsidy from Qadaffi. One must be realistic."

Rafalo led me through the airport checkout, past customs guards lackadaisically fingering luggage and out onto the tarmac, pointing toward one end. "The plane came to a halt at the end of that runway," he said as we walked out into the blazing subtropical sun. "The tires were blown. It could not take off."

"How long did it last?"

"Forty-eight hours. A nightmare. They allowed most of the women and old people to leave the plane, but there were still more than a hundred on board. The lavatories were overflowing. There was very little to eat or drink. The air conditioning failed. The plane was an oven."

"They wanted two million dollars and another plane to fly them to Damascus."

"Yes. We stalled, of course. That is the standard tactic. Stall and talk. The American embassy attempted to persuade our government to allow the Delta Force, your antiterrorist people, to assist us. We refused. For political reasons. However, since there were sixty Egyptians on the plane, people going from Cairo to Frankfurt, we agreed to accept help from them. The Libyans were being especially brutal to the Egyptians and to the Americans and Jews who boarded in Athens."

"Toward the end they began to kill a hostage each hour."

"Yes. They would bring the person to the door, shoot

them in the back of the head, and push the body out onto the runway. After the sixth execution, we were left with no choice but to attack the plane."

"How did they get away?"

"Mifsud took food and drink onto the plane periodically. He knew the attack was about to take place. He must have warned them. You must understand, Mr. Thompson. It was dark. The attack was about to begin. We did not expect the terrorists to attempt to escape. We turned off the spotlights to enable the Egyptians to approach in darkness. It was then that the terrorists dropped from the plane to the runway and slipped away. We believe they scaled the airport security fence and were picked up by vehicles of the Libyan embassy."

"All except Hildegarde Bohnerth."

"Yes. She apparently was hysterical about the killings, afraid to jump the ten feet to the runway. Before she could get up her courage, the attack began and she was wounded and captured."

"How did they leave Malta?"

"There was a Libyan freighter in the harbor. Witnesses saw a launch pick up three men and a woman on the dock and deliver them to it shortly after the plane was taken." Rafalo stopped. "This is the spot where the plane was parked." He pointed to barely visible stains on the concrete. "Blood from the victims."

"How do I get to Gozo?"

"I shall take you. If we hurry we can catch the last ferry from Marfa Point to Mgarr on Gozo." It took us an hour to traverse the island on its narrow winding roads, hemmed in by rough stone walls and fortresslike houses. Rafalo steered his Morris Mini through ancient villages and towns built of golden limestone, the sea always visible on our right, to the left tightly terraced fields cut out of the rocky barren landscape.

"A pity you cannot stay longer. As a historian the island would fascinate you. We are a microcosm of the history of the region. On Gozo there exists in a state of perfect preservation the world's oldest neolithic ruin, built four thousand years before Christ."

"The Maltese language is Punic?"

"Punic with a mixture of Greek, Saracen, Latin, Italian, French, and Arabic. And English, of course. The Maltese have submitted to their conquerors but survived them all."

The ferry, a modern ship with cars on the lower deck, open on both sides, and an upper passenger lounge, took a half-hour to reach the smaller island. Gozo is roughly ten miles long and five miles wide with a population of less than thirty thousand. Even more than Malta it gives the impression of living in a past time. The walled villages, perched on hilltops both for defense and to avoid using arable land, sit like golden fairy-tale fortresses guarding the valleys below.

"Victoria is the Gozitan capital. It was destroyed in a Turkish siege in 1553. Dragut the pirate, a corsair in the service of the sultan, attacked the island. The entire population, seven thousand people, retreated into the fortress. Dragut captured it, slaughtering the men and taking the women and children to Tripoli as slaves. They say there is even now a quarter of that city called Gozo. Old Victoria is still a ruin, the new city built below it. Dragut was later killed by a cannon ball in the Great Siege of 1565."

The Ta Xlendi was at the end of a winding road on one of the highest points of the island, a plush complex of stone cottages surrounding a central hotel with swimming pool and tennis courts.

"Mafia money," Rafalo said. "They bought a very large piece of rocky, barren land ten years ago intending to build a summer colony and a retirement home for aging gangsters. It didn't work."

"What happened?"

"The Mafiosi prefer to retire to Rome or Milan, although there are always a few hard ones in residence. Killers waiting for the heat to die down in Italy. You see, Gozo has nothing to sell but rock and sea. It is too far away. Too quiet. No discos. Few restaurants. Tourists want excitement. This is a peaceful little backwater."

"You sound as if you'd like to keep it that way."

"Yes. But David has been brought in to turn it into a popular resort and recover some of the investment. I hope he fails. It is my home. My village, Xewkija, is just down the road. David will be in the bar at this time of day. He makes his daily selection about now."

Mifsud stood at the elbow of a handsome German blonde, one hand resting lightly on her arm. He was tall for a Maltese. Tall and lighter skinned, with a mop of curly black hair and piercing blue eyes, the ancestral residue of some Viking ancestor. Or a by-blow of a British sailor. He stopped smiling at the sight of Rafalo, said something to the girl, and came over to us.

"Hello, Frank. I'm flattered by your presence. What brings you to our humble hostelry?" His English was different, lacking even the hint of a Maltese intonation, almost upper class in its British inflection.

"David. Meet Dr. Alec Thompson."

"Dr. Thompson. What brings you to Gozo?"

"You."

"He's working for Purvis, David. On the hijacking."

"Not another one?" the Maltese said. "I've told the police and dozens of newsmen all I know, Dr. Thompson. You are wasting your time and mine. Why not have a drink on the house and meet some of our charming guests?"

"I'm not interested in what happened. I need some background. A feel for the terrorists. You saw more of them than anybody else."

"You work for Purvis?"

"Yes."

"Why doesn't he give up? Forget the whole thing? What does he want?"

"The terrorists' heads. Mounted on pikes."

The big man threw back his head and laughed. "That's good. I like that. And you are supposed to deliver them?"

"Something like that."

He looked me over. "You're wasting your time. But since you're here, I offer you the hospitality of my house. Frank and I have known each other for, what is it, Frank?"

"Thirty-five years. Since we were born."

"And how is my sister? Pregnant again?"

"Better that you should marry and have children than spend all your time with those German cows you like so much."

"Frank should have been a priest. God knows we have enough churches. Three hundred of them at last count. But come. The hotel has excellent Gozitan and Italian cuisine. I will tell you what I can."

The restaurant overlooked a stark and barren landscape of rock and scraggly fields leading down to the distant sea. "A hard and difficult land, Thompson," Mifsud said. "Nobody knows it better than Frank and I. We grew up here, fighting the rocks for a living. And we both escaped. He to the cops and I"—he grinned—"I to the good life. But we both come back. Right, Frank? There is something about the place that haunts you."

"Why did the terrorists insist that you bring the food?"

"They didn't. I volunteered. Nobody wanted to go near them. They're crazies. They don't operate by any logic we can grasp. I was the senior British Airways representative on the island. It was my job to get on board, try to protect the passengers."

"Describe the scene."

The waiter had brought a bottle of Corvo, a dry, white, slightly bitter Sicilian wine, and snails simmering in a thick butter sauce. "I hope you don't mind. I ordered a special meal. It's not often we have such distinguished guests as my brother-in-law." He tasted the wine and nodded, frowning as the waiter poured.

"Gozitans don't make good servants. I'm not sure why. They want the work. But they can't seem to learn the manners of good waiters. They lack that essential servility.

But you wish a description of the scene on the plane, Dr. Thompson. It was pure hell. The stench was unbelievable. A hundred and fifty people had been cooped up for more than thirty-six hours. There was the smell of excretion, sweat, and fear throughout the plane. A dead body was still crumpled against the forward bulkhead when I came aboard. Later they threw him off the plane onto the tarmac."

"How many hijackers were there?"

"Three men and two women that I saw. But there might have been more. I was allowed only into the forward section."

"Can you identify them?"

"The Germans made no attempt to hide their faces. The Arab wore a facecloth, a sort of scarf, most of the time. And the Irishman a stocking. The Germans I would recognize."

"How do you know he was Irish?"

"The accent. I worked with the Irish in London. They're an underclass, like us, you know. His accent was very distinctive. An Irish Catholic from Ulster. A dangerous man."

"Wohlgemuth?"

"He was usually in the cockpit with the captain. Quiet. Chilly. In control. Very much the leader. The older woman, what was her name?"

"Skorzeny."

"Yes. Very brutal. I saw her pistol-whip one of the male passengers who lifted his head."

"And the young woman?"

"Nervous. Clearly not of the same caliber as the others. She was close to tears during my last visit."

"What did you see?"

Mifsud shrugged. "Not much. The Jews and the Americans were crowded into the front of the plane, forced to sit in an open space between tourist and first class. The Arab swaggered among them, occasionally kicking one for no apparent reason. The others patrolled the aisles, shouting at the passengers to keep their heads down, not to look at them.

Some of the women left on board were sobbing. It was not a pretty sight."

"Did you see Dolores Sindona?"

"I remember her. She was a lovely young woman with that special something one cannot describe. A mixture of sensuality and delicacy. The Arab sensed it, too. He would stop and talk to her. She ignored him. Very brave. Also very stupid. It wounded his vanity. She might be alive today if she had been a little more humble."

The waiter brought a platter of the small Mediterranean red fish, broiled to a perfect crispness, and linguine in a delicate sauce flavored with capers. "As you see, our cuisine is as much a mixture as our race, Dr. Thompson."

"How did you pass the message?"

Mifsud stopped in the process of serving the fish. "I am continually amazed at the rudeness of the Anglo-Saxon. Here we are in my house, eating my food, drinking my wine, and you insult me."

"Hildegarde Bohnerth told the Egyptians before she died that you gave information to Skorzeny on the timing of the assault. When the floodlights were doused it meant the Egyptians would hit the plane in forty-five seconds. The terrorists were told to drop from the plane onto the tarmac and head for the security fence in the confusion of the attack."

"Yes," Mifsud said, voice hoarse with controlled fury. "I aided them, Thompson. And do you know why? Because of arrogant Anglo-Saxon imperialists like you who think they own the world. You Americans are worse than the British. One can sometimes forgive them because of their monumental stupidity. But you are not stupid. You know what you do, looting the world and living in bloated opulence on the theft. Yes, Thompson. We will kill you wherever and whenever we can."

I pushed the plate away and stood up. "Your name just got added to the list, Mifsud."

Rafalo followed me out of the restaurant into the parking

lot. "That was very foolish, Dr. Thompson. David is a dangerous man. Very proud. You should not have threatened him."

"I'm not interested in Mifsud. He's a small boy, a messenger. But he's probably got a way of contacting Wohlgemuth. I want the message out that we're tracking him."

"Yes. That is the way we hunt birds on the island. We move across the fields flushing them into flight."

"A regular British shoot."

"Not exactly. You see we don't shoot them. We drive them into nets. And sell them into captivity. There is no ferry back to Malta tonight. We will stay at the house of my cousin in Xaghra, a village in the center of the island."

The roads were deserted. Rafalo pushed the little Morris through the night, bouncing in and out of potholes, gradually climbing toward the lights of the mountain-top town. The road narrowed to a single lane between two- and three-story buildings built like fortresses. Ahead, outlined against the sky, a massive cathedral loomed. Suddenly, the lights of a truck turned a curve and headed toward us, gathering speed.

"Hang on," Rafalo said, voice suddenly urgent as he floored the little car's accelerator. We were closing with the truck in a rush when he ripped the wheel to the right, sliding the little car into a narrow opening, bouncing it off a massive stone wall, killing the engine. Behind us the truck slammed down the road, disappearing in the night.

"Looks as if I may have offended your brother-in-law."

Rafalo shook his head. "No, Dr. Thompson. He would not have moved on his own. He was acting under orders. You have flushed the birds. I hope your net is strong enough to hold them."

chapter 5

I caught a Lufthansa flight to Frankfurt the following morning and a Pan Am shuttle which got me to Berlin in the late afternoon. The airport was located in the French sector of the city, commanded by a French Air Force colonel. But except for an occasional gendarme in the rounded kepi and distinctive French policeman's uniform, it was a German operation. The British, French, and Americans had occupied the western sector of the city since 1945, there by right of conquest. The last vestige of the Second World War. A world preserved in amber forty years later. Across the wall built by East Germany to imprison its people in 1961, three hundred and fifty thousand Soviet combat troops were camped in position to attack across the exposed northern plain of Germany. Behind them, in Poland and the Soviet Union, another four million were poised. Against this was ranged a NATO Alliance outgunned two to one in men, tanks, artillery, and planes, its only defense the unreal threat of nuclear war.

Nobody believed that, in the event of a Soviet invasion, an

American president would retaliate with tactical nuclear weapons. If he were to do so, the scenario was inexorable. The Soviets would answer, all central Europe would be incinerated, and an exchange of intercontinental missiles would begin, resulting in the death of three hundred million Russians and Americans. Europe wasn't worth it. Nothing was. But the fiction of nuclear reprisal was maintained, since the Soviets could never be completely sure that the Americans wouldn't, as a last resort, do the unthinkable, as leaders had throughout history.

So the surrounded city was a tripwire for war, and its people knew it. They had lived on the front lines so long that the wall, with its obscene graffiti, guard towers, and barbed wire had receded into their subconscious. It was here, in an international pressure cooker, that Dolores Sindona had worked as a stringer for *Time* magazine while deciding what to do with her life.

By noon I'd checked into the Kempinski, a quietly elegant hostel just off the main street, the Kurfuerstendamm, and resisted the impulse to dive into bed. The Reuters office answered on the second ring. An upper-class female British voice came through with controlled arrogance.

"Trevor is out to lunch. He may not be back today. Who should I say called?"

"I need to see him urgently. Where can I find him?"

"I'm afraid I can't give you that information." Her voice had taken on a chilly edge.

"Look. Call him and tell him a representative of Dolores Sindona's father is at the Kempinski." I gave her my name and number and hung up. She had to know where he was. Or he'd call in soon. Correspondents in Berlin were never more than a half-hour away from the telex. I'd almost dropped off when the phone rang.

"Myles here."

"Alec Thompson. I'd like to talk to you about the hijacking. Today if possible."

"Who are you?"

"I work for old man Purvis. He's planning to dig out the hijackers and waste them. I'm the gravedigger."

There was a long silence on the other end of the line. Myles sounded as if he'd already had a couple. "I'm at the Paris Bar. It's near your hotel. Why don't you join me for lunch? Just ask the waiter for my table."

The Paris Bar was a typical artists', writers', and actors' hangout around the corner on Kantstrasse. It had a vaguely French feel to it, walls plastered with posters, modern art, antique lithographs, photographs of Berlin personalities, and old theater programs. I found Myles in a corner near the men's john, a bulbous glass of Schultheiss beer in front of him. He was a slim man in his early thirties with blow-dried blond hair, regular, slightly coarse features, and a sensual mouth, weak around the edges.

"Trevor Myles."

"Alec Thompson."

"So the old bastard is going to waste the killers, is he? What a crock." He finished his beer and signaled to the waiter. "What'll you have? Best beer in the world, German beer. Can't do a fucking thing else, but they make great beer."

"Beer."

He ordered in elegant, accentless German. "What do you want from me? A description of the bastards? I've given it twenty times. Or do you want to hear the gory details again?" He'd been drinking more than beer. A couple of empty vodka glasses were off to one side.

"Tell me how it started."

"They came on with the rest of us in Athens. It was a British Airways charter to Athens and Cairo. You know. A package deal. Three hundred and fifty people crammed into a 747, no room for your knees. When we got to Athens we scattered across Greece. Dolores and I went to the Peloponnesus. Rented a car and went from ruin to ruin, stopping off at a beach here and there for a couple of days. It was bloody marvelous." The waiter brought beers and an iced glass of Wyborowa for Myles.

"The airport was chaos when we got back. There must have been four hundred people on the plane. Mostly Germans, but some Egyptians and Israelis. The bloody Greeks just lost control."

"What happened?"

"The cops said the guns were smuggled on board by the cleaning staff. Two of them were new hires. They disappeared after the hijacking. Used phony identity documents. Brought the guns and grenades on hidden in the cleaning materials and stashed them behind the paneling in one of the johns. When the plane was in the air, the terrorists broke them out. The leader, this chap Wohlgemuth, and that nasty-looking broad of his went up to the pilot's compartment. A stewardess tried to stop him, and he broke her jaw with a pistol butt. They had grenades with the pins out, holding down the lever. He kicked in the door to the pilot's compartment and told him to head south over the Mediterranean."

"What was going on in the main cabin?"

"The Arab was in charge. A fucking certified maniac. He spoke French with the other two, but the girl was German. The one the Gypos killed. And that absolutely mad Irishman in the stocking mask. They spread out, holding those fucking grenades without the pins, Uzis hung around their necks. Told everybody to bend over, put their hands behind their heads. Anybody who was slow got a whack with a gun butt on the head. It's a technique, don't you know? Total mindless brutality. Terrorize everybody. Get them under psychological control. Destroy their self-respect. They were bloody good at it."

"Then what?"

"Dolores and I were up front. We had aisle seats across from each other. They had a seating plan and a computer printout of the passenger list. They went through the plane pulling people out and herding them up toward us. Americans mostly. People with Jewish names. Israelis." Myles stopped and picked up the vodka, turning the thick iced glass in his fingers, feeling the cold.

"Then what?"

"Huh? Oh, yeah. They made announcements. Nobody was to move. If everybody sat still, nobody would be hurt except the Israeli and American fascists who had robbed the Palestinians of their homeland and were provoking the Third World War. Some such shit. It went on for a while."

"What language?"

"English. With a German accent. Bloody stupid, really, since everybody on board was German except for the few they'd gathered up front and about sixty Egyptian workers and students who'd used the charter to go home on vacation. I think it was Wohlgemuth himself, speaking from the captain's cabin. Sounded as if he was on a real ego trip. Then the skipper came on, telling everybody to remain calm and do what they were told."

I waited as he downed the vodka. "They told us their demands. Release the four terrorists in German jails. Broadcast some sort of declaration on German television. Deliver a couple of million dollars in hundred-dollar bills. Safe haven. They knew they weren't going to get any of it, of course. It was a grandstand play. What they really wanted was publicity. Humiliate the European governments. Show their power. That's what the Arab said. He talked a lot."

"Describe the scene in detail."

"They had maybe twenty Americans, about half of them Jews or people with Jewish-sounding names and four Israelis, up front. They'd pulled Dolores and the others out of their seats and shoved them into an open area between what was normally first-class and tourist, made them all sit on the floor in the aisles. The Arab pushed one big American and the guy turned on him." Myles finished the vodka.

"The Arab put the pin back in the grenade, dropped it in his pocket, pulled a switchblade, and stabbed him. He didn't even hurry, just stuck it in his guts a little below the navel.

People started screaming, and he yanked out the grenade again and pulled the pin. He ordered us to shut up and do as we were told or we would all be dead."

"What happened to the man he stabbed?"

"He took about fifteen minutes to die. Crawled up against the door and tried to stop the blood with his hands. Then he shit his pants and croaked."

"What was Dolores doing?"

"She was in the aisle, hands on the back of her head, like all the others."

"And the rest of the people in the plane? A 747 is the size of a basketball court. Wasn't somebody organizing some resistance?"

"They had guns and grenades. What could anybody do?" He was looking into some private hell.

"And then?"

"We flew around the Mediterranean for a couple of hours. They kept trying to get somebody to let us land. Rome and Athens refused. Beirut and Cairo, too. Finally, the plane was running low on gas. We were close to Malta. The pilot said he was coming in, permission or not. If you want my view, they'd planned on Malta all along. The Maltese put gas trucks on the runway to keep us off, but they moved them when he started his approach. We barely made it. The runway wasn't long enough for 747s. The pilot blew some tires and burnt out the brakes stopping it. We were way down at the end of the airport, almost off the runway. A bunch of Maltese cops in jeeps came driving up and started talking to Wohlgemuth through the front door. They palavered for half an hour, and he finally agreed to let some people go. Then they couldn't find a gangway tall enough. A real balls-up. Took more than an hour to get something rigged up. Then the terrorists let old people and women with kids go first, maybe half the passengers." He paused and waved for another vodka.

"Did you ever think about jumping them?"

"With what? They had these live grenades with the pins

out. You jump them, the grenades detonate and kill everybody in range. It would have been suicide. Nobody gave it a thought. Anyway, it got better for a while. They let people go to the johns. The stewardesses even served some orange juice. It was almost relaxed. We were allowed to sit up. They dumped the dead body out the door onto the tarmac. Then it all started going bad.

"They wanted another plane and crew, and the Maltese wouldn't give it to them."

I had a minute-by-minute description of the hijack in my notes. Myles was a good reporter. He was following it line by line.

"They wanted to go to Tunis with fifty or so hostages. Only trouble was, with the tires blown the 747 couldn't take off, and it was blocking the runway. Also, nobody was willing to give them a plane."

"Our embassy was negotiating to bring in the Delta Force to take them out, but the Maltese wouldn't let us."

"Yeah." Myles stared at me. "So they brought in the Gypos. Crummy fucking incompetent raghead bastards."

"The plane was on the tarmac a long time before the attack."

"Yeah. Eighteen hours."

"A Maltese came on board bringing food. He worked for British Airways."

"Mifsud. The treacherous son-of-a-bitch. He was one of them. Embraced the Arab like a long-lost brother, he did, when he came aboard the first time. Gave them the police plans. I told the investigators later and they ignored me."

"Why?"

He shrugged. "The Maltese were scared shitless. Afraid of Qadaffi, of losing their forty-million-dollar subsidy."

"What happened then?"

"After a while they started killing people, one an hour. The Israeli girl first, the one who was pregnant. Her husband. The American sailor in civvies. A Jewish housewife from Brooklyn." He stopped, gulping down the vodka.

"And Dolores."

"Yeah." His unruly mop of dark blond hair was damp with sweat now. "Listen, mister. Does old man Purvis really think he can find these bastards and waste them?"

"He's betting a lot of money that he can."

"What about you? You think you can find them?"

"Yes."

"How?"

I stared at him as he reached for the empty vodka glass, frowning and putting it back on the table, finally meeting my eyes.

"You'll pass the word that you're out to get them and hope they come after you. That's why you're telling me. So I'll spread it around. It won't work, mister. They'll ignore you."

"Not if I can get close."

"They'll go to ground in the East and wait it out."

"I doubt it. Wohlgemuth sounds like a typical haughty kraut intellectual. He'll come out of his hole if he's provoked. Particularly when he realizes it's just one man. He's on a massive ego trip. Got nothing but contempt for the opposition."

"Maybe." Myles hesitated. Made up his mind. "There's a tape, you know."

"A tape?"

"Yeah. I had a high-fidelity miniature recorder on board. I started running it toward the end when things really got bad."

"That's not in the police file."

"I didn't show it to the cops. It's got some stuff with Dolores on it. I didn't want the goddamn media broadcasting it all over the fucking world. You understand?"

"Yes."

"If you want to, you can listen to it."

"When?"

"Now." He moved with the caution of a drunk as he weaved through the tables, exchanging greetings in three languages.

"*Bonjour,* Trevor. *Ça marche?*"

"*Oui. Et toi?*"

"*Servus,* Myles. *Wie gehts?*"

"*Nicht schlecht. Wo ist Erika?*"

"*Auf der Buehne. Sie probt.*"

"Hello, Trevor. What's with that bit you did on the mayor's visit to London? Is it really on or are you just flanneling?"

"It's on. Fest will announce it tomorrow. He's seeing the prime minister. Gonna protest all those British soldiers raping sweet young German virgins."

"Whores who didn't get their money, you mean." We stepped out in the street followed by a roar of laughter from the restaurant.

His apartment wasn't far, off Savignyplatz around the corner from his office, a third-floor walk-up with high ceilings and big windows, sparsely furnished with a leather couch, glass dining-room table with four director's chairs, a Hausa blanket on one wall and posters of a Hundertwasser exhibit on another. A wall of books completed the decorations. Through an open door, a girl rolled off the king-size bed and disappeared in a flicker of bare flesh.

"You want a drink?"

"Beer."

He came back with two bottles of Berliner Kindl and extracted a tape recorder the size of a cigarette package from behind a pile of magazines, running it fast-forward and back until he found what he wanted.

"They'd killed five people by this time. The passengers were getting hysterical."

"And still nobody thought about jumping them? I mean, the odds were thirty, forty to one. You could have overwhelmed them, lost maybe a couple of people."

The young Englishman stared at me, shaking his head. "You don't understand. They were only killing Americans and Jews. They made it seem like it didn't concern anybody else but the hijackers and the Yanks and Israelis. And, anyway, something had happened. You read about it, but you have to live through it to understand. We'd become dominated by them. There was a''—he groped for the word—''a kind of symbiosis, as if we were part of the whole thing. I can't describe it. Everybody was paralyzed.''

''Play the tape.''

It was remarkably clear of background noise.

''You're pretty, you know that?'' the voice said in British-accented English.''

''That's the Arab. He'd been needling Dolores for a couple of hours. Coming on to her. Once he'd grabbed her breast and she swung on him, sort of. Really pissed off the young German girl, the one the Gypos killed. At one point she screamed at him to cut it out.''

''And?''

''He slapped Dolores hard, six or eight times.''

He started the tape again. ''Leave me alone. Please leave me alone. Please.''

I shut it off. ''You sure you want to listen to this? Why don't you let me play it?''

''He took her into one of the johns. You could hear her whimpering, begging him to stop. Then she screamed. He brought her out finally, pushed her over to the door, put the 9mm to her head and blew half her skull off. The impact drove her out through the door and onto the runway.'' Myles got up and walked over to the bedroom, turning at the door. ''The autopsy showed that he sodomized her.''

I played the tape half a dozen times, memorizing the intonations and speech rhythms of the Arab. He had a distinctive accent in English, flawless grammar but with the peculiar intonation of one not wholly comfortable with the language. He sounded exactly like my Palestinian students at Santa Cruz.

I shut off the recorder, and a minute or so later the door to the bedroom opened and a slim, dark-haired girl dressed in a beige shift carrying a pair of sandals came in, walking with the coiled grace of an athlete. ''What's with Trevor? If he keeps getting blitzed before noon, he'll soon be on the street."

I introduced myself.

"Hallo. I'm Jenny Blanton." She had an Oxbridge accent to go with an air of careless arrogance. "Get that look off your face. It's not what you think. I knew Trev years ago in the, ah, biblical sense when he was at the Polytechnic and I was at Cambridge. We met at a conference that was supposed to bridge the gap between us and the plebes in the red-brick universities."

"It seems to have worked."

"Well, not really. I mean, we screwed each other and all that, but it never really took. He's frightfully defensive."

"Probably with some reason."

She had light green eyes in a small, heart-shaped face. Not much above five feet with one of those compact bodies small women sometimes have. "Oh, God, not another American egalitarian. What a bore. Dolores was one. I think that's why she liked Trev. Even with his British accent and European cool she could patronize him. Also he was weak. American women like weak men."

"She was probably sick of Texas cowboys."

"Are you a cowboy? Trevor thinks you may be some sort of spook. He said so before he passed out."

"You knew Dolores?"

"Yes. Met her with Trev in London once. She was a rich, supercilious, spoiled little bitch with a nice overlay of good manners. Frightfully intelligent, though, in that special American way. You know, full of facts and figures and all that rot."

I grinned at her.

"No, I'm not jealous. Bitchy, maybe, but not jealous. Poor Trev was never much good in bed, and now he's absolutely done in. I'm just holding his hand like a sister, as it were. Are you hungry? I'm starved. Perhaps you'd buy me lunch? I'm dead broke and you look awfully prosperous. But, then, all Americans are, aren't they?'' She was grinning at me.

''Sure.''

We went to an Italian place I knew off Kantstrasse. The Borbone. She ordered for both of us. A mixed salad, shrimp in a piquant sauce, and a bottle of Orvieto reserve.

''And what do you do, Dr. Thompson? I mean, how do you make the money to buy that fabulous blazer and all that goes with it?'' I'd re-outfitted myself after the successful operation of two years ago, throwing away an accumulation of Sears Roebuck clothes that had seen me through graduate school and seven years of teaching, replacing them at Huntsman's in London. The wardrobe and decaying French ruin were all I had left of a hundred thousand dollars.

''I'm a university professor.''

''Where?''

''Santa Cruz. In California.''

''South of San Francisco? In the heart of the dope country? You don't by any chance have any samples with you?'' She was older than she looked at first glance. Late twenties probably, the small laugh lines around her eyes beginning to deepen, a wariness showing beneath the bubble.

''No. What's your story?''

She shrugged. ''Double first in classics at Cambridge. No interest in teaching. Went to work as a gofer for a fashion photographer and found out I liked it. He trained me in the technical side.''

''And you turned out to be better than he was at it.''

''Yes.'' The bubbles were all gone now. She looked at me over the glass of faintly greenish wine, eyes meeting mine with a sort of flat, impersonal self-confidence.

''So you came to Berlin to rescue an old lover?''

She started to laugh, throwing back her head, revealing a lovely muscular neck. ''You've got to be kidding. What was it your Satchmo said? 'Never look back. Something may be gaining on you.' No. I came to do a fashion show for Lorenz

Boelke. He's the hottest thing in German punk fashions right now. I'm doing an ad campaign for him in Britain. Trevor just happened to be here, and I looked him up for old times' sake." She sipped the wine. "He's not my cup of tea anymore, however."

"Cowboys?"

"More like intellectual truck drivers. And you, Dr. Thompson? Married, I should say. Two children in a semi-detached. Wife works in the university library part-time. European vacation every third year. Doing some sort of paper on terrorists. Not averse to a little recreational sex if there's no risk involved. A little worried about AIDS."

"Trevor didn't tell you?"

"Yes. He said you'd been hired to find and, ah, terminate the people who killed Dolores."

"You don't believe it?"

"It sounds wildly romantic. And not a little silly."

The waiter bought two metal trays of snails and with them a tall, slim man in his mid-thirties in a Brooks Brothers pin-stripe, muted regimental tie, button-down shirt, and highly polished wingtips. His face was as conventional as his clothes. He sat down next to Jenny without being asked.

"Hello, Thompson."

"Mr. O'Brien, Miss Blanton."

"You want to go to the ladies' room, Miss Blanton?"

"No. What a vile suggestion. Who is this rude person, Alec?" Her voice had taken on a chilly patrician pitch, the syllables swallowed and coughed up again as if wrapped in cotton candy.

"An old acquaintance. What do you want, O'Brien?"

"We want you out of town. There is a car out front with two of our men in it. We've picked up your bag. I've got you booked on the four o'clock flight. You get up and you leave. Now. I'll pay your bill and send the lady on her way in a taxi."

Jenny Blanton stared at us and lifted her wineglass to take

a sip. "Who is this individual? And what on earth is he doing wearing a Horse Guards regimental tie?"

"Works for the U.S. mission here. He probably thinks the Horse Guards are racetrack policemen."

"He can't just throw you out of town like this, can he?"

"We run the town, Miss Blanton. We're the law here. And we don't want this treacherous son-of-a-bitch around. Up, Thompson, or do I call my men in to take you?"

I stood up. He was an inch or two taller and twenty pounds heavier, but he wasn't really expecting trouble. It was a public place. In Europe. People observe the forms. I drove a knee into his balls, not hard enough to break anything but enough to bend him over. Then I hit him behind the ear, taking my time. I was out of practice and killing him would really have been bad news. I eased him into the booth as three Italian waiters converged on me. A five-hundred-mark bill stopped them in their tracks. Jenny and I were led through the kitchen to the alley with firm but exquisite courtesy.

"Please do not return to my restaurant, Dr. Thompson," the manager said. "I cannot afford problems with the occupation authorities. We will deliver the gentleman to his friends outside when he recovers."

"Come on," Jenny said. "Let's get the hell out of here." She hailed a taxi and gave an address in Dahlem, a suburb in the American sector. "I've got a working flat I can hide you out in. Now suppose you tell me what this is all about."

"I got crossways of the U.S. authorities here two years ago. They don't want me soiling their turf again. The computer at the airport coughed up my name, and they came after me. O'Brien is a spook."

"What kind?"

"CIA. I thought I'd have time to talk to Myles and get out before they caught up with me."

"Why didn't you just go with him? I mean, you'd already seen Trevor. Why arouse the animals?"

"If I had, they would have shipped me out and forgotten the whole thing. This way O'Brien has got to think I'm a possible problem. The town is too sensitive for problems. So they'll mobilize the machinery. Reports will go out. The Brits and the French will be informed. When they realize I'm looking for the hijackers, fifty or sixty people will know about it. The Soviets have sure as hell got a mole somewhere who will get the information across the wall that I'm looking for Wohlgemuth, and they'll warn him."

"And that's what you want?"

"It's easier that way. When they find me, I find them."

"Why are you doing this?"

"Money."

"You could get yourself killed. You're an amateur, and these terrorists are professionals. They'll snuff you out like a match if they find you're getting close." She turned and looked out the back window of the taxi, scanning the cars behind us. "Or is there a team backing you up?"

"You sound like a pro yourself."

"I read a lot of bad novels. Here we are." The taxi had pulled up in front of an old mansion built before the First World War. A confused mixture of neoclassic and neorenaissance that worked, in a weird kind of way. It had six apartments on three floors and one big one up under the roof.

"Lorenz rented this for me as a studio." She led me up to the top floor, opening a door into an immense room enclosed by uncurtained floor-to-ceiling windows. "It was some sort of orangerie when they built the place. Perfect for a photographer's studio. Natural diffused light." A jumble of camera equipment rested on trestles against the wall. Fashion props were pushed into another corner.

"Why aren't you working?"

"Because Lorenz is an indecisive clown. I did a series on the first part of the collection, and all of a sudden when he sees the proofs he doesn't like his own stuff. He's reworking the designs." She grinned. "It's chaos. All fashion stories are, but this one is worse than usual. Also I'm broke because I've just outfitted a new studio in London, and he hasn't paid me yet. I should get well on this layout, though. His clothes are really hot right now. It'll mean more work than I can handle."

"He's the one whose models have green and orange crew cuts and the coats have shoulders two yards wide?"

"If you fornicated with a bear in the middle of the Kudamm you couldn't be more sacrilegious. Lorenz is at the cutting edge of the Zoom look. You know what he did the other day?"

"What?"

"There was a party at a rival designer's. Wolfenbeutel. He dresses one of his models in a sort of jean miniskirt, nothing else, paints her legs orange and her upper body electric green. Her hair is already purple. Bare boobs with black nipples. He paints himself lavender and puts on a silver tank top and nothing else except little Peter Pan boots. His genitals are fire-engine red."

"Sounds sensational."

"Actually it was a flop. Everybody's so used to him, they sort of yawned." She led me into the kitchen, piled high with dirty dishes and glasses, and rummaged through the refrigerator, coming up with half a pizza, the dregs of a Greek salad, a couple of pieces of ancient chicken, a wedge of rank Stilton, two apples, and a bottle of Sancerre. "Let's eat."

She wolfed down the remnants, wiping her mouth with a swatch of gauzy material and talking nonstop. "What are you going to do?"

"Go see a fellow I know here. Runs a bar off Savignyplatz. Scotty's Place."

She put down the chicken bones and stared at me. "The black guy? Married to the German woman?"

"You know him?"

"Trev took me there. It's around the corner from his office. A hangout for black soldiers."

"Yeah."

"How do you know Scotty?"

"We served in Vietnam together. He knows some people who are wired into the German crime scene. The terrorists have some connections with them, mostly with fences and people who handle hot money and dope."

"They work through cutouts, Alec. You'll never get to them that way."

"You know a lot about it."

"Just what I read in the *Daily Telegraph*."

"Anyway, it's a way to get the message through."

"Then what?"

"I wait."

"In Berlin?"

"For a while. Until they're on the scent. Then I'll move on."

"Where to?"

"Listen, thanks for taking me in. I'll go see Scotty about finding a place to go under. Maybe we can have dinner sometime in London?"

"If you live that long."

I found a taxi at Saargemuenderstrasse and Clayallee, at the corner of the walled ghetto which housed the U.S. mission to Berlin. Behind the barbed wire and armed guards, a six-thousand-man occupation army, now calling itself a "protective force," ruled West Berlin, in conjunction with similar French and British units, like a Roman army in ancient Gaul. Its three major generals were proconsuls whose word was law. Over the years a facade of local government had grown up with a ruling mayor and his twelve-man cabinet carrying on the day-to-day government of the city. But within each of the occupation complexes, Allied diplomats and military officers oversaw and approved all their actions, much as the politburo and its party apparatus in Eastern European countries rules over the governmental sector.

Scotty's place looked superficially pretty, much like any

other German bar. Massive wooden tables polished to a gleam, a big oak bar along one side. A tiny kitchen in the back serving sausage and sauerkraut, pigs' knuckles, Westphalian ham, goulash, and a few pork dishes. And barbecued ribs and cole slaw. There was one difference. The walls were covered with posters from the U.S. Over the bar a knock-off of the famous Steinberg drawing of New York showed Scotty's home state of South Carolina occupying nine-tenths of the United States with the rest in miniature around the edges. Next to it was a picture of Scotty in a confederate cavalry officer's uniform being greeted by a senatorial candidate once noted for his virulent racism and now a fervent supporter of black civil rights.

The bartender hadn't changed.

"Hello, Jason."

"What'll you have, Dr. Thompson?" Jason had dreadlocks and the bulging biceps of a bodybuilder. Like Scotty, he'd put in his twenty years, married a German girl, and stayed on in Berlin. He taught weight lifting part-time in a German yuppie gym where I had occasionally wrestled, and once in a while he gave a demonstration on television.

"Beer. Scotty around?"

"Naw. But some of your friends have been coming by regular."

"O'Brien?"

"Him. Couple of his studs. They ain't real friendly." He drew the beer the way the Germans do, slowly, watching the head rise to the top of the glass and sink before adding another dollop. It was real beer. Water, hops, sugar, and malt. No additives.

"Where can I find him?"

Jason polished the bar, which didn't need it, in that automatic gesture of bartenders and short-order cooks, circling his bulging forearm across the worn, gleaming wood.

"Man, why you don't leave Scotty alone? Every time you

come in here, we got trouble. Last time they almost close us down. If the general hadn't known Scotty in 'Nam, his ass woulda been grass."

"Scotty's a big boy, Jason."

"He's a romantic, Alec. An adolescent romantic living in the same dream world all you men inhabit." I looked over my shoulder and found Scotty's wife at my elbow.

Christa was about forty, tall, blond, blue-eyed, a little hard-edged, but with the classic beauty of a German woman of the nineteen twenties. I stood up and kissed her hand. She held it out like a countess, making me bend my back.

"Buy you a beer?"

"I drank my last beer in 1965," she said. "Give me a Perrier, Jason. What do you want with Scotty?"

"I need a place to stay for a couple of days. Some information."

"The town is full of hotels, Alec."

"And CID men."

"What have you done this time?"

"Nothing. Just looking around. How are things going?"

"The bank is booming." She worked as an accountant at the Deutsche Bank days and kept books for Scotty in the evening. They'd been married for fifteen years. I had the feeling he was still a little dazed. And Christa had what she wanted. "And the bar breaks even. Keeps Scotty busy. He should be back any minute."

He walked in as she spoke, a tall, elegant, café-au-lait man with that grace the French call being *bien dans sa peau*. "Hello, Loot." I'd been "loot" to Scotty since 'Nam. "Stickin' your head in the devil's lair again, huh?" He had big hands with the delicate grip of men who know their strength.

"Scotty. How's it going?"

"Can't complain. Government ain't stopped paying pensions, Christa's making out like a bandit, and the bar's doing real good. 'Course, John Henry ain't what he used to be, but you can't have everything, huh?"

Christa finished the miniature Perrier and got up to go, brushing Scotty's cheek with hers, moving against him as his hand slid down over her back and across her behind. He watched her go until the door closed behind her, took the beer Jason had drawn, and led me to a table in the corner.

"I was playing racketball with a guy from the JAG office." Scotty had spent his last two years as an MP attached to the Judge Advocate General's Office in the city. "He tells me you beat up O'Brien, and they got an all-points out on you. Man, you can get your ass in a crack without half trying. How come you pick that paleface to beat up? He's head spook here now. Real bad news, Loot."

"Is Xerxes around?"

"Naw. Got himself transferred. Head honcho in Paris, I heard. O'Brien's the main man. Spooks run things in Berlin. You ain't got no rabbi in this town anymore. What you onto anyway?"

I explained what Purvis wanted, leaving out the details of the hit team. Scotty whistled soundlessly. "Sounds like a real mean old redneck."

"He is. You know anybody with a line on the Brigade of the Fifteenth of January?"

Scotty shook his head. "You hear things here and there in this business. Like when they need money, they'll knock over a jewelry store and fence the merchandise. Mostly they like banks, though."

"Why?"

"Like ole Willie Sutton said, 'That's where the money is.' But the banks are marking the bills electronically now, taking numbers and running them through computers. These freaks knock over a bank, they have to launder the scratch through a money broker, guy who can sit on it for three, four, five years. He gets twenty, thirty percent for the service. Only thing is, they use cutouts. Associates, I think they call them. Not people who pull the jobs, but hangers-on. They're insulated real good, Loot. You gonna have a hard time getting close. Who you looking for?"

"Guy named Dieter Wohlgemuth. Born in Regensburg. According to the file, his mother and sister still live there. Only thing is they don't show up in the housing register."

"Yeah. People change their names."

"You know anybody in Regensburg who could nose around for me?"

"Money no object?"

"Within reason."

"Hey, Jason. Bring me the black book, will ya? And another beer for the Loot, here. You hear anything from your ex-wife?"

"Christmas cards. She's working on her first million."

Scotty whistled soundlessly. "Ain't no justice. Chick who looks like she does and brains, too. You scrambled up with somebody?"

"No."

He shook his head. "Time to be settlin' down, Loot. You gettin' a little long in the tooth be chasin' poontang all the time. Wears a man down. If you ain't careful, AIDS will getcha."

Jason brought the beer and a black looseleaf address book. "He's trouble, Scotty. We oughta kick his honky ass outta here. You gonna lose the license if you keep messin' with him."

"Jason don't like you," Scotty said, flipping through the book. "He thinks you're a bad influence on me."

"Here he is. Lothar Clemens. Ex-detective lieutenant. Knew him during that tour I spent in the CID here. He got in a fight with some of the local politicians. Some sort of corruption investigation. Got himself transferred down to the zone. Yeah. Here it is. Regensburg. He's retired there now. Got a private license. Does industrial security, insurance claims."

"Thanks. What about in town? Somebody who might fence for them. Sell guns. Provide local muscle."

"Lemme check around. Where you stayin'?"

"I'm not."

He nodded. "Go to the Hotel Bulgaria on Uhlandstrasse. Off the Kudamm. Ask for Guenter. Owes me one. He'll give you a room. Forget to register you. It's kind of noisy, what with the girls and their customers going in and out, but he's got protection. When I get something I'll give you a call."

chapter 6

I walked through town for twen[...]
bratwurst and a piece of black [...]
stands, washing it down with [...]
the city, soaking up the pa[...]
surrounded by a wall and thr[...]
Soviet troops, it had mainta[...]
humor and slightly degener[...]
famous in the nineteen-twen[...]

Guenter turned out to be an aging, [...] pot belly, pallid complexion, and a ci[...] the corner of his mouth. "Scotty called. I[...] marks a night. Three days. No more. You wan[...] sent up or a girl, call me." I paid him three days in ad[...] The room was minimal. An ancient double bed, chest o[...] drawers, and a bathroom dating from the previous century. I lay down to go over my options and went out like a light, jet lag catching me by surprise. Scotty's call pulled me out of it hours later. It was dark outside. Almost midnight.

He was talking over the background noise in the bar. Big Bill Broonzy came through behind him:

[...]teenth-century
The Zur Henne[...] [...]th stuffed boars' heads
[...] old soccer and rifle teams in
Germa[...]s of soldiers in World War One and Two
[...]; mirrors advertising beers not made since th[...]
twenties and a massive oak-and-marble bar with the lo[...]
brass handles used to pump beer up from barrels in[...]
cellar. The building abutted the wall, nestling in a cr[...]
niche of the twelve-foot-tall, graffiti-stained concret[...]
dividing the city. Its clientele, scattered over its t[...]
sitting around scarred wooden tables on ricke[...]
chairs, self-consciously bohemian in blue je[...]
jackets, and beards. You had to book a tab[...]
advance.

"Reservation?"

"No. I'm looking for Herr Mittenwa[...]"

"Is he expecting you?"

"No. Tell him Scotty sent me."

"Wait here, please."

I wandered over to the bar and[...]
the big glass stein fill with suds[...]
It was a ritual only a people w[...]
uses of time would put up w[...]

The waiter motioned to[...]
threaded my way through[...]
table set aside for regu[...]
Mittenwald looked lik[...]
hundred pounds, vir[...]
out of his should[...]
massive paw wit[...]

"Mittenwald[...]

"It's priva[...]

He had b[...]
examined[...]
Scotty. [...]
no?" [...]

"Y[...]

[...] yup[...]
[...]rde film [...]
[...]e, and quiche[...]

He motioned for his two bodyguards to leave and indicated a chair. "Well, what can I do for you?"

"I need information."

"What kind of information?"

"My employer's daughter was killed by terrorists on an airplane. The one in Malta. He intends to find the people who did it and eliminate them."

"Why do you come to me? I run a bar for young intellectuals. What would I know about such people?"

I sipped my beer. It was superb. Light and full-bodied at the same time, heavy with nourishment, lifeblood of the ancient Teuton warriors surging out of the dank northern forests into the Mediterranean light, battering the wine drinkers into submission. Only to be corrupted by them.

"I don't expect you to know anything. But you may have some friends who do. Somebody who wants to make some heavy money."

"How much?"

"Ten thousand."

"Dollars?"

I nodded.

"What do you want to know?"

"Where I can find Dieter Wohlgemuth."

"That is worth more than ten thousand dollars."

"That's a down payment. You come up with him and we'll deal."

"Who are you?"

"Just a friend of the family."

He heaved himself up from his chair. "Wait here. I must make a phone call." I sat with my back to the wall, taking an occasional sip of the beer, watching the handsome young men and pretty women pose like characters in nostalgic movies, cigarettes dangling from their fingers in archaic imitation of Bogart and Bacall. Europeans still haven't heard of lung cancer. Or cholesterol. Or maybe they just didn't care.

Mittenwald took his time. I ordered another beer and

listened to the conversation between a dark, hazel-eyed girl and a blond, bearded young Visigoth at the next table.

"Eric, I am not your property. You cannot treat me the way you do that BMW, polishing me every day and parking me in a heated garage when I'm not needed."

"What was he doing in your apartment?"

She shook her head in exasperation, looking over the crowd, bored. "I've told you four times. I'm doing the illustrations for his book on Berlin wit. We were going over some of the sketches."

"In your underwear?"

"I wasn't in my underwear. It was hot. I had on a summer robe."

"You had been screwing. I could smell it."

She had long straight hair, halfway down her back. She ran her hands through it now, combing it out. "Eric, you know something?"

"What?"

"You're a jealous fool. You're also beginning to bore me. Oh, there's Ursula. I'll be right back." She leapt up and weaved among the tables, taut behind rotating in skintight jeans, exchanging greetings and hugs here and there before dropping into a chair at a table full of clones across the way.

Mittenwald waddled back and sank into the heavy armchair at the end of the *Stammtisch*. "You are, how should I say, bad news, Dr. Thompson." I hadn't given him my name. "The Amis are looking for you. They have given the German police your picture. You are, how do they say in American gangster movies, hot?"

"Are you interested in the proposition?"

"I am always interested in money. Who is not? Only people who are bewildered. However, I am a known quantity here. A little dope, a few girls, a little fencing, some smuggling. You understand? I am respectable. I do not get rich, but I do not exaggerate. I cooperate with the police. They allow me to survive. How do you say, live and let live?"

"And I'm out of your league."

"You are dangerous. Much too dangerous for a small man like me. I must ask you to leave." I got up to go. "Oh, and, Dr. Thompson."

"Yes."

"I would not go back to the hotel. My informant tells me it is staked out by the police."

"How much for the beer?"

"On the house, Dr. Thompson. On the house. A business expense." He laughed a short, strangled chuckle, looking like a cross between Alfred Hitchcock and the wrestler Battling Barsky.

On the way out I went down the steep stairway to the cellar john, half a gallon of beer pressing heavy. As I finished, immersed in the usual graffiti offering various forms of anal and oral sex in three languages, the two bodyguards came in and leaned on either side of the door. The one on the left had the broken nose and crushed ears of an ex-boxer, scar tissue woven in clumps around his eyes and lips. It suddenly had the makings of a long night.

I dried my hands and turned toward them. There wasn't much point in delaying it any longer. I kicked the boxer in the balls, just missing putting him away as the toe of my loafer bounced off his inner thigh. It doubled him up, and I broke his nose again, smashing a knee into his face. It was a mistake. The unmarked one was the hard case. He caught me behind the ear with a stiff-armed karate chop as I turned, and spun me across the room up against the stalls, moving after me on the balls of his feet, swinging his shoulders. At two hundred or so, he outweighed me by thirty pounds, and there was no place to run. Behind him the boxer was methodically stuffing toilet paper up his nose to stop the bleeding. Outside, a third one was turning people away from the john. Politely.

I feinted with a left as the big guy came in, and he didn't even bother to block, moving his head a touch and smashing out with twisting straight-armed karate punches like pistons.

I slipped the left and he splintered the two-by-four framing the door to the stall behind me. My thumb found his left eye socket as I got inside, digging in and almost popping it loose before he bellowed with pain and flung me across the small room, bouncing me off the urinals. The boxer caught me on the first bounce, landing a right hook a little below the belt. After that it was downhill. I passed out in the middle of it, curled up on the floor as they kicked me methodically, avoiding my head, trying not to mark me.

It was getting light when I came to in the park across the street. Two young Turkish kids were going through my wallet, extracting the money, throwing it back to me, and taking off as they saw me move. I was surrounded by modernistic stone sculpture which served as a playground. The lights from the East German side, illuminating the killing ground between the two walls, cast a pale green glow over everything.

They'd been careful not to mark me up too much. One eye was almost closed, and my left arm was semi-paralyzed. A couple of ribs felt fractured, but they'd done a professional job. From neck to knee I was pulped. It took a while to get to my feet, but once I was moving, the pain merged into a steady, bearable kind of monotony. I walked six blocks to the U-Bahn stop across from Checkpoint Charlie and caught the train to Wittenbergplatz, changing there for Dahlem. Berlin subways use an honor system. You bought a ticket and punched it on the platform each time you rode. If an inspector caught you without one, you paid a fine. Nobody checked me, and I got off at Oskar Helene-Heim in Dahlem and walked through the lightening dawn to Jenny Blanton's apartment, leaning against the bell until a window on the top floor flipped open.

A tousled head appeared. "Who the hell is it?"

"Alec Thompson."

"Go away. My God. It's five o'clock in the morning."

I leaned against the bell, not moving. It took her a couple

of minutes. She opened the gate and stared at me. "Oh, shit. Can you make it upstairs?"

"Yeah."

She walked beside me, not offering to help as I pulled myself up on the heavy wooden banister.

"You need a doctor?"

"No. Nothing's broken. I just need a couple of hours. Do me a favor."

"What?"

I extracted a couple of Eurocheques and signed them. "Couple of kids rolled me. I need money. Can you cash these?"

"Sure. God, you're filthy. What did they do to you?"

"Stuffed me down a toilet, probably. Trying to bring me around, so they could have some more fun."

"Strip. I'll get your clothes cleaned. There's a place near here that will do it in a couple of hours. Get in the tub."

The water was cold when she shook me awake. I pulled myself erect, left arm functioning again. "Jesus Christ," she said, staring at the long, folded flesh of the old shrapnel wound winding up my back. "Where'd you get that?"

"Unfriendly natives."

She led me to her bed, a rumpled mass of pink sheets smelling of woman. "Get some sleep. I'll try to get back around noon with your clothes. I've got a meeting with Lorenz this morning. He's finally got the fucking collection ready. Here, take these."

The yellow pills wiped out the pain and enveloped me in a golden cloud. Weightless, I moved through disembodied space until the gold began to darken into blackness, and I was back in a familiar place. I'd been there three hundred times before, a hooch in a nameless village, the girl lying beside me, murmuring endearments in broken French, running her hands over my body, following them with her lips, feathers of indescribable delicacy, bringing me to the edge, stopping, smiling, enveloping me in her slim, muscular body, lying full length on top of me, hardly moving, gripping and releasing, prolonging, gasping little cries of half-pain, half-delight, small breasts thrust insistently in my mouth, the knife suddenly appearing in her hand, aimed at my throat.

"Alec, wake up." Jenny Blanton was shaking me, face hovering over me in alarm. "You were having a nightmare. It seemed to start as an Oriental wet dream and wind up in a snake pit," she said. "That's an impressive collection of scars. Vietnam?"

"Yeah."

"Bloody ridiculous war. Why did you fight in it?"

"I was drafted."

"Your clothes are hanging on the back of the chair. There's a razor in the bathroom. You can use my toothbrush unless you've got a vile disease." She caught my look. "You're wondering why I'm doing all this for you?" She grinned. "My mother always said that I could never resist a wounded animal. I always had birds with broken wings, mangled rabbits, and smashed cats recovering around the house. Typical Brit. To hell with people, but beware of damaging one of our four-footed friends."

"So I'm an honorary animal?"

"Something like that. There are two thousand marks in your wallet. I bought you a new tie." It was silk. Pink polka dots on a light blue background. "The one you had was in shreds. Also a shirt. So you're about a hundred marks short." She hesitated. "Are you going to tell me what happened?"

"I don't know."

"I beg your pardon?"

I told her of the meeting with Mittenwald.

"Why did they beat you up?"

"Warn me off. He may be in deeper with the brigade than just laundering money and fencing goods."

"What are you going to do now?"

"How about that lunch?"

She stared at me. "In a restaurant? Are you crazy? That spook O'Brien will have the town covered like a blanket."

"He wants me off his turf. I've done what I can here. I'd rather be somewhere with a little more running room. So we'll let him pick me up."

"Where will you go?"

"Regensburg."

"Regensburg? El touristo trapo. Why Regensburg?"

"Wohlgemuth's birthplace. His mother and sister still live there. I'll pay them a visit. Push him a little more. His psychological profile reads very macho. Maybe he'll get irritated and come after me. It's like seducing girls. You push all the buttons until you hit the one that works."

We drove to the French officers' club in her rented Peugeot convertible, top down, absorbing the pastel Teutonic early-summer sun. "You're driving on the left," I said as we headed for a bus which had veered off to the right to avoid us.

"Oh, shit," she said, wrenching the little car over to the right, almost wiping out a bicyclist. "Why can't these bloody continentals learn which side of the street to drive on?" She left behind a trail of enraged hornblowing Germans as she weaved through the midday traffic at high speed, squeezing the little car into tiny spaces, ignoring the stolid, disciplined traffic patterns of the natives, turning left into the deep forest where the French recreation area was located. The squat mass of the officers' club overlooked the Tegelersee, a glittering expanse of blue water flecked with sails like a Dufy painting.

Theoretically only members of the three allied powers could use the restaurant, the best in the city, but nobody ever asked for identification if you looked British, French, or American. I had used it for years on my research trips to the city. The headwaiter, a German, greeted us in impeccable French.

"Dr. Thompson. Delighted to see you again. The usual table?" He led us through the light, airy room to a spot by the window and pocketed his usual ten marks concealed in a handshake.

"How can you get in here?" Jenny asked.

"Easy. I bribe him."

We started with snails in the little white porcelain milk jars washed down with half a bottle of Puligny Montrachet and moved on to steak au poivre and a bottle of 1979 Pommard. The French army had expert wine buyers who got everything at cost. The room around us was filling up with graying French colonels, slim and dessicated Brits in Sam Browne belts and gaudy headgear, and a sprinkling of Americans in their drab uniforms. Seeded among them were civilians from the three powers and a few prominent Germans who had permission to use the place. Politicians, media, and cultural figures. An occasional actor.

Xerxes appeared with the coffee, a big man, running to fat, his stomach beginning to bulge, the jacket of his expensive British suit not quite closing across it. The headwaiter led him to our table, trailed by O'Brien.

"Hello, Thompson," he said, dropping into an empty chair. "You going to introduce the young lady?"

"Jenny Blanton, Frank Xerxes. He's a spy." She looked from one to the other of us.

"What's going on?"

"I think these gentlemen want a word with me. Maybe we could join you in the bar for a coffee in a few minutes?"

Xerxes heaved himself an inch off his chair as she got up to go.

"I thought we told you to stay out of this town, Thompson," he said as he watched her walk away. He lit a Gauloise as he spoke, the yellow stain of the cheap French tobacco spreading across his thumb and first two fingers.

"I thought you were in Paris."

He coughed a hacking smoker's cough. "Fucking things are going to kill me. What? Oh, yeah. I'm what you'd call the company's regional manager for Europe." He grinned, revealing blazing white teeth. Young and slim, he would have been handsome in a sleek Mediterranean way. Middle-aged and overweight, sweat showing through the armpits of his jacket, he looked like a retired NFL tackle gone to seed. Or a traveling salesman in ladies' lingerie. In fact, he was one of Langley's last enforcers, the old breed. Devious, paranoid, dispassionate, ruthless. The perfect spy.

"Thompson, you assaulted O'Brien. You realize we could throw you in the German slammer without charge and let you rot? *Untersuchungshaft*. Investigative custody. Krauts never heard of habeas corpus. They threw the guy who owns the *Spiegel,* the *Time* magazine of Germany, in jail back in the sixties for four months. Then they let him go without ever saying why they were holding him. We don't take kindly to having our agents battered by amateurs like you."

"We're even."

"What?"

I looked over at O'Brien. "You want to tell him?"

"Mittenwald's goons took him apart last night."

"What the fuck were you doing with Mittenwald?"

"Passing a message. I didn't know he was one of yours. Buster Brown here told him to have some fun with me."

"Fucking informer. Doubled and tripled. Useful slimeball." Xerxes said. "Makes sense. Going to him. He'll let one of Wohlgemuth's hangers-on know you're looking for him and why. Only the brigade is not stupid enough to fall for that. They'll lay low until you wear down. Ignore you. How much time did old Purvis give you?"

"All summer."

Xerxes shook his head. "He's wasting his money. We've been trying to make them for three years. Every time we get close, they fade into the East. The Soviets have major terrorist training camps in Moscow, Tashkent, Batumi, Odessa, Baku, and Simferopol."

"Simferopol?"

"Yeah. The major base for the Soviet Academy for Military Training, with special emphasis on military intelligence. They give them training in sabotage, kidnapping, explosives, you name it. In return they get KGB and GRU training in intelligence gathering and pass on anything they pick up. They go for rest and recreation and refresher courses to camps in the satellites. Pankow and Finsterwald in East Germany. Varna in Bulgaria. Karlovy Vary and Ostrava in Czechoslovakia. Place near Lake Balaton in Hungary."

"So if I get close they'll just fade away?"

"Yeah. Six months later, they'll resurface. Hijack a plane, rob a bank, kill some kraut industrialist, bomb a French department store. And it starts all over again. They've got a couple of hundred passive helpers. People who run errands and act as messengers. There's always a cutout. We've gotten close fifty, sixty times without making a hit."

"Infiltration?"

"We've tried it. They only take people they've known for years into what they call the front-line cell. Or they recruit for specific projects from other groups. Action Directe in France, the PLO or the Red Brigades in Italy, the PROVOS, ETA. Even some of the Latin groups. A new face is automatically suspicious. Also, a new member has got to make his bones."

"How?"

"Same way the Mafia does it. He hits somebody. We can't ask our people to kill an innocent man just to get on the inside."

"You haven't got a chance, Thompson," O'Brien said. "If we can't nail them with the assets at our disposal, how the hell do you expect to?"

I ignored him and ordered a Remy Martin. The kind in the clouded bottle that tastes like marinated money. "You got any objection to my trying?" I asked, turning to Xerxes.

He exchanged looks with O'Brien. "Here in Berlin, yes. It's too touchy. We can't afford to get crossways of the Soviets in this town. We operate under a tacit truce. Espionage is okay. No violence. We control our assets and they control theirs."

"What about that disco bombing?"

"Aberration. Bunch of Syrian crazies."

"I need twenty-four hours to clean things up here. Then I'll move on."

"Where?"

"Trailing them. Digging out family and friends. Putting together a mosaic."

Xerxes nodded. "This time we're on the same side, Thompson. I might be able to help you. But not in Berlin. I want you out of here. I'll pick you up at the girl's place at 7:15 tomorrow morning. We'll both be on the eight o'clock flight to Frankfurt." He lifted his big body out of the chair and stared down at me. "What makes you think you can pull it off when we can't?"

"You play by the rules."

chapter 7

Lorenz wants me to do a session on some new designs this afternoon. You want to watch?''

''Sure.'' We were standing in front of the French officers' club watching Xerxes' Mercedes disappear. There was nothing left to do in Berlin. On the way back to her apartment Jenny turned a few more German drivers into fear-crazed pulp, maneuvering the little French car in and out of the disciplined German traffic like a predatory fish. The big, airy room had been transformed. Two young Brits, slim and effeminate, were moving with the speed of light, setting up cameras, arranging lights and white canvas reflectors over a bordellolike set which occupied the center of the floor. A fire-engine-red fake leather couch was the centerpiece. Draped carelessly across its back was a Mexican serape straddled by an impossibly tall, emaciated young woman wearing some sort of filmy black teddy which kept sliding off her shoulder to reveal the pink tip of her left breast. She was drinking a diet Coke from a can and reading *Vogue*.

''Can't you hurry it up? This goddamn blanket scratches like hell.'' Two other models in black stockings, garter belts, wisps of white string bikinis, and brassieres leaving the nipples free sat cross-legged on the floor reading. One was eating an apple, wiping the juice from her lips with the back of her hand. Hovering over it all was a gray-haired man in a pink tank top and purple corduroy jeans, neck weighted down with gold chains, a large chunk of uncut jade dangling from his left ear.

"Well, thank you, dear, for deigning to show up," he said in a withering, faggoty voice. "Your assistants have been most helpful. Makes one wonder whether you're really necessary to this operation."

"Fuck off, Renzi. If you would quit dithering and get your act together we could have had the story done in three days. We have to get off the dime. I've got to take this circus to Paris in three days, or have you forgotten?"

"Of course I haven't forgotten, my dear. You're doing children's fashions with that disgusting homophobe Maurice. Be calm. We're virtually ready to shoot."

She looked over the scene. "What in God's name is this all about? Are we advertising clothes or a whorehouse?"

"My garments have already vastly improved the German birth rate, my dear. Women buy clothes to make men screw them." He spoke English with no trace of an accent. "The trouble with my competitors is that they've been listening to liberated lesbians who want women to buy clothes that turn men off. Also those half-assed sociologists who think women dress for women. Women say they dress for women. In fact, they dress to get screwed but don't want to admit it."

"You're a male chauvinist faggot, Renzi. But you may be right."

"Of course I'm right. Those stupid polls are useless. People always tell lies. My research shows that panty hose were a disaster. The garter belt is the single most erotic invention of the fashion trade since eye shadow. Not just any old rag to hold up your stockings, mind you. Stand up, Sheila." One of the models rose with a graceful dancer's movement and dropped into a pose, legs spread, hands on hips, pelvis thrust forward, a sullen, challenging look on her face.

"That's what turns men on. Not all that punk crap we're seeing."

Jenny stared at him and started to laugh. "Renzi, you're the one who invented punk. Your 1977 collection was the beginning of it. You took hot pants off the hookers and put them into society. And now you're saying it's crap?"

"My dear, genius is the ability to admit error. And spot trends, of course. Also everybody's closet is full of those vile clothes that nobody in her right mind is going to buy anymore. No, my dear. Punk is passé. Oh, the lower classes will continue with it for a couple of years, and I don't intend to give up my mass-market line yet. But old-fashioned perversion, with a modern touch, of course, is what people want now. It appeals to the new conservatism. The virgin courtesan. Discreet pedophilia. That's what will sell. Everybody's so jaded with promiscuity. Listen carefully. We're going to start with shockers."

"Jesus, Renzi. Let me off this fucking blanket. It scratches like hell."

"As soon as they get the lighting right, my dear. Patience. All in life is not champagne and screwing. Where was I? Oh, yes." He waltzed across the room and came back with a sketch book, rapidly flicking a black felt-tipped pen across the paper, outlines of conservative women's suits suddenly appearing one after the other.

"We start with the underwear. Lace, black and white, no other colors. Simple, elegant, immensely suggestive. Stark makeup. Georgette," he screamed above the babble of voices, and a small dark woman in a white smock appeared from one of the back rooms.

"How is the makeup coming?"

"Wilfrieda is almost finished. You want to see?" She turned and shouted for the model, who came out wearing a white wrapper stained with the drippings of makeup, her face a pale mask slashed by lipstick so purple it was almost black, eyebrows etched broadly, eyes made to slant in semi-Oriental mystery.

"She looks like the Dragon Lady."

"I beg your pardon?" The German designer moved on, ignoring Jenny's attempted explanation. "This is the shocker. We'll open the layout with Sheila like a fist in the face." I drifted over to the tiny kitchen looking for a beer as he sketched the scene for Jenny. They called him the Fassbaender of Fashion in Germany, after the homosexual drug-addict film director who had burned himself out at thirty-six and died of an overdose of heroin. He had made dozens of films portraying postwar Germany as a society suppurating with corruption.

Beginning a decade earlier, Lorenz had flamed across the European scene, first as a militant student demonstrator, artist of the absurd, and talented publicist with a flair for organization. He had turned to fashion after his so-called anal sculptures of toilet bowls and urinals had palled, and had been on the cutting edge of the industry ever since. Each new collection was more outrageous and popular than the one before. His success was fueled in equal measure by calculated extravagance and steely efficiency. Now a millionaire, he was a major backer of the radical Greens in their assault on Germany's conventional political parties. His antics garnered reams of publicity in magazines and on the tube and didn't hurt sales of his trendy clothes.

"You can't do it. It makes her look cheap."

"Sheila? Cheap? My dear, she could make almost as much selling herself in Frankfurt as she does as a model."

The girl looked up and frowned. "You think?" She had a lower-class British accent which sounded like Liverpool. "God, it would sure as hell be less work than this."

"The way the Brits do it, darling, it certainly would," one of the German girls said, grinning.

"Fuck you, Berthe. In ten years you'll be modeling as a stand-in for cows if you keep swilling beer and eating sausage."

"Stop talking, you two," the makeup artist screeched. "It will crack your maquillage." She moved from girl to girl with a soft towel to soak up the sweat which popped out in seconds under the lights.

They worked for six hours, repeating take after take, the big cameras clicking rapidly as each scene was set, Boelke compulsively meticulous, arranging the slivers of underwear to hint at, without actually revealing, the girls' genitalia.

"If you weren't such a raving faggot, Renzi, I'd accuse you of copping a feel," the English girl said as he pushed and pulled at her bikini panties to make them crawl up her crotch.

It was ten P.M. before they broke, everybody soaked with sweat, the models relaxing into deep exhaustion as the makeup woman cleaned their faces, revealing the starved anemia beneath. In jeans and tank tops, without makeup, they looked like normal young women, a little thinner, faces a little finer boned than most, nothing special. They skipped down the stairs chattering in a wild mixture of English, French, and German.

"When can I see the prints?" Boelke demanded.

"Tomorrow afternoon. Jess," Jenny called to one of her assistants. "Be here at six tomorrow. We should have some decent contacts by noon. How big do you want the blow-ups?" They discussed details, and Lorenz left with the two young assistants, arm around the shoulder of one, whispering in the ear of the other.

"Well?" Jenny asked.

"Impressive."

"Yeah. And a royal pain in the ass. But he's immensely talented. Even better, he's a fanatic for detail. Do me a favor?"

"Sure."

"Massage my neck and back. I'm cracking with tension."

She stripped off the man's T-shirt soaked with perspiration and stretched out on the red sofa. "Start with my neck." I dug my fingers into the lateral ridges, bunched with muscle, and worked down the back. "Where'd you get all the muscle?"

"Gymnastics. There was a big fad a few years ago. Remember? Olga Korbut and the Romanian. My mother made me. I also do a little karate here and there." She moaned. "Not so rough. Just rub me."

She moved in sudden sensuality beneath me. "Hey. You've got great hands. Where'd you learn to do that?"

"Vietnam."

She half-turned to face me. "I hear the girls are fantastic."

"It's a poor country run by men. The girls do what the men want."

"And you like that?"

"It's a novelty." I turned her over and began massaging her stomach, unbuttoning her jeans and running my hands up from the edge of her pubic hair to her throat, avoiding the small breasts, using my fingers the way the Vietnamese masseuses had.

She reached up and ran her hand over the bulge in my pants, isolating him, running her fingers up and down the edges. "I have an idea."

"What?"

"Why don't we take a shower?"

I followed a trail of underwear and jeans into the tiny bathroom, joining her under the steaming water. She pushed her short hair back and draped herself against me. "Jesus, you are a mass of scars," she said, running her hand along a welt down my left side and across my stomach, gripping me gently. "Come on," she said, jamming off the water and grabbing a towel, running it over me and herself alternately as I let my hands float over her body.

The bed was a huge circle in one corner of the studio. She pushed me down and leapt astride me, stroking my chest, entwining her fingers in the black hair. "You are a furry beast, Dr. Thompson," she said, stretching out full-length on top of me, lips moving along my jawline, down my neck and side, small muscular hands stroking me, mouth flicking across my stomach, taking him in her mouth gently.

Looking up at me, she said, "You come and I'll kill you."

I pulled her up and flipped her over on her back, feeling her writhe in protest beneath me, finally becoming quiet, grinning as I pinned her. "Foreplay later, huh?" she said, gasping as we moved together, her body reacting to every nuance, sensing when my control was slipping, stopping, moaning in little gasps as she came over and over, forcing me over on my back.

"Not so rough, love. Oh, yes, yes, yes. Now, love, now, now, now.

"Well, well, well," she said, leaning her elbows on my chest, holding him inside her with her thighs. "I really did underestimate you."

"Crude macho Yank? Wham, bam, thank you, ma'am?"

She fell asleep in my arms, exhausted, turning her back, nestling against me like a small, tired child. Next morning I slipped out of the immense bed and dressed quietly as she lay sleeping, entangled in the pink sheet.

Xerxes was waiting in the dark blue Mercedes 280 with German license plates. The driver got out and opened the door for me. Xerxes looked me over. "You seem to have recovered."

"Good makeup man. What have you got?"

He handed me a beige government folder. "Not a hell of a lot. The Maltese hijacking was their last known hit. It's been six months. They should be about ready to move again."

"How did they get out of Malta?"

"Libyan freighter. The *Al Ashram*. It was anchored in the harbor. A Maltese police van picked them up after they went over the airport security fence. The ship was moving out an hour and a half later. We should have expected it. The Libyans pick up the tab for about half the Maltese budget every year. They get consideration."

Xerxes lit a Gauloise and coughed. "A Polish LOT Airways flight flew them from Tripoli to Warsaw. We lost them then. They usually go to ground at a spa on Lake Balaton in Hungary. Keszthely. Play tennis, go on hikes, practice shooting, brush up on new explosives, polish their techniques. There's a training camp with all the latest gadgets nearby. Mock-ups of planes, banks, embassies. Everything laid out down to the last detail."

"So they could be anywhere?"

"Read the file. They follow a pretty rigid MO. Very German. Very disciplined. Solid preparation. Everything routinized. Even the variations are patterned. It's their one weakness. So far they've concentrated on banks, planes, and embassies, with an occasional sideline bombing or assassination."

"That really narrows it down."

Xerxes grinned. "Any one of ten thousand targets. But we're reasonably sure it will be a bank this time. The kitty must be getting low. The Malta operation cost a fortune."

"The Soviets don't finance them?"

Xerxes shook his head, lighting his third Gauloise as the Mercedes made the turn off the highway into Tegel Airport. "They get access to material, a place to go to ground, transport. But they pay for all of it. In valuta. And they've got to be getting short."

"Okay. A bank. There are thousands of them in Europe."

"Nobody ever said life was a bed of roses, Thompson. You've got a couple of hours with this file. Make no notes. I'll pick it up from you when we get to Frankfurt." The Mercedes dropped me off at the Pan American boarding gates and moved off, heading for a VIP area. The Allies had a monopoly on flights to Berlin, one of the rights the victors still enjoyed. Pan American, Air France, and British Airways were your only options. My flight to Frankfurt was on time for a change. I checked through the tough-looking German customs police and settled down to read the CIA file on Wohlgemuth and his band. He had begun serious operations as a gofer for the Venezuelan terrorist Illich Ramirez Sanchez, better known as Carlos the Jackal, in the early days following his gradual metamorphosis from a student activist and nonviolent demonstrator into full-blooded terrorism.

Wohlgemuth was in Vienna at the time of the kidnapping of the OPEC oil ministers, living in a small pension in Sievering, acting as outside man for the group. Carlos and his band had infiltrated the OPEC meeting area using false credentials and coldbloodedly gunned down three guards, one an aging Viennese policeman shot in the back as he ran toward an elevator. Gabrielle Kroecher-Tiedman, Carlos's deputy, had dropped him like a rabbit as he scuttled away. She had then walked calmly over to his body and put another bullet in his head from a 9mm Russian Makharov.

Wohlgemuth's first major independent action had been the kidnapping of a French Airbus which landed at Entebbe in July 1976. His luck held there, as it had ever since. He had left the plane to make contact with two Lebanese leaders of the hijacking when the Israeli rescue team hit the plane with its seventy-eight Jewish hostages. They killed all the hijackers in a surgical strike which still stands as a model for such operations. Quick, ruthless, brutal, giving no quarter, taking no prisoners. As the Israeli spokesman had pointed out, terrorist prisoners were an inconvenience. Better by far to execute them on the spot.

The rest of the file was a litany of bank robberies, kidnappings, murders of German politicians, and attacks on American military bases in Europe. All interspersed with rest periods at one of a series of safe havens in Eastern Europe or the Middle East. The members of the band fluctuated, only Wohlgemuth and Gudrun Skorzeny seemingly constituting the core. They recruited, as needed, members of the Japanese Rengo Sekigun, the Italian Red Brigades, France's Action Directe, and the Irish Provisional IRA. An endless stream of embittered young Palestinian gunmen came out of the Eastern European training centers, equally eager to bed down the aging female German terrorists as to kill capitalist western pigs.

Xerxes fell into step with me at the Frankfurt airport. He'd made the flight in a closed-off compartment next to the pilot's cabin. "What's your next move?" he asked as I passed the folder back to him.

"Regensburg. Wohlgemuth's mother and sister live there."

"Waste of time. He was cut off, driven out of the family a decade ago. His mother thinks he was responsible for the heart attack that killed his father." He glanced at me. "You're a hustler, Thompson. You know you can't pull this off. You're squeezing old Purvis for all you can get, and then you'll walk away from it, taking as much of his money as you can."

"Yeah, well, it was his idea. And there's no law against it." I watched him turn and move away, remarkably light on his feet for a big man. I stopped at the biggest of the car-rental agencies and drove off with a BMW sports coupe, a bomb on wheels, capable of hitting two hundred kilometers an hour and cornering like glue. Out on the autobahn I let it out gradually, getting the feel of the taut suspension, pickup, and gearshift, a little stiff from lack of use. I settled in at a hundred and seventy-five klicks and focused on the ribbon of road, clogged with cars hurtling along at the speed of light. Fat German burghers, stomachs pushed against the steering wheels of their Mercedes, cigars clamped between their teeth, hands at ten and two, drove with the fanatical efficiency of Fangios and the ruthlessness of a Panzer Group leader, flicking their lights imperiously to clear the track, tailgating to within inches when you reacted too slowly to their commands.

I was wrung out when I slowed for the Regensburg turnoff late in the afternoon. A beautiful medieval city, virtually untouched by war, it began as a Roman garrison town, Ratisbon, guarding the frontiers of the empire. Its dominance of the Danube waterway made it a major power in the Middle Ages, but its strategic and economic importance declined in the seventeenth, eighteenth, and nineteenth centuries, leaving its center almost undamaged by war or modernization. Today the former free imperial city is a tourist attraction and site of a large university, its narrow streets lined with picturesque fourteenth- and fifteenth-century buildings carefully preserved for the alien hordes who stream through it in the summer. It is a fairy-tale place in the failing pastel light of a German spring.

I parked in the narrow courtyard of a gasthaus just off Gesandtenstrasse, the main boulevard of the city. Der Rote Falke was pure German kitsch. A small reception desk fronted on a long hallway. On the left, a back door to the butcher shop which was part of the complex, farther along a massive modern kitchen, and to the right a big rectangular restaurant and bar decorated with the inevitable heads of dead deer and boar. A wall of beer mugs with the names of their owners occupied a third of the space behind the bar.

Lothar Clemens, the former cop, had recommended the place when I'd called from Berlin. The receptionist told me he was waiting for me in the bar. It was full of tourists. A table of American students in identical University of Colorado T-shirts drinking beer out of huge gray earthenware steins, a smaller group of older British tourists in the multicolored shirts Americans used to be laughed at for wearing, and assorted Germans in leather shorts and sandals wolfing down mountainous plates of pork, sausage, sauerkraut, and boiled potatoes.

"Herr Thompson?"

He was a small, wiry man, about five feet seven, all gray. Hair, eyes, skin, and suit. "I have a table in the corner." He glanced around. "My apologies, but I haven't been here in years. It used to be a quiet neighborhood bar. Now"—he shrugged—"the whole town is full of tourists in the summer. I recommend the beer, however. It's from a small brewery on the outskirts of town. Not the stuff they make in steel vats. And how is Scotty?"

"Well. Retired. Getting older."

Clemens nodded. "Yes. They forced me to retire three years ago at sixty-five. My wife died last year. My son lives in Hamburg. I am, how do you say, superfluous.'' He smiled, revealing gleaming false teeth.

''Scotty says you consult on security and do some insurance investigations.''

My beer came and we touched steins. ''Occasionally. More and more occasionally. In former times, Germans respected the experience of age. No more. We have been infected with the mania for youth. People blame you Americans, but I don't believe it. I think the war, machines, and the speed of modern life have tended to break down the old traditions. But I ramble like the old man I am becoming instead of getting down to business.''

''Have you had any success finding Wohlgemuth's mother and sister?''

He passed across a folded piece of paper. ''She lives at Schillerstrasse 18, a small house, with her daughter, Elizabeth. Both women changed their names to her maiden name, Hopf, after Wohlgemuth became notorious. She works as a pathologist at the Virchow Clinic. Her daughter is also a doctor. Gynecologist. Unmarried and unattached. The two women live quietly and have almost no friends. They travel once a year to Minorca, where they stay in one of those organized villages.''

''Club Med?''

''Something like that. Only more sedate. The daughter had an affair several years ago with a married colleague but broke it off when it became clear he would not leave his wife.''

''Politics?''

''No obvious affiliation. The daughter was part of the rebellious left at the university, but she has no record of violence.'' He hesitated. ''She's rather dim. A mouse.''

''The father?''

''Died of a heart attack in the early seventies. Brought on by a row with his son, apparently.''

''About what?''

''Politics, what else? The old man was a typical German

martinet. Joined the army at eighteen in 1938. Shifted to the Waffen SS in 1940. Fought the whole war in the Leibstandarte Adolf Hitler. Came out an obersturmbahnfuehrer. A major, I guess you would say."

"Prisoner?"

"Not him," Clemens said, muscular hand tightening around the beer stein. He was deceptive. Under the age wrinkles, his neck was thick with muscle. "He deserted at the end, submerged in East Germany, joined the Communist Party and was well on his way to becoming a big wheel when somebody recognized and denounced him in 1949. He got away a jump ahead of a one-way ticket to Siberia. Came west and joined one of his old SS comrades in an electrical repair business."

"His mother?"

Clemens consulted his notes. "Nothing much of interest. A typical bourgeois girl. Father killed in the war at Stalingrad. Mother remarried in 1950. Finished medical school. Began a promising career. Went to work. Met Wohlgemuth in 1949 when he came out of the East and married him almost immediately. An inappropriate marriage, but a woman in her age group was lucky to marry at all. Fifty percent of the men who were suitable died in the war." He looked up. "A fairly conventional history."

"When was Wohlgemuth last seen in Regensburg?"

"Nineteen eighty. He was already underground but the police weren't actively looking for him. He was still small fry. Came back in the spring to see his mother, and nobody has seen him since."

"Letters?"

"The police still watch his mother's mail. They've seen nothing from him. But, of course, there are other ways of getting letters. Through friends, or post office boxes. He wouldn't write them at home. Not with every antiterrorist force in Europe after him. There's a reward, did you know? Fifty thousand marks."

"Find him and it's yours. Plus another fifty."

Clemens whistled silently through his teeth. "Somebody wants him bad, huh?"

"The father of one of his victims."

"So that's what you are doing?" He looked me over, gray eyes focusing. "My apologies, Dr. Thompson. I'm losing my touch. I mistook you for someone, or something, else. When one is no longer in the business one's perceptions lose their sharpness. As to your offer, I do not particularly need the money, but I am offended by these privileged young people who believe they have all the answers to society's problems and have set out to terrorize and kill anyone who disagrees with them. Germany will disappear from the map of Europe if it is torn apart by another paroxysm of foggy political romanticism."

"So you think Wohlgemuth and people like him are a modern version of the Nazis?"

"Too simple, but with a grain of truth, Dr. Thompson. They believe in cosmic solutions, like Hitler, like Lenin, like all the star-gazing fanatics of history." He sipped the beer, staring across the room at the young Americans. "Look at them. Young savages, full of good humor and health and high spirits. Observe the expressions on the faces of the young Germans at the next table, the contempt and feelings of superiority they show." He shook his head. "In Germany one must be miserable to enjoy one's youth. Miserable, guilt-ridden, and full of fire in the belly to make over one's fellow man into some ideal of perfection. And if he resists, kill him. That is the German crime."

"Sort of a nation of cosmic *Besserwisser*." It was an expression in German meaning "knowing better than someone else." It carried with it the connotation of overwhelming pomposity.

"Exactly. But I bore you with my simple policeman's analyses, Dr. Thompson. I was never able to finish the university. The war. Prison camp. The bad years."

"Where were you?"

"Siberia. A place called Tobolsk. In the Imgyt marshes in Western Siberia."

"What did you do?"

"At first I worked with a hundred others on a kolkhoz, a giant farm. There were almost no men. They had either been killed in the war or deserted their families. We moved in with the women. There was no place else. The Russians wanted them to breed cannon fodder for the next war. Three of my children still live there. I help them as much as I can. I worked on the farm for seven years. The first winter was the worst. When we arrived in the fall, they told us to harvest the potatoes. Like good Germans, we organized into work battalions."

He grinned over the beer, shaking his head. "God, what pride we had. We cleaned the fields, working like demons, brushing off the dirt and eating the potatoes raw, like apples. At the end of the first day, we expected to be complimented, since we'd picked four times as many potatoes as the Russians on either side of us."

"And?"

He laughed, a dry chuckle. "The head of the work battalion screamed at us, red in the face, beside himself with fury."

"Why?"

"We had picked every potato. Everything would go to the Central Kolkhoz Station, and there was nothing left for the local collective to eat in the winter. The Russians picked only every other row, leaving the rest in the ground, digging them up over the winter and surviving on them. But you have been in a war, too, Dr. Thompson. In Vietnam with Scotty."

"Yes."

"A bad war. Like ours in some ways. Always looking over your shoulder, surrounded by hatred and fear."

"Where were you? Other than Russia."

"I was drafted in 1938. Into the infantry. Took part in the Polish campaign, France, Italy, then back to Russia. I was lucky. A bad wound"—he touched his side unconsciously. "Lost part of my liver. I'd been commissioned by then. A friend arranged a transfer to Paris in early 1943. I spent eighteen months on the staff there."

"How'd you wind up in Siberia?"

"Stupidity. I could have remained in Paris. I had French friends who would have hidden me until the resistance stopped killing Germans who surrendered. But like an obedient fool, I left. And wound up in Koenigsberg when the Russians surrounded it."

"How long were you a prisoner?"

"Eight years. I was lucky when I came back. In Berlin they needed French-speaking policemen. I rose to the rank of detective lieutenant and retired to an honorable old age."

"I'm going to call on Frau Hopf tomorrow. Once I do, Wohlgemuth is going to know I'm tracking him. I could use somebody to watch my back."

"I am an old man, Dr. Thompson. Of what use could I be to you?"

"Yeah. An old man with an expert rating in nine-millimeter automatics and a former instructor in unarmed hand-to-hand combat. You look like you stay in shape."

"I helped train the police recruits here until a few months ago. They released me for age." He grinned at me, false teeth glittering as they reflected the dim light of the bar. "It would give me pleasure to accompany you tomorrow."

"Have you got a weapon?"

"Yes."

"You realize these jerks would waste you without giving it a thought?"

"I am an old man, Dr. Thompson. I live in one room, am no longer allowed to eat and drink what I like, have no interest in women, and most of my friends are dead. What have I got to lose?"

chapter 8

Frieda Wohlgemuth lived in a sixteenth-century row house which listed slightly to the left, its dark brick stained by centuries of coal dust. An ancient Volkswagen in impeccable condition was parked with its right wheels up on the narrow sidewalk. Clemens knocked on the door sharply, sending reverberations through the old house. Only cops knocked on doors like that.

"Who is it?"

"Police."

The door opened a crack, revealing a pale, ravaged face, luminous light blue eyes leaping out of it, a remnant of youth. She glanced at the badge Clemens flipped open, not noticing that it was an honorary one issued to retired policemen, and unhooked the chain, standing back to allow us to enter.

"What do you want? Is it Dieter? He hasn't been here in years. Why don't you leave us alone? I've told you all I know."

"What is it, Mother?" The young woman was a replica of her mother, twenty years younger. Thin, almost desiccated, face beginning to show stress lines, dominated by the same brilliant blue eyes. "Tell them to go to hell," she said as she saw Clemens. "We don't have to talk to the police. We've done nothing."

"Your brother is wanted for murder," Clemens said. "For savagely executing unarmed hostages. We have reason to believe that he has been in communication with you. If he has, and you have not informed us, you can be arrested and tried as his accomplices."

The older woman held her hands interlaced in front of her, gripping the knuckles almost in an act of prayer, focusing on Clemens a look of pure hatred. Her daughter circled her thin shoulders with an arm. "What is it you want from us?"

"When did you last hear from your brother?"

"Two. No, three years ago. A postcard."

"Where from?"

"Kuwait, I think. Or perhaps it was Yemen. We tore it up and threw it away. He has caused us nothing but grief and misery since he was a student. We want nothing further to do with him. And he killed my husband," the woman said.

She stood aside and motioned us into a tiny sitting room crowded with heavy late-nineteenth-century sideboards and overstuffed furniture too large for the room, walls hung with copies of romantic paintings of thunderstorms and fake ruins by Caspar David Friedrich, every inch of space packed with porcelain figurines interspered with family photographs. The largest showed an imposing young man in an SS uniform, hat tilted at a cocky angle, ribbon of the Iron Cross folded at his neck, legs apart, fists on hips, boots polished to a high gloss.

I walked over and stared at the face, a younger, tougher version of Dieter Wohlgemuth. "His father," the woman said. "Dieter killed him."

"You exaggerate, Mother," the younger woman said.

"He killed him just as if he had pulled the trigger of one of those pistols he loved so much."

"What happened?" Clemens asked.

"He came home from the university in Berlin. It was

Easter 1973. There were student riots every day. Over Vietnam. Over nuclear weapons. Over American imperialism. He had hardly entered the door when his father began to scream at him. 'Canaille,' calling him a communist." The woman put her head in her hands, rocking back and forth. "Dieter screamed back at him, accusing him of being a petit bourgeois, a lackey of the fascist capitalist state."

"And?"

The younger woman replied. "They fought. My father slapped him, very hard, as he used to do when we were children. I can still hear the sound. Dieter grappled with him. They fell"—she indicated one of the heavy armoires. "My father was very strong, but he had a bad heart. He was pressing Dieter against the doors there, slapping him across the face, back and forth, when he suddenly turned pale and fell. He slid to the floor, his eyes still open." She turned away. "But you know all this. It's in the police files. Why do you persecute us? Who are you? This man"—she pointed at me—"he is not German."

"He is an American policeman. Many of the people your brother killed were American. One was a young woman like you."

Wohlgemuth's mother sat up suddenly, looking at us with dry eyes. "What is it that you want?"

"The letter," I said, taking a stab in the dark.

"Letter?"

"The letter he sent through a friend. We want it."

The older woman's already pale face drained of all color and she turned in panic to her daughter, whose eyes flickered for an instant toward an antique rolltop desk in the corner. Clemens caught the look and moved across the room, trying the closed top. He turned to the woman. "The key, please."

She shook her head, reaching for her daughter, terror squeezing her face. Clemens shrugged and extracted a heavy pocket knife, inserting it along the wood at the lock, working it back and forth, springing the ancient mechanism and pushing up the well-oiled wood. It took him a couple of minutes, the two women standing frozen in the small, dark, crowded room.

The envelope was postmarked Paris, the seventh arrondissement. April 12, 1987. No return address. There were two small handwritten sheets. Clemens handed them to me.

> Dearest Mother and Lisabet,
>
> All goes well with us. Gudrun was quite ill with appendicitis, but she was operated on two weeks ago, and is now feeling quite well.
>
> The last attack was a great success. We caused an immense international uproar. American television showed nothing else but our action for three days. The Jewish capitalist conspiracy was revealed for even the stupidist American to see. Even the Israeli-controlled media had to carry our message. They are terrified of us now. Soon support for the criminal Israeli state will begin to erode, and the European fascists will sicken of cooperating with their American masters. We will once again dominate our own house when they are thrown out. Then the revolution can finally begin for which we have all waited for so long.
>
> Our cooperation with our Moslem brothers will mean that Germany will have reestablished its historic ties with the Arab world. The symbiosis between Germany's fine technology, managerial genius, exceptional educational resources, and human potential will combine with the Moslem world's oil wealth to make us no longer need the mongrelized support of the arrogant American barbarians.
>
> I know the police are persecuting you. Be courageous. Especially Lisabet. Ignore the jibes of your colleagues. Their sons and daughters in the university will soon turn against their reactionary parents and will be with us. Never fear. It is inevitable. Logic is with us. We have captured the world's attention. We

are revealing the brutal, savage greed of the capitalist bastards who are oppressing us, and, soon, everyone, not just the intellectuals but the betrayed workers as well, seduced by the opium of consumerism, will awaken and join us in destroying the cynical blood-suckers.

I looked up from the letter at the two women standing like statues. "Does he really believe this? It reads like something written in the last century. German workers drive Mercedes and go on vacations to Sri Lanka. They're hardly proletarian revolutionaries."

"You Americans are such naive primitives," the young woman said. "Living in your silly dream world of unlimited opportunity, believing all that pap about freedom and democracy. You are manipulated by concentrations of capital that dictate to your government and rearm to destroy the progressive and peace-loving socialist countries. You sound like my idiot father. Ignorant, uneducated, a prisoner of his prejudices and his petty little hatreds and fears. Brutalized by his society until he had become a monster, beating us in frustration and torturing my poor mother"—she put her arm around the older woman protectively—"until Dieter finally killed him."

"Killed him?"

The two women's eyes met. "It doesn't matter now, Mother. If they find him they will shoot him down like an animal." She turned to face us, slim body rigid with suppressed rage. "Dieter had suffered beatings all his life from my father. When he came back from Berlin for the holidays, my father had beaten my mother as well. Her face was a mass of bruises. Dieter was furious. He had just spent six months in a special camp in Lebanon training to be a freedom fighter. He screamed at my father, who hit him." She stopped, luminous blue eyes circling the room, seeing the scene again. "He was strong, my father. A bull of a man.

We had always been terrified of him. Now Dieter fought back."

"How?" Clemens asked.

The girl shook her head. "I don't know. It was all so quick. He hit him in the throat, I think. And my father couldn't breathe. He stumbled across the room clawing at his neck, trying to get air. And then he died."

"The death certificate said he died of a stroke."

"Yes. Dieter had a friend. A lawyer." She was defiant now, the words coming in a rush. "A sympathizer. He arranged for a doctor in the movement to sign a false death certificate. There was no autopsy. My father had high blood pressure. We are a respectable family. There was no suspicion."

"Crushed larynx," Clemens said. "Probably no visible bruises. No reason for the police to become involved. Who is the lawyer?"

The two women were silent. I looked down at the envelope of the letter. It was addressed to a post office box. Clemens nodded imperceptibly and the girl caught the exchange and screamed at us. "Get out. Get out of our house. You have no right to harass us."

Outside, Clemens took out his pad and wrote down the number of the box. "I'll have to move quickly. The woman will warn him. It would be much more effective to take him by surprise." It took fifteen minutes, calling an old friend in the post-office security service. We sat in a nearby bar nursing Steinhager, Germany's answer to drinkable kerosene, until the call came through.

"Lothar? Franz here. The box is registered to Dr. Otto Skierka. He's a lawyer. His office is in his home. Goethestrasse 15, Apartment One. Ground floor. What's he done? Falsified an insurance policy?"

"Something like that. I owe you lunch at the Lindenmueller, Franz. Next week?"

"The Lindenmueller? My God. Retirement must be

lucrative. I will await your call. I expect a Beerenauslese, perhaps a Johannisburg, if this is on the expense account." Clemens hung up, frowning.

"Do you know the name?"

"Skierka? Yes. He's a radical. He had some connection with Wohlgemuth, but I forget the details." He shook his head. "My memory is not as good as it once was. It will come to me."

I told him what I knew of Wohlgemuth's jailbreak and Skierka's suspected complicity.

"Yes. Of course. I remember now."

"What's the matter, Lothar?"

"The family. Monsters, all of them." He shook his head. "Even after thirty-five years as a policeman I am always surprised at what you find when you lift the rocks."

"There's always a reason. If you grow up in postwar Germany with a brutal ex-SS man for a father, you're going to rebel. Or become a clone."

"Yes. You are right. That is the problem. These young terrorists think they are progressive. In fact, they are using the same techniques as the Nazis. The same justification. The ends justify the means. And hidden behind the verbiage of peace, ecology, and humanity is a glorification of the romantic German mission."

"It may even be simpler than that. In a modern industrialized society there is no room for the dreamer, the idealist, and the perfectionist. Your people are unwilling to settle for a high level of mediocrity. You go for the final five percent. And fuck it all up."

"*Plus ça change, plus c'est la même chose.*"

Dr. Otto Skierka regretted he could not see us immediately and gave us an appointment for the next afternoon at four P.M. "You realize the women will have already contacted him?"

"So why is he seeing us?"

"Taking your measure, probably. So he can report back to

Wohlgemuth." He glanced over at me. "You have an evening free in this lovely city, Dr. Thompson. What would you like to do?"

"I saw an advertisement for Wallenstein."

"Ah, yes. A superb production by a company from Munich." We had dinner at a cellar Weinstube and walked through the city to the classical theater, a gem of a building in seventeenth-century baroque, where Schiller's great drama of hubris and its tragic result was being shown. The Austrian nobleman struts across the stage in conflict with his emperor, spinning dreams of empire until, betrayed by his own men, he is stabbed by the Scottish mercenaries in his service.

"Well," Clemens asked, "what did you think of it?"

"Sensitive production."

"Yes. But a stupid play. It's inaccurate as history and makes this superstitious upstart general into a sort of moody heroic figure instead of the traitorous servant he was. All very German in his vaporous romanticism."

"You spent too long in France surrounded by their phony Cartesian logic. Bloodless elegance devoid of substance."

"Perhaps. But these people you are tracking grew up on this romantic nonsense. The French are fed on the cyncism of Molière and the British on Shakespeare's dark realism. You Americans have an instinct for the empirical. Germans enshrine misty sentimentalism and Visigothic heroics."

He bowed slightly as we parted at the gasthaus and disappeared down the ancient cobblestoned streets, walking very erect.

We met the following afternoon at Skierka's plush offices. They occupied a rebuilt medieval ironmonger's, a solid, squat brick structure on Ludwigstrasse. Silk wallpaper in muted beige patterns provided the backdrop for original Renaissance lithographs of the ancient city. His secretary was an athletic-looking woman with her bleached blond hair done up in a heavy braid, contrasting sharply with coal-black eyebrows and hazel-flecked brown eyes in a pointed face. She was confronting an IBM portable PC word processor as we entered, clearly intimidated.

"Yes?"

Clemens identified us. "Dr. Skierka will see you shortly," the woman said, returning to the computer's book of instructions. I walked over and stood beside her.

"I've got an identical machine. Perhaps I can help you?"

She looked up, eyes locking on mine. A woman in her early thirties with a taut figure encased in a dark green suit. "It's very difficult to understand the instructions. They use"—she made an impatient gesture.

"Code."

"Yes. Code. For example"—she typed a sentence on the screen. "I want to double-space, but it keeps telling me press 'Y.' Why should I press 'Y'?" We played with the machine for ten minutes as I tried to translate the IBM arcania into understandable German.

"You are really very kind," she said as the buzzer from the inner office sounded and Skierka's voice came through, inviting us in.

He was dressed in an expensive pinstriped three-piece suit, patterned blue silk handkerchief in his breast pocket matching his tie, thinning hair combed forward and around his ears, wire-rimmed glasses, a gold Piaget watch, and English wingtips shined to a glow. He remained seated, letting us stand.

"I hope you realize, Clemens, that you have endangered your pension with your actions yesterday. My clients can bring a court action against you for violation of your trust as a former state functionary. It is not excluded that you could be sent to prison."

He hadn't changed much in the five years since Wohlgemuth's spectacular jailbreak. Skierka had evaded prosecution for supplying him with the gun and had never looked back. After moving to Regensburg and setting up a law office, he had been elected to the federal parliament on the radical Green Party ticket and become a major political figure.

Clemens produced the letter from Wohlgemuth. "You are being used as a letter drop by the most dangerous terrorist in Germany, Herr Skierka. If you want to pick up the telephone and denounce me, please do so."

The lawyer ceased fiddling with his silver letter opener and motioned us to take seats. "What is it you want from me?"

"I've been hired by the father of one of Wohlgemuth's victims to locate him and set him up for execution. You are in contact with him. We want his address."

Skierka laughed. Not loud and it didn't go higher than his mouth. "And why would I do that? Assuming that I know where he is."

"A variety of reasons. You're respectable these days. On the verge of obtaining real power. If the Greens and the Socialists win in the next election you could wind up a cabinet minister. Your revolutionary days are behind you." I glanced around the opulent office. "You're obviously representing some large and powerful German industrial concerns who hire you as a form of insurance against being kidnapped by Wohlgemuth or others like him. You probably kick back some of the scratch to the brigade. But you're beginning to like the good life. Being fawned on. You wouldn't want it all to come tumbling down around your ears. Also, Wohlgemuth is increasingly an anachronism. Violent terrorism has probably had its day except in Lebanon. He's an embarrassment. Why not let us solve your problem? And if this isn't enough reason there's another one."

"And that is?"

"Purvis Oil Corporation is the thirteenth largest industrial complex in the world. Wilbur Purvis owns most of it. He could step on you like a bug, Herr Dr. Skierka, if he chose to do so."

The lawyer held the silver letter opener between his two

index fingers, hands very quiet. "So Purvis is behind this. We wondered who had hired you. What exactly does he want?"

"Wohlgemuth's head. His and the rest of the Brigade of the Fifteenth of January. Preferably mounted on pikes."

Skierka shook his head. "He won't get them."

"Why not?"

"First, because they are too clever. They've developed a body of expertise which is impressive. Second, they have access to virtually endless funds. Money buys protection, safe houses, corrupt policemen, and information. And third"—he threw the silver knife on the desk—"the Soviet Union finds them useful and offers a haven when things get too hot."

"You sound like you regret it."

"Your analysis is partially right, of course. Dieter and people like him were useful to the movement in its initial stages. As Lenin said, 'Terrorism is justified as long as it fulfills a political and revolutionary purpose.' The terrorists disrupted the stolid self-satisfaction of the German burgher. They set the scene for the Green movement to develop. They proved that a small minority, indeed a tiny one, could panic a bourgeois society, revealing its fundamental weakness and insecurity."

"Setting the stage for revolution?"

"Germany is not ready for revolution. The objective conditions do not yet exist. But they will come. Perhaps violence will again be useful."

"To push the democratic state into repressive measures in order to survive, eventually leading to a takeover of the government by totalitarian groups that in turn arouse the population to revolt by their brutal actions. Even you don't believe such theoretical nonsense."

"I see you have read Carlos Marighella's *Mini Manual for Guerrillas,* Dr. Thompson. Exactly. The classic final destruction of the bourgeois state through increasing levels of internal conflict is our goal. For such a scenario to work, we need economic recession, unemployment, and universal discontent. Given the anomalies of the capitalist system, we will eventually be able to provoke such conditions."

"And until then?"

"We work within the system, subverting, taking power with the Socialists, and through discipline, logic, and ruthlessness, eventually dominating the coalition. At the same time we will seed our sympathizers in key positions throughout the bureaucracy, the police, and the military."

"Where's Wohlgemuth?"

He shrugged. "In Paris, I assume. He doesn't give me an address. When he needs something he calls." Skierka glanced at his watch. "And now, gentlemen, I have another appointment. It was entertaining meeting with you. I will let Dieter know you intend to kill him. He will be amused." Skierka stood, not extending his hand, a slim, steely figure, short stature enhanced by cleverly concealed lifts in his heels, and led us to the door.

I stopped at the secretary's desk on the way out. "How's it going?"

She glanced up, brushing a lock of hair out of her eyes. "It's very simple really, once you get the hang of it. It's just"—she looked helpless—"I'm intimidated by machines."

"Me, too. I'm much more interested in your beautiful city. Perhaps you could recommend some things I should see?"

She looked me up and down then. Not exactly like a side of beef, but calculating what was in it for her. "There really is too much. I wouldn't know where to begin."

"Perhaps with dinner. At the Lindenmueller?"

She pushed back the errant curl of blond hair, hazel eyes meeting mine. She smiled. "Why not?"

"I'll pick you up here after work," I said, introducing myself. Her name was Annemarie Witzleben.

"Perhaps it would be better if we met at the Koepernick. It's a bar. Just down the street. At six."

Clemens turned to me on the street outside. "What do you expect to get out of her?"

"She's a mature young woman, pushing thirty-five, in a country with a critical shortage of men. If she works for Skierka she's bound to be to the left of Lenin. She may even know Wohlgemuth."

"So you ply her with wine, make love to her, and take advantage of her gratitude?" The golden late-afternoon sun reflected off his plastic teeth as he grinned.

"Best case. Worst case just the first two. In any event, we aren't doing so badly. Wohlgemuth mailed that letter in the seventh district. He's definitely in Paris. Foreigners have to register if they live in France for any length of time. Gudrun Skorzeny had an operation. There will be a record of all this on the ministry of interior and ministry of health computers. I need access. Can you arrange it?"

Clemens frowned. "It would cost money. I know a French functionary in the interior ministry. He worked with us during the occupation."

"A collaborator?"

Clemens smiled. "A survivor. Moderately corrupt. He always needed money and probably still does."

"We'll leave for Paris tomorrow morning. Not together. I'll drive via the Saar. I want to talk to Hildegarde Bohnerth's family.

Skierka worked late. It was almost six-thirty when I watched his chauffeur-driven Mercedes 300 pick him up and disappear into the evening traffic. She came out ten minutes later and strode across the narrow cobblestoned street with the arrogant self-possession of handsome women everywhere.

The Koepernick was a wood-paneled café and bar with an elegant graying pianist playing fifties ballads softly in one corner and waiters in dinner jackets moving discreetly through the German yuppie crowd.

"I used to come here with my husband," she said, joining me at a window table, ordering a scotch and water. "Only it was a student bar, then. We were all revolutionaries. Long hair, jeans, leather jackets, beards.'' Her lip curled with contempt. ''We learned it from you Americans, watching the civil rights riots in the sixties and the anti-Vietnam demonstrations in the seventies on television. Like parrots, we copied what we saw. Not really understanding it.''

''You sound bitter.''

''Wouldn't you be? The men went on to get their precious degrees, becoming lawyers, doctors, professors. Now they are driving Mercedes, buying ski chalets, and vacationing in Tibet. Marrying obedient vapid younger women. And we are bringing up their children in poverty.''

''Some aren't.''

''You mean Dieter and Gudrun? Yes. At least he's consistent. He was crazy then and he's crazy now.''

''You knew him well?''

''Well enough. He and Gudrun were different from the rest of us. Even Skierka was a dilettante. But they were genuine revolutionaries.'' She drank down the scotch, and I motioned to the waiter for a refill.

''You wouldn't be trying to get me tipsy, Dr. Thompson? Pump me for information?'' She looked amused. ''I should warn you that I could always drink most men under the table. It might be a costly evening for you.''

''My motives are thoroughly dishonorable.''

She laughed. ''All right. Then let's go to the Lindenmueller. I've always wanted to. But you're wasting your time if you think I can tell you anything even if I wanted to. Dr. Skierka keeps his revolutionary connections totally separate from his business.''

''But he told you why I visited him.''

''He dictated a note for the files. Dr. Skierka is very careful.'' She hesitated. ''And of course I told him of our rendezvous.''

''What was his reaction?''

''He told me to enjoy myself.''

She took my arm as we walked through the ancient streets

to the Alter Kornmarkt and climbed the worn stone steps of a fifteenth-century mansion to the Lindenmueller. Its vaulted dining room, lighted by ornate chandeliers, overlooked the medieval Romanesque tower which dominated the square. Gleaming crystal, fresh flowers, and crisp starched linen covered the tables. Ancient battle maps decorated the walls. Under one the legend proclaimed the defeat of Varus's Roman legions by Hermann the Cheruscan in A.D. 9, the first time a legion had lost its eagle. Another celebrated the defeat of the French at Sedan in 1871.

"What exactly are you after?" she asked after we had ordered two manzanillas and were studying menus the size of small blankets.

I explained for the fifth time the job Purvis had hired me to do.

"And you will kill him when you find him?"

"Somebody will."

She shivered slightly and sipped the golden wine, its bitter dryness reflecting the semi-desert of its southern Spanish origin. "If he doesn't get you or your friends first. They must be paying you very well."

"Enough."

We ordered. The menus were in French, mirroring the restaurant's eighteenth-century pretensions. Escargots and boeuf Stroganoff for her, crudités and a steak for me. A bottle of overpriced Pommerol '79.

"You understand," she said. "Dieter didn't start as a murderous fanatic. He was a rather gentle soul in the beginning, battered and browbeaten by that monster of a father. At first he was only a messenger boy for Baader-Meinhof. It was a sort of game for all of us. You know how Germans are. Romantics. Seekers after the holy grail. Then he met Gudrun." She finished the manzanilla and I ordered another.

"The female is more lethal than the male?"

"In this case, yes. Gudrun was, how can I describe her?

Serious. She wasn't interested in the men's interminable debates about the nuances of Maoism or Trotskyism. She wanted something simple. To kill the rich. Take over their factories. Establish socialism. And, above all, destroy the Americans."

"Any special reason?"

"Yes. She was illegitimate. Her mother worked on the American base in Wiesbaden." The woman's face twisted with rage as she spoke. "She slept with the soldiers. Became an unpaid whore. Gudrun had no idea which one was her father. But she hates all Americans with ferocity. There are many Germans like her. People who watched their parents grovel before the insolent, self-righteous conquerors."

"You, too?"

"No. But my husband. His uncle was the famous general, von Witzleben. If he had had the courage he would have been a terrorist as well. Almost all the members of the Red Brigades come from families brutalized by the Americans."

"Scratch a political fanatic and you almost always come up with a personal trauma. Che Guevara was beaten up by an American sailor in a Buenos Aires bar. He swore vengeance."

"Yes. But here it is more profound. We are all ridden with the guilt of our fathers. My whole generation resents being blamed for what they did. Especially since some of them are still in power."

"Who?"

"Helmut Schmidt and, of course, Richard von Weizacker, the federal president. They both spent six years in Hitler's armies. Von Weizacker was in the Kursk salient when his battalion leveled their 88s at a *kessel* containing three hundred thousand Russian prisoners and killed them all. And the murderous swine now gives pompous speeches telling Germans to accept their guilt. He, who defended his Nazi father from charges of war crimes at Nuremberg. A man who served as the highest-ranking official in the Nazi foreign ministry for ten years. It's obscene for his unctuous son to be preaching to us, who are innocent of anything except being born."

"So you rebelled."

"Yes. Unfortunately we cannot escape being Germans. So we lashed out at all the old traditions. Obedience, discipline, patriotism. Family. All authority was evil." She put her head back and laughed, beautiful face breaking through the mask of makeup. "And it was a lot of fun. You could sleep with anybody you felt like, stay up all night, throw rocks at the police. And everything was paid for by the state if you were a university student."

"What keeps Wohlgemuth going now when everybody else has made his peace with the system?"

"Power. He wants to rule. It was Gudrun in the beginning, pushing him, mocking, forcing him to be a man. Then, once he had killed, he got a taste for it. He was like a dog once it has copulated. Then all other dogs are his enemies. Also there was the excitement of risk and danger. It's like a drug once you start. You get hooked. But you wouldn't understand that, Dr. Thompson. You're a scholar, hidden away in your world of books. I suppose you avoided going to Vietnam like all the bourgeois in America, hiding out in the universities while the lower classes fought your dirty little war. Pretending to be idealists when you were really simply cowards."

"Brandy?"

"Of course. But first I must make some repairs." Her voice was slurred, and she swayed slightly as she threaded her way through the tables on the way to the john.

The room was full now, impeccably turned out older couples, middle-aged men with striking younger women, and a table of Japanese and German businessmen in dark suits getting politely blasted in a semi-private alcove.

Her hazel eyes were out of focus and her lips were slightly slack when we left an hour and three brandies later and caught a taxi to the large glass-and-concrete apartment block where she lived on the outskirts of town. In the elevator, she moved against me, arms circling my neck, mouth soft and frenetic, hips grinding against mine. We got off at the fourth floor.

I took the keys from her fumbling fingers, opening the door into a severely modern room, all glass and white leather, with a Beuys drawing on one wall and a copy of Warhol's Marilyn Monroe poster on the other. It was, like most German apartments, a combination living and dining room. A miniature kitchen gleaming with appliances looked out through a square service window.

"Come," she said, taking my hand and leading me into the bedroom. "I'll only be a minute."

She took ten. The room was a combination bedroom and study, the bed, neatly made, a fold-down sofa during the day. I went through the Rolodex file next to the phone, finding no names that spoke to me. The drawers were organized with ferocious neatness and efficiency, everything in its place.

She was a stunning creature in the dim light of the bedroom, big without being fat. And she was no longer blond. The heavy blond braids were gone. Her hair was cut close to her head, almost as short as a man's, black as her eyebrows. "How could I have deceived you into thinking I was blond?" she said, laughing and running her hands down over her flat stomach across the swelling pubic mound. "You didn't undress, *Liebling*. Here, I will help you."

She pulled off my coat and began to unbutton my shirt, hands moving down to my pants, unzipping, running her hand inside, stripping me.

"That's better," she said, suddenly shivering against me. "Hold me, please. I'm cold." I slipped into the bed beside her, feeling her body fit itself into mine, mouth moving along my neck in a gentle caress. "Just hold me. Do you mind? Don't be impatient. I haven't had a lover in two years. My son, you know. He's twelve now and in boarding school, but before that it was difficult. Children do not understand."

She lay against me, body gradually relaxing as I stroked

her back, running my hands through her hair. She pulled back a little, letting her fingers move over the mortar wound. "So you were in Vietnam? Why didn't you tell me?"

"Didn't seem important."

"It must have hurt."

"They give you drugs."

"Did you kill a lot of people?"

"No. I was in the supply corps. Got hit by accident."

"So you weren't a real soldier?"

"No."

"I'm glad. I would have trouble sleeping with someone who had killed poor innocent Vietnamese women and children."

I turned her on her back, running my mouth down her jawline and neck, over her breasts, and down her stomach. "Oh, my God. Don't do that." She moaned involuntarily, her body arching to meet the caress, then pulled me up and over her, opening herself, gripping me with big, muscular legs. "Let me do it," she said, holding me still against her, rotating her hips ever so slightly, stopping as she felt the excitement in me grow.

"Be calm, *Liebling*. Let me take my time." In a quick movement, she turned me over. "Be still," she commanded, giggling. "I will do the work." She was an expert, using her body like a machine to optimize her pleasure, sensing when my control was slipping, easing up just in time, beginning again, lips tight with concentration. Suddenly she slipped loose, body moving up over my chest until she was over my face, supporting herself against the wall with her hands. "Kiss her. Gently, lover, gently." She moaned as I stroked her thighs, and quivered as I ran my tongue lightly over her.

She slipped back down, face tense with strain, and reinserted him. "Kiss my breasts, Hard. Bite. Bite," she gasped, shuddering against me in a final spasm.

"The neighbors must be having a ball next door," I said as she collapsed in my arms, body still trembling.

"Was I loud?" she asked, laughing against my chest,

twining her fingers in the hair, nipping at my neck. "I'm very good, no?"

"Yes."

She lay on my chest, a fine film of perspiration covering her body. "So are you, *Liebling*. What a pity—" She broke off in midsentence.

"How do you mean?"

"Oh, nothing. Only that you will be leaving soon, no?"

"Tomorrow. But once this business is over, I could come back, if you like. Spend a week."

"You really think you will find him?"

"He's in Paris. Skierka knows where."

"And you want me to help you? Because we had a good time in bed?" She shook her head, smiling. "Americans are sentimental halfwits. Life doesn't work that way. It's true, I like you. But I wouldn't risk my job. Or getting killed to help you. In any case, I agree with Dieter and what he is doing. Germany and the West are corrupt."

"Think it over. Mr. Purvis will be extremely generous to anybody who assists us."

"God, it's true. You Americans are all such materialists," she said, turning on her side. I ran my hand along her stomach, stopping at the small scar I'd noticed earlier.

"Appendicitis," she said, out of bed now, slipping into a filmy blue silk nightgown. "You had better get dressed. I'd love to have you spend the night and have a reprise in the morning, but this is an apartment building full of bourgeois. It's all right to have a lover as long as he doesn't spend the night. Then you are a tramp. I'll make us coffee."

There were two of them. A slim, handsome young Arab with a toothbrush mustache decked out in a tight-fitting Pierre Cardin suit which made him look like a thirties Italian gangster, and a wild-looking character with the face of a hawk and a mop of curly black hair flecked with gray. Deep blue eyes, surrounded by laugh lines, stared out from under thick unkempt eyebrows.

"Sure and look at the lover boy," he said, a silenced twenty-two caliber Ruger zeroed in on my breastbone. "Be a doll, Gudrun, and run your hands over the lad to see whether he's holding a piece or not, that's a good girl."

She did a thorough job, moving up and down my legs, feeling my crotch, grinning up at me as she did, stepping back. "Nothing. But then he wouldn't be armed. He's an intellectual. A wimp."

"Well, what have you got to say for yourself, Dr. Thompson? Have a seat, man. Don't stand there trembling like a girl. Is it the weapon that bothers you? Sure, and Paddy O'Faolin was never one to frighten the lover boys." He slipped the gun inside the ancient blazer with gold buttons and the crest of Dublin's Landsdowne Rugby Club on its breast pocket, gesturing toward the white couch across from him.

"Now you'll be good enough to tell us all about yourself, lad, and how you planned to put us in our graves. You will, now, won't you? We'll be wanting to know who hired you, why, and just how it was you were going to do the dirty deed."

"Yes." The Arab leaned forward. "Tell us, Thompson. We are insulted, you see. That someone would send an incompetent such as you after us. It's like a bad joke. So tell us everything. If your memory slips"—he smiled—"we have here a marvelous mnemonic device invented by the French in Algeria. We call it Attila. It's similar to your cattle prod, the one you used on the blacks. Only much more powerful." He held up a thick baton with a metal tip. "When I ram this up your anal orifice and touch the button, you will go into orbit."

I sat down and glanced at the woman, who leaned against the wall, arms crossed under her breasts. "What happened to Skierka's secretary?"

"She took the day off," Gudrun Skorzeny said. "I played the part brilliantly, no? Poor little me, deserted by my callous husband. Bringing up my son alone." She started to laugh. "You accepted it all, panting after my body. Blinded by lust. God, men are fools."

"Are you going to make coffee?"

She looked inquiringly at the Irishman, who grinned. "Sure and the lad has spunk. By all means, make us coffee, Gudrun. Perhaps we will have him drink it through his nose. Now, Thompson." He stopped and frowned. "That name. Scots, is not? You're one of the Protestant scum the Sassenach chased out of the highlands, who landed in our fair land and polluted it, are you not?"

"I'm half Polish and a quarter Creek Indian. The other fourth is probably Scots Irish."

"Not Irish, me boy. Scots. There's no Irish in that tight-assed Pictish breed. They just landed on our lovely turf for a while and stole our land. But never fear, me boy. We'll soon be rid of them. Now tell us about the ones who'll be killing us."

"The team leader is Sam Hoffman," I said, naming a Green Beret I'd known in Vietnam who was now a dentist in Albany, New York. "He's got a mixed team of ex-German Bundesgrenzschuetz and Mossad specialists, four or five, I think. They're holed up somewhere in Austria. I've been given a telephone number to call once I locate Wohlgemuth. Then they'll stake him out and kill him. The touch will be made by a specialist from the States, probably with a sniper rifle if it can be done. If not, one of the team will knife him in a crowd. Or they'll blow his car."

"And you really think you can find Dieter?"

"I already have."

"How so?"

"I've found you. You know where he is. It's just a question of squeezing it out of you."

The Irishman's seamed face tightened with concentration. "Sure, and you're not precisely what you seem, are you, laddie?"

Gudrun Skorzeny came in with a tray of coffee cups and a white plastic cylindrical thermos jug of coffee and placed it between us. "Have your coffee," O'Faolin said. "Then Ibrahim will give you an exam using Attila to jog your memory."

I picked up the coffee canister and glanced at the Irishman, who was watching me, frowning. "Like some?"

"Sure, and I believe I will, Yank." He leaned forward and picked up a cup. "It's a cool one you are for a scholar."

I thumbed up the flip top on the plastic cylinder and threw the boiling contents in his face, following the motion of my arm, going over the coffee table, slamming him back in his chair, my elbow going for his throat, jerking the Ruger free from his belt and snapping a shot at the Arab, who did a quick back somersault and landed out of sight behind a couch. Gudrun Skorzeny had dropped to the floor, yanking loose the cord of the Bauhaus lamp, plunging the room into darkness. I moved for the door, ripping it open and rolling out into the corridor as an automatic pistol stitched holes in the wall above my head, coming up with a fix on the door, putting two shots through it to slow them down, then heading for the fire stairs, down three flights, and out into the street.

Clemens opened the door of his ancient Opel and waved me in. "The police are on their way here. I just picked up a call on the radio. A neighbor complained about shots. We've got to get out."

"Pity."

"Why do you say that?"

"Three of the four are up there. Everybody but Wohlgemuth. If the police weren't on their way, I might have been able to take a couple of them out. How come you followed me?"

"Something about the girl struck me as false. I went back to Skierka's office and talked to the concierge. She was a temporary, hired for the day. His secretary was sick. Then I remembered, she looked vaguely familiar."

"Gudrun Skorzeny."

"Yes. Your plan was almost too successful, my friend. You let them know where you were and what you planned to do. Skierka delayed seeing us for a day, allowing them to arrive here, look you over, and set up the hit. Gudrun took the secretary's place, and you played into their hands. What happened up there?"

I told him briefly.

"You are lucky to be alive."

"Stop for a minute." He pulled over and I wiped the Ruger clean before throwing it over a wall into a garden.

chapter 9

"You must leave Regensburg immediately, Alec. It's too dangerous to stay here."

"I could call in the team. Lay an ambush." We had met in a café on the Gesandtenstrasse for breakfast.

"No." Clemens carefully buttered one of the hard rolls the South Germans call *Semmel*. "They are not fools. Outside talent will be brought in to kill you. O'Faolin and the others have already gone to ground somewhere, reevaluating the situation. You are clearly too dangerous to be left running loose. The game has changed. It's you who are now being hunted."

"I doubt that they'll try to kill me."

"Why not?"

"They want the hit team. Identities. Location."

"Without you the hit team is toothless. No, my young friend, they will snuff you if you stay here. It is, how do you say, their turf? And a matter of honor and prestige. Go to Paris. That's where they are holed up. They cannot operate with the same confidence there."

"A level playing field? Okay. I'll be staying at the Hotel

Esmeralda on the Square Viviani in the fifth. That is, if you still want a piece of the action?''

"Yes."

"I'll book you a room. Once you get there, see if you can get your French ministry contact to check the hospital records for April. They must be computerized. It shouldn't be difficult. That's when Gudrun Skorzeny was operated on for appendicitis. Isolate any foreign women between twenty-five and thirty-five. She's probably using a fake German passport, but it could be Scandinavian."

"How do you know?"

"It's in the file. They have sympathizers in the German, Swedish, and Danish foreign offices who steal passports for them. I'm going to look up Hildegarde Bohnerth's family in Rastatt on the way to Paris. What have you been able to get me on her?"

"Very little. She was quite young. There is not much of a trail. She apparently joined the brigade only recently." He passed over a three-by-five card with scribbled notes. "Graduated with a teacher's certificate from Heidelberg, where she lived with an Arab medical student, Ibrahim Assad, from 1983 to 1985. Arrested for demonstrating against the emplacement of Pershing missiles and against your president's visit to the cemetery at Bitburg. Mother deceased. Father a high school teacher in Rastatt." There was an address.

"The Arab Assad. He's almost certainly the terrorist on the plane and in the apartment last night."

"You aren't sure?"

"No. Assad's picture was shown to the passengers, but they couldn't make positive identification. You know how it is. All ragheads look alike." Clemens looked pained.

I pulled into Rastatt in late afternoon. The small city is an ancient ducal capital of about thirty thousand near the French border, once a powerful regional force in pre-Wilhelmine Germany, long since reduced to living on its architectural treasures. These consisted primarily of a massive redstone palace built in the eighteenth century by a buccaneering duke known as Ludwig the Turk. I stopped at a gasthaus off the main street built in Ramada Inn plastic and bought a map of the town, locating the house of Hildegarde Bohnerth's father. It turned out to be a street of one-story cottages with small gardens, neatly fenced, flower bedecked, and immaculately kept. Little ceramic dwarfs guarded most of the enclosures. A man in his fifties was picking aphids off a rosebush at number twelve.

"Herr Bohnerth?"

"Yes?"

I introduced myself. "I'd like to talk to you about your daughter if I may."

He stood up, a tall, slim man with a slight pot belly, wearing the blue overalls of a workman. "My daughter? My daughter is dead."

"That's what I want to talk to you about."

"Who are you?"

"Another man's daughter died on that plane, shot in the back of the head," I said. "I represent her father."

A look of pain flitted across his face, dominated immediately. "The Sindona girl? Yes, of course. She must also have had a father. Curious, I never thought of it. Who are you and what do you want?"

"I'm trying to find Wohlgemuth and his group."

"To what purpose?"

"We plan to kill them."

He nodded. "Yes. I can understand that. When I heard of my daughter's senseless death, I was overcome with rage. It was such a stupid waste. If I could have gotten my hands on those Egyptian savages at that moment, I would gladly have strangled them. They tortured her to death as she lay wounded. Cold-bloodedly." He glanced down at his muscular hands and clenched them into fists. "However, everything passes. Vengeance is a useless emotion. In any event, I don't see how I can help you, even if I were prepared to."

"The Egyptians didn't kill your daughter. Wohlgemuth and his gang did."

"Yes. Of course, he's ultimately responsible for perverting her childish idealism. What do you want from me?"

"Can we talk?"

He stepped aside, opening the door to his house. "Forgive the disarray, Dr. Thompson. I am a man alone. My wife is dead also." The house was spotless. He stripped off his coveralls, revealing pinstriped trousers, shirt and tie, and slipped on a suit jacket. "I usually have a schnapps at this time of day. Made by a farmer I know out of apples and cherries. Perhaps you will join me?"

He poured the clear liquid into two tiny glasses and held it up in a formal, wordless toast. "Now, what is it you wish?"

"Tell me about your daughter. I need information. Anything that might lead me to Wohlgemuth and his group."

"She was a normal young woman, or so we thought. Very studious. She was kept from entering medical school by favoritism and prejudice against women. It made her a little bitter, perhaps, although not excessively so. She seemed happy to be preparing her teacher's credentials."

"Do you know Wohlgemuth or any of the others?"

"You have come to the wrong man, Dr. Thompson. I knew absolutely nothing of my daughter's activities until the German consul in Malta called to tell me she was dead and to offer assistance in returning her body. Until that moment I thought she was vacationing in southern France." He refilled our glasses. The clear alcohol had a deadly bite, leaving a faint whiff of cherries on the tongue.

"Did you know her friend, Ibrahim Assad?"

"Yes. Of course." He straightened in his chair. "Are you saying he is a terrorist?"

"We're not sure. He may have been on the plane with her. Tell me about him."

"She met Ibrahim in Heidelberg. He was studying medicine. A Palestinian refugee. I believe his father is also a doctor. They were driven out of Haifa in 1948. He grew up in the refugee camps." He shrugged. "What can I say? Hildegarde's mother was not happy with her choice, but we had brought her up to be nonracist, a good social democrat. And he was a cultivated young man. Very gentle. Superb manners. So we accepted him into the family. They planned to marry when he finished his studies."

"Did he speak much about politics?"

"The usual. You must understand. I oppose your country's imperialist foreign policies as did my daughter. Assad hated you for your support of Israel and your looting of the Arab world's oil through your multinational corporations. I must say I sympathized with the Arabs. That fat Israeli general"—he searched for a name.

"Sharon."

"Yes. He looks just like Goering. And acts like some Prussian junker. And the wars. It's a bit like you Americans slaughtering the Indians, isn't it? A modern industrial western state against an essentially medieval people?"

"Did Assad ever speak of terrorism?"

"Yes. I disapprove of it, of course, as I disapprove of any violence. Ibrahim explained why the Palestinians had no alternative. The Jews had taken their land and driven them into exile. Intruders. Strangers to the place for two thousand years. He didn't think of it as terrorism but as a resistance movement such as the French against the Germans in the Second World War."

"You seem to agree with him."

"I am a German. I feel great sympathy for the Jews. I admit to our guilt. My guilt, although I was too young to have taken part in the Nazi crimes. But two wrongs do not make a right."

"What about your daughter? How did she wind up with a gun in her hand on that plane in Malta?"

"You are insulting her memory."

"I'm trying to take a bunch of bloodthirsty fanatics out of circulation and keep them from repeating senseless massacres like this one. Do you want to help, Dr. Bohnerth? Or do you want the blood of more innocents on your hands? In addition to that of your daughter, of course."

"You are cruel, Dr. Thompson. What have I done to deserve this?"

"You're a mushhead. The type of idealist who is oblivious to reality. You want something to be true, therefore it is. And you brought your daughter up in the same sort of blind egotism which passes for idealism. Stubborn, stiff-necked, and self-righteous. Isn't that the way Heine described the Germans?" I quoted him the verse:

They walk about so stiltedly
So sprucely bolt upright
As though they've swallowed the whipping rod
That bloodied their backs last night

"And you regard these qualities as a virtue." I stood up. "Thanks for the schnapps."

He waved me back toward the chair. "Sit down, Dr. Thompson. Sit down. I do not necessarily agree with your, and Heine's, simplistic analysis either of me or the Germans. But I concede that Wohlgemuth and his gang must be stopped. What is it that you wish?"

"Tell me about your daughter. Sometimes seemingly unimportant details can be useful. I need a profile of her."

"She joined the Green Party last year. Over my protests, I might add. When her mother died, I lost what little control we had over her. After all, she was a woman, not a child. She could do as she wished. She was attracted to the Greens because they oppose American imperialism, spoiling the environment, and the materialist excesses of the German bourgeoisie. She did not recognize the dangers of their program, its lack of democracy, and their intolerance for the points of view of others." He refilled our little glasses.

"Why would she have joined Wohlgemuth's group? You obviously believe in nonviolence. What made her reject you?"

"The young seek solutions. They are impatient. In her eyes, Germany has become the mirror image of America. A nation of consumers. Lacking in ideals, a greedy society totally betraying the great innovative German thinkers who dreamed of making over the world into a gentle, disciplined, civilized place where people of goodwill could live out their lives in fulfillment and peace."

"I'm not sure what massacring innocent people on airplanes has to do with all that."

"The ends justify the means. As Marx said, 'Force is the midwife of an old society which is pregnant with a new one.' Thus terror in the service of revolution is justified. These young people think of themselves as soldiers in the service of a better world."

"Hitler thought the same thing."

Bohnerth shook his head. "No. He used evil means to seek evil ends. My daughter, and all leftist idealists, believe in the use of brutal means in the service of mankind. You can argue that they are wrong. But there is a difference, Dr. Thompson. There is a difference between cruelty as a means to a better world and simply as a tool for some dictator to enrich himself." He was getting a little drunk. The bottle of schnapps had diminished by a third. We were getting nowhere. I got up, feeling as if the cartilage in my left knee had begun to dissolve in the alcohol.

"Well, thanks, Dr. Bohnerth."

He stood, a tall, lost figure, gentle face set in a mask of pain, staring at a picture of his daughter on the mantelpiece. "She was a beautiful, gentle girl. I cannot believe she is gone." Tucked in the corner of the studio picture was a snapshot of a group of Arabs grinning into the camera, Hilegarde Bohnerth in the center. In the background, a banner proclaimed "Bienvenue Chez Shariff."

Next morning I dropped the car off at the Hertz affiliate and caught a train to Paris. The Hotel Esmeralda was located across the river from Notre Dame overlooking the Square Viviani and its twelfth-century church, St. Julien le Pauvre. The hotel, in a building not much younger than the church, was a narrow five-story edifice slanted back from the street, its fourteen rooms shabby cubicles favored by academics, students, and people who believed Fodor when he said you could see Europe on ten dollars a day. Its minuscule lobby was dominated by a romantic portrait of Victor Hugo's Esmeralda looking over her shoulder at a ghostly Quasimodo. A stack of backpacks filled up most of the reception area.

The owner, a troglodyte of Albanian extraction who vaguely resembled Dracula, greeted me in impenetrable French. His cauliflower ears marked him as a former professional wrestler. We'd worked out together in the same gym for a couple of months when I first came to Paris in the late seventies when he'd still been in the ring. He'd retired a few years before and married the widow who owned the hotel. I always stayed there when I was in Paris.

"Mathilde. Come. Alec has arrived." She was Marseillaise, about half his size, with a dark Mediterranean face suffused with sleepy sensuality. Her first husband had been a small-time pimp and gangster who had taken her out of a Toulon brothel and brought her to Paris. Ivo had replaced him after he bought the farm in a knife fight five or six years before.

She embraced me, kissing me on both cheeks. "*Tiens*, the professor begins to have gray in his hair. And how is your charming wife?"

"Divorced and rich."

"But of course. She was much too beautiful to waste herself with a poor professor. Women such as her do not remain poor, Alec. You are devastated, no?"

"No."

"You are a cold man. Like all Anglo-Saxons, you lack passion and romance. But that one was"—she grinned lewdly—"sitting on a fortune. She married a rich man, no?"

"No. She's in Washington. Runs a computer firm test-marketing cosmetics and other products for women. They just made her a partner. She's some sort of a genius with computers."

The Frenchwoman shook her head. "American women are fools. So much work when she could have it for nothing. And what are you doing in Paris?"

"Tracing down some members of the Charlemagne Division for an article on French fascism," I lied.

Mathilde's eyes arched. "The French SS? My mother told me about them. Some of her friends from the bordello went to Leningrad with them. And died there. When are you going to give up Nazis and do something a little more cheerful? Bordellos, for example. You could do the history of bordellos in France. Interview me, my mother, and grandmother. Perhaps makes some money."

"Four thousand three hundred and twelve young academics are already working on the subject. A recent dissertation dealt with the graffiti on the urinal walls of a fourteenth-century house of ill repute in Sarlat in the Dordogne. Another traced four thousand cases of syphilis in the eighteenth century to one active young lady in the Drome. Whole families became infected by her. He postulates that a miniature economic recession in the area was directly attributable to her activities and the resulting lost production and health-care costs."

"Well, I hope they are enjoying their research," she said, throwing back her head and laughing. "Priests and professors. Always the ones who tipped the least."

Ivo showed me to a fourth-floor room, the biggest in the hotel, with a view of the Square Viviani and Notre Dame across the river. A windowless bath lifted the price to twenty dollars a day. I hauled out the Paris telephone book and checked through the restaurant names. Chez Shariff was in the Rue Mouffetard, in the midst of a warren of streets in the triangle between the Boulevard St. Michel and the Boulevard St. Germain. A student quarter now shared with the Algerian underclass that cleaned the pissoirs of Paris and collected its garbage.

I cracked a bottle of Duque de Alba, sat in a broken-down overstuffed chair in front of the French window, propped my feet up on the iron railing, and soaked up the weakening spring sun, watching the shadows around the great church lengthen as it cast a golden glow over the ancient stones. Down below, in the square, a young American played the guitar and sang "Georgia on My Mind" in an uncanny imitation of Willie Nelson while a plump young blonde in jeans sat at his feet knitting, the coffee can between them ringing with an occasional contribution as the crowd surged around them. Students, arm-in-arm, stopped every few feet to grapple in embraces just short of copulation. Black, brown, and Oriental faces were salted with pale Vikings towering over the dusky stream. The French moved among them like mobile scenery, lugging briefcases and groceries, oblivious.

It was eight before Clemens knocked. He joined me at the window and accepted a glass of the mellow Spanish brandy, frowning slightly. "Too sweet. I prefer the dry bite of Hennessy."

"Any luck?"

He extracted a small red notebook from his shirt pocket and perched a pair of rimless glasses on his nose. "Madame Erika Ladenkampf, née Bokorny, Mainz, November 3, 1955, occupation teacher, French Residence Permit Number 1,232,403 Z, domiciled as subtenant Rue St. Antoine 108"—he looked up—"in the Marais near the Place de la Bastille. Operated on by the surgeon Martin de la Gard at the Salpetrière Hospital August 13, 1986, for acute appendicitis. No complications. Released on the fifth day after the operation. Next of kin, husband Hans Ladenkampf, teacher." Wetting his forefinger, he turned the page. "The apartment is in the name of Eliane de la Margerie, a professor at the Lycée Louis Le Grand, member of the

Communist Party. Arrested on seven occasions for disturbances of the public order. Released without charge. Activist in the Friedrich Engels Cell of the lycée. Thirty-five years old. Divorced. No children.'' Clemens looked up.

''She is the daughter of a famous family of diplomats and soldiers. Protestants, as are many French functionaries. Her uncle, with whom she lived after her father died, was ambassador to Peru and Venezuela. She is believed to have met and been influenced by Carlos Ramirez Sanchez while her uncle was stationed in Caracas.''

''Carlos the Jackal.''

''Yes.''

''Action Directe?''

''The police have no such proof though they suspect a connection. The apartment is clearly a false address. Wohlgemuth and Skorzeny do not live there, but the de la Margerie woman could certainly lead us to them. Do you want me to stake it out? There are several cafés close to the entrance. I can move from one to the other and keep her under surveillance.''

In the square below, two clochards were arguing violently near the church. Suddenly they assumed boxers' stances and danced around each other in a slow-motion caricature of a prize fight, throwing punches in slow motion that didn't quite land.

''You think it is too dangerous?''

''We don't want to spook them. Is there a hotel across the way? You could rent a room and watch them from there.''

Clemens nodded. ''Above one of the cafés. A pension. The Flandin.'' He folded his notebook. ''I will move there immediately. No point in paying for two rooms. Did you have any luck in Rastatt?''

''I'm not sure.'' I told him about Chez Shariff. ''It may lead to nothing. I'm going there for dinner tonight.''

''You want me as a backup?''

''No. I don't want us connected.''

Clemens obviously had not unpacked. He appeared below

five minutes later with a small cloth suitcase and walked across the square headed for the metro station, pausing to drop a coin in the singer's coffee can, gray figure merging with the evening crowd.

Graham De Crecy answered my call on the third ring.

"Yes?"

"Thompson."

"Welcome to the city of light, professor. Any luck?"

"Maybe." I outlined the plan.

"Sounds doable, old boy. Let's just hope for your sake they don't have any other ideas."

chapter 10

Chez Shariff was on Rue Mouffetard near the corner of Rue Epée de Bois, down four steps into a half-cellar, a typical North African bistro decorated with Bedouin blankets, a couple of camel saddles, wooden-handled Turkish coffeepots and a garish painting behind the bar of Boumedienne in desert dress. A beaded curtain blocked off a private dining room at the rear. I ordered couscous, a demi of Beaujolais Villages, and settled back to read the *Herald Tribune*. The Iraqis had fired an Exocet missile into a U.S. destroyer, killing thirty-seven sailors. Testimony in the Irangate hearings was bogging down in tedious details of schemes to support the contras, Gorbachev was visiting Romania, and a tornado had wiped out the town of Saragosa, Texas.

The clientele of Chez Shariff ranged from students of all ages and races to morose, solitary Frenchmen of indeterminate age and profession and occasional tourists. Tough-looking young Arabs would occasionally enter and disappear behind the beaded curtain at the rear.

The manager, a slim, middle-aged man with a shock of

gray hair and a pockmarked face, moved among the tables with a bottle of Raki, offering drinks on the house.

"Bonsoir, monsieur. Are you enjoying our couscous?"

"Yes. Excellent. Your place was recommended to me by a friend."

"Ah, really?" He was politely bored. "Yes, we are well known among a restricted circle. May I ask your friend's name?"

"Dieter Wohlgemuth."

He twisted the bottle deftly after filling the small glass to the rim, not spilling a drop of the colorless liquid, black eyes meeting mine. "Enjoy your *dégustif,* monsieur."

I gave him a half hour and left at eleven, taking a roundabout route back to the hotel, staying on the well-lit main boulevards, cutting over to the Rue Claude Bernard into Guy Lussac to the Boulevard St. Michel. They were good. Two of them in dark coveralls and running shoes. We moved together, separated by fifty yards, up the Rue Soufflot, past the Pantheon and into the Rue Clothilde. They closed in, then, under the walls of the Greek revival monument to France's heroes, separating slightly, moving in on me at an orthodox forty-five-degree angle, light reflecting off the blades.

De Crecy slipped out of the shadows as they tightened the triangle around me, curling an arm around the face of the one on the left, pulling his head back, cutting his throat as his scream died in blood. His companion spun in a half circle and crouched, confronting the Englishman. I hit him in the back of the neck with a straight right, hoping the roll of bronze ten franc pieces in my fist wouldn't break either my hand or his spine. He went down on his knees and De Crecy was on him, stuffing a handkerchief in his mouth and taping it shut, tossing me the roll of coarse medical tape to secure his hands. Malhe brought a blue Peugeot 505 alongside and we flipped him into the trunk. The whole thing took about fifteen seconds. We drove in silence through the city's back streets into the suburb of Neuilly, pulling up at a small two-story nineteenth-century pavilion whose carriage house had been converted into a garage.

"Costing Purvis a bloody fortune," De Crecy said, grinning. "But it's very private. Thick walls and a nice deep wine cellar to muffle this chap's screams." He was right. Steps led down off the kitchen into a combination wine cellar and storage area, empty racks on all four walls. Eric Malhe taped the Arab to a wooden chair and freed his mouth, fishing out De Crecy's handkerchief.

He was young, not much over twenty, with the startling blue eyes of the Bedouin in a handsome, aquiline face. "My God, he's lovely," De Crecy said in French. "What a pity." He shook his head regretfully. "Well, old boy, do you want to conduct the interview, or shall I?"

"Go ahead. Just try not to enjoy yourself too much."

"You understand me, Mohammed?" De Crecy asked.

The youth spat in his face, saliva dripping down the Englishman's cheek in a whitish glob. "Oh, I say. That's really not nice at all, old sod." He hit him, open-handed, methodically, the sound echoing through the cellar. Ten, fifteen, twenty times, until the youth's head rolled on his shoulders.

"Be careful. Don't kill him. They're delicate, these Arabs," Malhe said.

"Quit playing, De Crecy. We haven't got all night. They'll find that body soon and figure out we've got him. We've got maybe four or five hours to get Wohlgemuth's address out of him and make the hit. After that they'll be gone."

"The team is still in Scotland," Malhe said.

"Then we'll do it without them."

"Since when are you in charge of the mission?" De Crecy asked, watching the Arab recover.

"We get paid on results. When they find out we've taken these two, it could spook them into going to ground in Eastern Europe. Would you rather make the hit there or here?"

"You have a point, professor," De Crecy said. "Eric, be a darling and get Halloran on the line. Scramble it with that infernal machine. Tell him we may have to move tonight. He should get here as quickly as possible. There will be a fair mess to tidy up before we're through." He turned back to the Arab.

"And now to serious business," he said, lapsing into French. "You understand, Mohammed, that we don't really want to hurt you." The boy snapped his head away as De Crecy stroked his cheek. The Englishman laughed. "However, we simply must have Herr Wohlgemuth's address, and quickly. You can make it easy on yourself or you can force us to hurt you. Which will it be?" The young Arab stared at him impassively.

De Crecy turned to me, slim face pale under the bare bulb of the cellar. "Are you familiar with the psychology of torture, Thompson? No, of course not. Why should you be? The military are addicted to such crudities as cattle prods and dental drills." His French was excellent with only the slightest touch of a British intonation. "In fact torture is primarily a way of breaking your opponent's will rather than his body. Of course, the Chinese did have some rather exquisite purely physical techniques. The rat, for example, placed under a brass bowl on the subject's stomach with a fire built on top of the bowl. Sooner or later the wretched animal would begin to chew his way through living flesh to escape the heat. Our young friend here would probably be babbling if we had a rat and a brass bowl. Pity. I've always wanted to try it." He turned to the youth, whose light blue eyes were riveted on his face now.

"You are aware, Mohammed, that you are going to die? We will have to kill you once this is all over. So your choices are really rather limited. You can die quickly and humanely after giving us the information we need. Or you can die painfully and slowly, giving it eventually anyway. I realize it's not much of a choice. Of course"—he paused and looked at me—"perhaps we could arrange it so our young friend could live after all. Not quite the way he anticipated, but then, life is imperfect."

He jerked the young man's black silk shirt loose, undid his belt, and deftly pulled down the tight pants, raising his eyebrows appreciatively. "Charming. Really, the young ladies must regard you with favor, Mohammed." He held out his hand, twisted it slightly in a magician's turn, and the knife appeared, flicking open. "You are from the city, Mohammed, but perhaps you have seen sheep or camels castrated? You know the method? First you tie off the scrotum tightly to stop bleeding, then with a special curved knife you slice off the balls." De Crecy spread the youth's legs, holding them apart with his knee, and slipped the knife under his gonads, lifting them delicately with the blunt edge.

He let them drop, talking to me, ignoring the youth, whose face was damp with sweat. "You know the Arab culture, of course, Thompson. Without his manhood, this youth would be treated with the same casual contempt as a woman. In fact, he would automatically be used as a woman. With his beauty, initially at least, he could find himself a keeper, some aging pederast, to protect him. But the excess estrogen would soon erode his muscles, give him breasts. That taut muscular young ass would become flabby like an old woman's. Then he would have to sell himself to toothless old queens in the market." He spoke softly to the youth.

"You know you will talk once you've lost your balls, Mohammed. All your virility will be gone then. You'll be a woman. We'll break you easily then. Why not die with your manhood intact?" The youth snarled a guttural Arabic obscenity. De Crecy stooped and deftly extracted a lace from one of the Arab's shoes, wrapping it around each hand and pulling it tight. He slipped it around the scrotum, looped it, and pulled it tight in a sudden brutal gesture. The scream of agony tore through the dense air of the cellar as Malhe descended the stairs.

"Get on with it, De Crecy," the Pole said. "Quit getting your kicks. Halloran agrees. We have to go after them on our own or they might slip through our fingers. He'll be here sometime tomorrow. We're to move whenever we think we have to." The Arab was contorted with agony, body straining against the tape.

Malhe moved over and loosened the shoelace, stepping back, winking at De Crecy. "*Pauvre petit*. Betrayed by his own people and yet still willing to die to protect them."

The Arab looked up at him. "What? What did you say?"

"They sold you to us, *petit*. Your own people. How did you think we knew you were going to attack Thompson? Somebody had to tell us, no? To set you up for us."

Confusion fought with pain behind the youth's eyes. "Why?"

Malhe shrugged. "Who knows? Perhaps because the Germans have become too dangerous. Too crazy. Also they will not follow discipline. They are arrogant. When your leader realized we had been hired to kill them, it was perfect. We would solve his problem as well. But betrayal is dangerous. If the Germans found out and we failed to eliminate them"—he drew a hand across his throat. "So you're the sheep, *petit*. They sacrificed you. If things go badly, they can say we forced you to tell them where the Germans are." De Crecy stepped forward and tied the lace again, drawing it tight, listening to the scream. Again, Malhe released it, pushing the Englishman away.

"There is no need to die for your betrayers, *petit*. We will kill them, then come back and release you. And you can take your revenge."

"I don't know where the Germans are. They deal through Ibrahim."

"Assad?"

The young Arab nodded.

"Where is he?" Malhe hunkered down in front of the youth, his slavic face open with sympathy. "Tell us, *petit*.

Your leader has betrayed you. And to protect these foreigners. You were the sacrifice.'' De Crecy wound the lace around his hands again.

He gave us the address then. Eighteen Rue de Sevigné. ''It's in the Marais. Near the Place des Vosges.''

Malhe looked at De Crecy, who nodded. ''We'll have to take the risk that he's not lying, Thompson. We must move quickly. They may already have missed this boy.'' Malhe stepped behind the youth, caught his head in a modified full nelson, and snapped his neck with a quick twist. He cut the tape and tore it from his arms and legs, lifting the body effortlessly onto his shoulders.

De Crecy unlocked a cabinet in the front hall of the house and handed me a silenced 9mm Beretta with an extra clip. A small arsenal of pistols, submachine guns, and explosive devices was arranged with military neatness.

''How many do you expect?''

''One. Two at most. They split up when they're not working. Contact each other through cutouts.''

Malhe took the Peugeot and we followed in a Citroën, an old rebuilt DS-19, winding through the deserted streets to the Bois de Boulogne, empty except for the occasional whore who had still not made her quota. The Pole pulled over on a deserted stretch of road and dumped the Arab's body onto the pavement. De Crecy put the big Citroën in gear and drove over it, grimacing. ''What a pity. One does not see a specimen like him very often.''

The Rue de Sevigné was located in one of the city's oldest quarters. Number eighteen was a two-story fifteenth-century building with a faded sign over two huge wooden doors advertising ''Charbon.'' A smaller door was cut into one of the two big ones, and Malhe went to work on it with a small crowbar, deftly springing the ancient lock. The door opened onto a dark passage which ended in a cobblestoned courtyard. On the left, a spiked iron fence set off a ruin that might once have been the house of the owner of the coal yard, which extended some fifty feet back to a large warehouse. A

"You're pretty, you know that?" I said, standing in front of the Arab. He frowned, puzzled.

"Repeat it."

He shrugged. "You're pretty, you know that?" It was the voice from the tape, the same silken insolence, the same intonation. He remembered then, dark eyes narrowing momentarily, fear flickering in the depths.

"He's a pro," De Crecy said. "It will take hours to break him. Shall we try the woman first?"

"Sure."

"Well?" De Crecy said to the woman, a once-handsome blonde in her late thirties, twenty pounds overweight, beginning to sag, the marks of alcohol and drugs marking her face.

"Well, what? What the hell are you doing breaking into my studio in the middle of the night?"

"We're looking for his friends."

"What friends? He doesn't have any. You've made some sort of a mistake." She glanced at Assad, who had picked up a metal drafting ruler and was twiddling it in his fingers. "He's a medical student. Broke. With no place to stay. I picked him up in a bar a month ago. What do you want with him?"

"The Germans," De Crecy said. "Where are they?"

"What Germans? I don't know any Germans. And neither does he. You've got the wrong man."

I showed her a photograph, slightly blurred, taken with a telephoto lens of Assad looking out the pilot's compartment of the hijacked plane. It was the only picture of him without the stocking mask. She stared at it. "Where was this taken?"

"On a hijacked airliner in Malta last year. He'd just thrown the body of an American girl with a bullet in her skull out onto the tarmac."

"I don't believe it." She looked at Assad, who was balancing the metal ruler on his forefinger.

"How long have you known him?"

"A month. Six weeks maybe."

"Where did you meet him?"

"In a café. Over in the sixth. He bought me a drink. The last thing he ever bought me." She looked defensive. "I usually avoid Arabs. They're nothing but trouble. But he was different. He spoke English like an American. And he bought the drinks, that evening anyway." She looked from one to the other of us. "I need a man now and then. It's not easy for a woman alone in this city. When you're twenty you have to fight them off. Now"—she shrugged letting it die.

"Is he living here?"

"I suggested it. He was"—she stared at the photograph lying on the table—"gentle and kind."

"And good in bed," De Crecy said.

"What would a faggot like you know about that?"

I stopped De Crecy as his hand flicked toward her face. "We're looking for his friends." I described Wohlgemuth and Skorzeny.

She shook her head. "I've never seen them. He usually took me to Arab places. I never met any Germans with him."

"Chez Shariff?"

Her eyes flickered. "No. I've never heard of it."

"You really must not lie to us, darling," De Crecy said, slapping her across the cheek and jaw with the barrel of the Beretta, leaving a red welt. She spun out of the chair onto the floor. Things began to come apart then. The telephone started ringing and, as Malhe's eyes momentarily turned toward it, Assad jammed the metal ruler through the fluorescent bulb into a socket, blowing a fuse, plunging the brightly lit room into darkness.

The Palestinian lashed out with his right arm, hand held like a blade, catching the Pole on the temple, smashing him back against the wall. Assad moved in a crouch through the statuary as De Crecy fired at his weaving figure, the silenced Beretta's guttural cough counterpoint to the bullets ricocheting off the iron sculptures.

"No, don't kill him!" the woman screamed, throwing herself in the line of fire, taking a slug in her throat just as Assad, outlined against the dim light of the sky, crashed through the glass, body in a tuck to avoid the splinters. The dark in the courtyard was impenetrable as I looked down. There was no movement.

"Eric, you fucking incompetent," De Crecy said quietly. "We'll pay for this one." The Pole sat up, back against the wall, eyes glazed.

I picked up the phone, which had continued to ring.

"Ibrahim?"

"Yes."

"Dieter here. Listen. This American Purvis has sent after us has gotten his hands on Mustafa. He will crack. We're moving now. You can reach us through Eliane. You'd better get out of there quickly. He's becoming a nuisance. We'll have to eliminate him before the next action."

"Yes."

"Ibrahim?"

"Yes." There was a silence on the other end. The phone suddenly went dead.

"Wohlgemuth?"

"Yeah."

"Shall we wait for him?"

"He won't come. He made me on the phone."

"Then we'd better get the hell out of here. He'll alert the police."

"We've got to clean the place up. Make sure there are no prints. Nothing we can be traced to." I did a methodical search as Malhe and De Crecy checked out the apartment. For a supposedly poverty-stricken Arab he dressed superbly in Pierre Cardin suits and handmade Italian loafers. His wallet showed the BMW registered to one Addul Hassan. He had a Tunisian passport in the same name. The spiral notebook was tucked away on top of the wardrobe. It was full of sketches and notations in Arabic.

As we came into the courtyard, Malhe touched my arm

and pointed toward the iron fence in front of what had once been the owner's house. Ibrahim Assad was impaled by the throat on one of the iron spikes, his body twisted in death.

"Well, well. The gods do work in mysterious ways. One down and three to go."

Malhe quickly inserted the silenced Beretta in the dead Arab's hand and fired two shots into the night sky, letting the weapon fall to the pavement.

"That won't fool anybody."

"Perhaps not. But police are the same the world over. Give them an excuse to solve a crime easily and they will take it. In any case, who cares about an American tramp artist and a destitute Palestinian?"

chapter 11

"So you fucked it up."

"Yeah. But the trigger man is dead. That ought to make old Purvis happy."

"He wants them all. If you'd kept the slope alive, we could have wrapped it up in a couple of days."

"He's a nut."

"De Crecy?"

"Yeah. He enjoys his work too much. Remember those kooks in 'Nam who liked it?"

Halloran tasted the beer. "Fuckin' French suds taste like weak horse piss. Yeah. I remember them. Get you killed if you stood near them. What the fuck you expect me to do? Hire boy scouts? Sure he's playing about five cards short of a full deck. People who go around killing other people for money are generally a quart low. So what do we do now?"

"I've got another lead. May not amount to much. Have you seen this?" I pushed the morning edition of the Paris *Herald Tribune* across the table opened to page three. The headline read: "Suspected Terrorist Found Dead."

"Yeah. Story says they think there was a shootout among

rival groups. Somebody wasted him and made it look like suicide. So what's wrong with that? We're in the clear."

"The French politicians have a deal, Mike. They leave these guys alone as long as they don't pull anything in France. It's a gentlemen's agreement. We're a wild card. The cops here don't like wild cards. Chances are there will be an anonymous phone call giving them some information."

"Yeah. And they know who you are." He grinned suddenly. "Well, amigo, looks as if life could become kind of interesting for you. You want I should put one of my boys on you? Give you a little protection?"

"Why not just give me a signboard?"

"Uh-huh. They are a little conspicuous. So what do we do?"

"Hunker down in Neuilly with your army. You better split up, though. Seven of you in that house are going to arouse curiosity. Put a couple in hotels. And don't pile cars up in front. This may take some time. We can't afford having the French cops on your ass."

"We could move out to the country."

"No. When it breaks, it'll break fast. You've got to be close. Wohlgemuth is used to being tracked. It looks as if they move regularly, whether they feel pressed or not. Once I get a fix, we'll have to nail them quick. Keep somebody near a phone twenty-four hours a day. Set up a watch. You're going to have to be ready to move on a half hour's notice. Steal a couple of cars and alter the plates. Keep them stashed in the garage. How do you plan to get out once the hit is made?"

"Motor yacht at Cherbourg. No problem. Old Purvis's shipping manager has one of the port officials in his pocket. We'll get clearance automatically. Out to sea and onto one of his small tankers, which is standing by in Amsterdam, supposedly under repairs. You want to come along?"

"No."

"Suit yourself, amigo." He finished the beer and stood up. At the bar one of the team watched him in the mirror. "You let us know when and where. Meantime, I'm sending the boys out by twos to get used to the local slopes." He laughed. "Goddamn French drivers are the most dangerous things we're gonna face, hoss."

I watched him leave, trailed by his bodyguard, a nondescript man of medium height, short, thinning blond hair and wire-rimmed glasses, wearing a blue windbreaker and chinos. He might as well have had *American* tattooed on his forehead. But except for the roll of muscle at the base of his neck and the bricklike solidity of his body, he could have been any tourist rambling aimlessly through the city's ancient streets.

I got up and crossed the square to the Beaubourg and climbed the stairs to the Matisse exhibit, where I had arranged to meet Clemens. It was a reprise of his middle years in the hot sun of Provence, full of lush women, brilliant colors, and, in the drawings, the strong, simple line with the force of eternal truth.

Clemens was studying a brilliant red female figure, legs slightly spread, on a blue sofa. Through a window behind her, the sea, all flat planes. "Remarkable how he does it so effortlessly," he said. We shook hands, the German inclining his head in a slight bow.

"What have you got?"

"Last night. The death of Assad?"

"A bad mistake."

"Unfortunate. However, I think we can confirm that Madame de la Margerie is indeed their contact. Four people visited her apartment this morning before seven o'clock."

"Wohlgemuth?"

"No. But one fits the description of the fourth hijacker."

"He wore a mask. How could you identify him?"

"His hair. One of the hostages noticed that he had a heavy mop of curly black hair." Clemens passed over a photograph taken with a long lens, a little grainy, showing a tall, lean, hawkfaced man with light eyes, a swarthy pockmarked face, and a great beak of a nose.

"Who is he?"

"He's registered at the Hotel de Suede in the Rue Vaneau as Edward Patrick O'Grady. Citizen of the Republic of Ireland. But born in Belfast. The description in the file mentions that one of the hijackers had an Irish accent."

"The others?"

Clemens shrugged. "I had to make a choice of who to follow. He seemed the most interesting. We could use more people. Members of the hit team, perhaps."

"No."

"Too conspicuous?"

"They're killers, not trained for surveillance. Wohlgemuth and his people would make them in five minutes. What about you? Did he suspect he was being trailed?"

Clemens smiled. "Aging men are invisible. Anyway, I simply followed him to the taxi stand and listened to the address he gave."

"You got his name from the receptionist?"

"No. It's a small hotel. I inquired about a room. They file a name card by each room key. I waited until he came out and watched where they filed his key. I then checked him out with my friend at the ministry of the interior." Clemens consulted his little red notebook. "He arrived in Paris from Munich yesterday via Aer Lingus."

"Anything else?"

"Only that he is a dangerous man. I can smell him. A killer."

"What about the de la Margerie woman?"

"She spent an hour at a judo and fitness club in the neighborhood last night. It is run by a German. Volker Loewe, a former Olympic judo champion while a student at the University of Bonn, and his wife, Gerda." He thumbed through his little red book. "They have been in Paris for three years. Known radicals. Their clientele is international. Among them Arabs, Germans, Italians, Spaniards, Latin Americans and"—he looked up—"Irish."

"Lothar. You're getting too close to them. If they're as good as I think they are, they're going to make you."

"Clearly the death of Assad has agitated them," he said, ignoring me. "They will be preparing either to run or to fight. I have the feeling they will fight. This leaves them vulnerable."

"Like a boxer who starts to punch."

"Yes. They cannot come out of their shell without offering some openings. This may be your best chance. Assad's death will have rattled them. They should not be allowed to regain their poise."

"I'll start with the club. What's the address?"

"Rue de Charles. Number Thirty. It's in a sort of half basement. Do you want a backup?"

"No. Stick with the de la Margerie woman. She just might lead us to somebody."

"Unlikely. They have certainly scattered into safe houses by now. Standard operating procedure. They will contact each other only through messengers and cutouts until an operation is meticulously prepared. They will be even more cautious now, since they will suspect a *Spitzel*. How do you say in English?"

"An informer. They're going to have to have a meeting, Lothar. It looks as if they're planning to rob a bank." I showed him the sketches and notes from Assad. "There's no address, but your ministry friend might be able to locate the site from the sketches. Assad mentions a special collection point for foreign exchange receipts for the Le Guenedahl exchange house. Foreign currency gives them more flexibility. Saves laundering charges."

"The Le Guenedahl branches are mostly in the center of town. Around the Champs-Elysées, the Opéra, the Faubourg

St. Honoré, the Latin Quarter. Where the tourists congregate. It should be possible to find their central collection point. You think they will go ahead with it?''

''It's worth a try. They're arrogant, Lothar. Their hubris is high. Nobody has been able to touch them. And they need money.''

''Yes. They're also enveloped in a mystique that the Socialist God will not allow them to fail. They're romantic fools, of course. Otherwise they would not be what they are.''

''No Socialist God, Lothar?''

''No God at all. When will you check out the judo club?''

''Tonight.''

''Good luck. I will contact you tomorrow morning.'' He moved off, stopping before each painting, consulting the thick catalog, examining each canvas at a distance, then close up with a small jeweler's glass.

At the Esmeralda, Ivo was surrounded by a half-dozen American students all talking at once in impeccable southern-accented French, Vanderbilt emblazoned on their backpacks. The troglodyte passed a note to me over their heads.

''Call 260 38 30. Room 325.'' It was the Ritz Hotel. The clipped, educated British voice came over the line like ice cubes banging against the side of a glass. ''Alec. I made it. That maniac finally got his act together. How are you?''

''Fine.''

''What about lunch?''

''Sure.''

I walked across the Petit Pont past Notre Dame, across the Ile de la Cité, and turned left on the quai, soaking up the early summer sun, watching the young lovers locked in each other's arms as they leaned against the stone balustrade. At the Louvre I cut right past Pei's silly glass pyramid and walked under the arcades, threading my way through the slow-moving mass of tourists, turning right on the Rue Castiglione into the heart of the city's gold coast, past

Cartier's into the Place Vendôme with the little Corsican on top of the Egyptian obelisk gazing eternally at the discreet headquarters of the Morgan Guaranty Trust Company. I wondered what would have been his fate if he had been six feet tall and equipped with normal genitals.

Jenny met me in the Ritz bar wearing one of Renzi's more muted creations, its wide shoulders stressing her slim waist and boyish hips, the lime green bringing out her dark hair, repeating and deepening the color of her eyes. She kissed me on the cheek, half rising from the leather chair.

"Well, you're still alive and relatively undamaged. Does that mean failure?"

"How's Renzi?"

"Ecstatic. The proofs came out just the way he wanted them. We'll get a ten-page spread in the British *Vogue,* and my price will go up."

"What are you working on here?"

"Maurice is doing his late spring collection."

"Another Lorenz?"

"Maurice? My God, no. He's a satyr. Exercises droit de seigneur over all his models. Indefatigable lecher."

"But the same sort of weird clothes?"

"Hardly, although the theme is the same. Pedophilia. He's frilly whorey where Renzi is punk whorey. You know, lace and flounced skirts and high heels with silk straps."

"Sounds like 474 A.D. in Rome."

"What happened in 474 in Rome?"

"It fell to the Goths two years later."

"Oh. Well. Two years is a long time. Anyway, the modern Goths are into fashion, too. Have you seen Madame Gorbachev lately?"

"So you think you'd survive the decline of the West?"

"Sure. You would, too. We're survivors, not heroes. Speaking of survivors, are you going to buy me a drink?"

The waiter hovered discreetly at my elbow. "I guess we should have martinis since this is Hemingway's old hangout."

"White wine for me. I'm in training for the showing tomorrow." She looked around the room, furnished with discreet bourgeois elegance. "So the old man hung out here, huh?"

"He liberated it in 1944. They found a whole bunch of his manuscripts in the attic not so long ago. Stuff he'd forgotten about."

"You haven't told me what's going on."

"Not much."

"I read in the *Tribune* about a terrorist being killed last night. One of the hijackers of the Malta plane."

"The story didn't say that."

"Oh? Really? Then I must have heard it on the news. Drink that vile concoction and take me to lunch. I'm famished."

The martini was superb, a whiff of lemon peel lingering on the rim of the glass, the Boodles gin dominating the vermouth, chilled crystal keeping out the heat. I drank about half of it and followed her through the understated elegance of the lobby.

"Where shall we go?"

"I know a little place near here. Unpretentious and expensive. Don't look so chagrined. I'm buying this time," she said, taking my arm, dragging me to the show windows of the Rue St. Honoré. "Look at that," she said, giggling at a display of black lace panties with openings in strategic places. "The French are obsessed. All they think about is sex."

"Yeah. But they just talk. They never do it. Except in books and films."

"Unlike you strong, silent Yanks who just do it and never talk?"

"How long are you going to be here?"

"At least three days. The collection goes on tomorrow and the next day, but I'm going to do at least a day of pictures in the boutique. Intimate stuff."

"Won't Renzi be irritated? I mean, you work for him and the competition?"

"They're not competitors. No woman who bought Renzi's creations would be seen dead in Maurice's and vice versa. Here it is."

We turned into an archway between a jewelery store and a shop selling switchblade knives. The La Fourchette was at the back of a courtyard. One square room and a smaller alcove. A typical cashier's lectern next to the door opening onto the kitchens. Tables for two rimmed the room, crammed against each other. In the center bigger tables for four. It was already filling up with businessmen and women from the quarter, prosperous-looking middle-aged keepers of the expensive shops with the well-fed, hard-eyed faces of the bourgeoisie.

"You like?"

"It's real."

"Yeah. Somebody will ruin it soon with an article in *Gourmet*. Then thousands of your countrymen will descend on it, they'll raise prices, get a star, drive out the locals, and go broke."

"You sound like you're against greed."

"Only in other people."

The trout amandine was fresh and flaky. Purvis Oil bought us a bottle of Puligny Montrachet, and we were both pleasantly blitzed when we left two hours later.

"Your place or mine?"

She looked at her watch and frowned. "God, lover. I'd adore to, but I've got a meeting. And I hate quickies. Can we see each other tonight?"

"Sure. When will you be free?"

"Around eight. Why don't I come by your hotel? We could explore the Latin Quarter." She pecked my cheek and disappeared through the ornate brass-rimmed doors of the Ritz, and I headed back across the river to pick up my gym gear. I didn't need much. A jockstrap with a built-in cup and a wrestler's singlet. In any big city in Europe you could find a gym where the wrestlers worked out. They bore little resemblance to the new fitness centers full of arcane machines, hot tubs, and a bar to socialize in.

In lower-class neighborhoods, unpainted, with rust-stained showers, reeking of stale sweat, they usually accommodated both boxers and wrestlers. My normal routine was thirty minutes on the medium weights, two hundred situps, and some serious stretching followed by a couple of intense six-minute sessions on the mat with the local tigers.

Eliane de la Margerie's club was French yuppie. It was called the Club Jahn after a nineteenth-century German health fanatic and occupied a large basement space under some small stores on the Rue Charles. The anteroom was thickly carpeted, its walls decorated with framed Olympic posters of gymnasts, muscles etched with tension. Place of honor was given to a photograph of the throw that had won the owner his Olympic gold in judo. A kinetic shot, slightly blurred, the agonized face of his opponent staring into the camera just before landing on the mat. A handsome young blond receptionist in a skintight leotard cut to her navel was touching up her makeup when I came in.

"Yes?"

"I'd like to get a workout."

"You wish a membership?"

"No. I'm in town temporarily. I'd like to come in on a day-to-day basis."

She quoted me the price, took my money, and handed me a towel and the key to a locker. The place looked like a clone of an upscale American health club. Mirrored walls, chrome universals, Nautilus, stationary bicycles, and a few gimmicks special to the French. About a third of the room was given over to a karate arena where a dozen or so young studs were posturing, kicking the air, and grunting impressively.

I did a few stretches and checked out the clientele. An aging faggot, slim and wiry, worked methodically on the weights, dyed hair belied by the matrix of wrinkles around his neck and eyes. Two young women, fifteen pounds overweight, pushing bicycles up imaginary hills. A slim girl of eighteen or so in purple tights lying on a padded bench lifting ten-pound weights. A normal sight except that she was bare-breasted.

I ground out two hundred situps and had started on the weights when the German appeared. Six feet, one eighty-five, compacted like cement. A Visigoth right out of a Hitler Youth poster, blond, almost white hair curling down over his neck. He had the long, lean muscles of the true athlete rather than the bulging protein- and hormone-fed bulk of the bodybuilder.

"You are a new member? Welcome to our club." He spoke excellent, slightly accented French. I took his hand, which lay limp in mine. He was good and he knew it. He didn't have to push it. "You are wrestler?" he asked, noting the faded logo on my singlet.

"Used to be."

"I do judo."

"I saw you win the Olympics on television."

"Yes. I was lucky. The karate class is finishing. You would perhaps like a workout?"

"I'm not much good at judo."

"We will wrestle." He changed into a singlet and joined me on the mat, moving with the loose grace of the top-flight jock. Judo and wrestling have some things in common, but not much. He outweighed me by twenty pounds and took me down without too much trouble, but on the mat he tried simple cross-body moves exclusively. It wasn't pretty, but I broke out of a guillotine, using his weight against him, slipped free, and landed on my feet again.

He grinned up at me from the mat, handsome features suddenly turning coarse. "Very good move." He was on me then, turning me right and left, using his weight and strength, jamming a leg behind my knee, slamming me to the mat, landing on top, grappling for a pin, clamping me in a cradle, one arm through my crotch, the other around my neck, punishing, wearing me down. I jammed the heel of my left hand under his jaw, forcing his head back, and rolled to the right. He was too strong and too quick, slowly muscling me toward the inevitable pin, when a voice cut through the chatter of the spectators who had gathered around the mat.

"Volker."

He stood over us, staring down at me. Not much different from the photographs. Hair shorter, small mustache, a little heavier, but no real effort at disguise. "Come into the office," he said to the German, turning on his heel.

"You're lucky," the bare-breasted girl said, offering me a hand up from the mat. "He likes to hurt people."

They were waiting when I came out of the shower. Two slender, Middle Eastern types, one holding a silenced Makharov on me. They were professionals, never getting within reach, big snout of the silencer never wavering from my breastbone as I dressed. A door gave off the dressing room into a narrow, windowless corridor, on one side the ancient stone of the original basement. The office was down some steps past broken rowing machines and some ancient weights, a cramped, windowless room with a big metal desk and a couple of cheap chairs. The walls were crowded with photographs of Loewe battling in various championship bouts. A half dozen silver trophies and his Olympic gold medal were in a dusty glass case.

Wohlgemuth sat behind the desk, feet up, leaning back in a big leather executive chair. "Volker, you are a stupid, dangerous fool." He threw a picture across the desk to the judoka. It was a grainy shot of me on a street in Regensburg, slightly out of focus, but recognizable. "We gave you this two days ago. Did you look at it?"

The big German nodded, saying nothing. Wohlgemuth turned to me. "My congratulations, Dr. Thompson. I'm not sure how you found us, but your efficiency is truly impressive. Perhaps you could tell us your secret."

The two Middle Eastern types had stationed themselves behind me in the corners of the room. Loewe sat on the edge of the desk. Gudrun Skorzeny and Paddy O'Faolin leaned against the wall, the Irishman looking like an aging hawk with his beak of a nose and piercing blue eyes.

"We now know a good bit about you," Wohlgemuth said. "You are, for example, a respected scholar of the Nazi period. I have glanced at your book on Sepp Dietrich. Excellent work, considering the abysmal lack of culture of your country. It even shows some ideological sensitivity." He glanced down at some notes in front of him.

"Your military record is a bit foggy. A combination of rather baroque heroics culminating in your being very nearly court-martialed. Then there is the bizarre episode two years ago in Berlin." He affected a slight British accent overlaid with a German inflection.

"Most American academics with your background are, if not active supporters of our tactics, at least sympathetic to our goals. So we are a little puzzled that you accepted the job of hunting us down. Why?"

"Money."

Gudrun Skorzeny laughed. "At least he's honest, Dieter. How much are they paying you?"

"A hundred thousand."

"For what?"

"To deliver your bodies."

"And you think you can do it?"

"Ibrahim is in the morgue."

One of the Lebanese stirred, and Wohlgemuth shot him a warning look. "So you do not risk your life for a belief, as we do, Dr. Thompson, but for crass materialistic gain."

"You're not fighting for an ideal. You're a spoiled bourgeois intellectual. Arrogant, intolerant, hungry for power. A neurotic eaten by guilt at having murdered your father. A clinical Oedipal case."

"So, you are an amateur psychologist as well. Do you lump all of us in this category? Ali, Hassan, O'Faolin, Gudrun?"

"The Arabs want respect. Their pride is wounded.

Gudrun''—I shrugged—''I guess mostly she wants to be a man.''

''And me, professor? The poor Irish laddie. What makes me the murderous beast I am?''

''You're programmed. An Irish maniac. Brought up with your mother's milk to hate the British and the Protestants. And, like everybody who starts killing, it gets into your blood, like a drug. You can't live without it. Rebellion is just an excuse to get your kicks.''

''You disappoint me, Thompson. I would have thought an intellectual, even an American, would have some understanding of the objective realities. Instead you fall back on the old Viennese fraud, personalizing everything, contemplating your navel. You clearly don't believe that 'the history of all hitherto existing society is the history of class struggle.' ''

''Sure I do. But it didn't take the *Communist Manifesto* to convince me of that. I knew it by the time I was eight years old.''

''And you don't believe in the validity of revolution in order to develop a truly classless society.''

''No. The old cliché is right. A revolution is nothing more than a change in the governing class. You trade the capitalists for a Communist bureaucracy which is in some ways even more overbearing and corrupt than the capitalists because it's so monolithic.''

''So you give up hope and remain in the morass and filth of capitalism?''

''Or you work at governing yourself. Reforming where you can, putting restraints on power, dividing it up so that nobody can dominate. You chip away at the margins of injustice, use the capitalist motor and human greed to increase the pie, and government policy to divide it more equitably. You look for ways to improve incrementally. You're patient.''

''The slave mentality,'' Gudrun Skorzeny said, voice dripping with contempt. ''Dieter, we're wasting time.''

The German nodded. "Yes. I'm afraid you are no more than a conventional myrmidon of the capitalists, Thompson. Now we need some information from you. First, who are the other members of your group? Second, where are they? And third, a detailed outline of your specific plans."

"And if I tell you to screw off?"

"You tortured Ali's cousin"—he motioned to one of the Arabs. "Forced him to reveal Ibrahim's location. He would like nothing better than to return the favor."

"Better let him get started, then."

I wasn't expecting it. The big judoka kicked me in the side, spinning me around and slamming me up against the wall. I was bent over, hardly able to breathe when the slaps started, methodical, mind-numbing, open-handed, turning my head right and left. He got a little careless after the fifth one, taking too long a backswing, and I came up driving my fist into his throat in a stiff-armed semi-uppercut. He spun away, eyes bulging. As I turned toward the door my luck ran out. A searing explosion of pain at the back of my head pitched me forward into a well of blackness.

chapter 12

The smell was the first thing I noticed. A combination of stale sweat, soap, and chlorine. Then the pain in the back of my head. I pried my eyes open and tried to move. They had trussed me like a chicken, binding my hands with a nylon rope, pulling my legs up against my back and tying them to my hands. A bright bare bulb burned overhead. It was the club's laundry room. Piles of dirty towels, wet bathing suits, and sweaty gym clothes in net bags with plastic name tags were stacked around three industrial washing machines sitting on wooden two-by-fours. On one wall a massive dryer hummed, its contents beating against the glass window.

The room was a windowless stone box dating back to the fifteenth century, the gleaming equipment incongruous against the stone walls encrusted with the grime of centuries. A whiff of the city's ancient sewers overpowered the other odors.

Boxes of detergent were ranged on a shelf above the washing machines. A half-empty glass bottle of bleach stood at the end of the shelf. It took twenty minutes to inch my way across the floor to a sponge mop, grip the handle in my already numb fingers, slide back to the machines, and probe upward for the bottle. On the fifth try it tipped, shattering on the concrete.

I cut through the rope and began a methodical exploration of the room, finding the square metal manhole cover under a pile of wet towels. I pried it up using a doubled wire coat hanger and stepped back from the rush of stale air. An ancient rusted iron ladder led downward. I was slipping into the hole when the voices stopped on the other side of the door.

"Are the last clients gone?"

"Yes."

"And the girl? The receptionist?"

"She just left."

"Very well. Ali, bring him to the office. We don't have much time. He can scream all he wants now. Nobody will hear."

I came up out of the hole and flattened myself against the wall by the door. The Arab came through alone, gun in his belt. I kicked the door to behind him, wrapping an arm around his throat, tightening it as he groped for the gun. His body writhed momentarily, both hands tearing at my grip. The gun fell to the floor and skidded out of sight under one of the washing machines. He kicked in a final despairing spasm before he passed out. I picked him up and threw him into the now quiescent dryer, punching the start button. The machine coughed into life, overload buzzer beginning to scream in protest at the weight. It should buy me time while they pulled him out.

I dropped into the open hole, yanking the manhole cover over it behind me, and descended into the darkness. O'Faolin's muffled voice followed me down.

"He's gone into the sewers. Get a flashlight, Dieter. We'll go after him."

It was pitch black. The iron rungs gave out ten feet down, and, hanging from the last one, I let myself go. The drop was about four inches onto a curving cobblestoned surface. The ancient storm sewer was a rough circle, a rivulet of water from some underground stream flowing sluggishly down the center through the detritus of centuries. I moved along the curved wall, hand touching a furry mass which skittered away.

Behind me a flood of light streamed down the shaft. "Quick, Hassan. Once he's in the sewers we'll never find the bugger."

I felt my way down the dark tunnel out of the glow of light. It curved gently to the left and descended in a very slight grade in the direction of the Seine. Behind me O'Faolin's voice echoed off the walls. "Go right, Hassan. I'll take the left. He can't move fast without a light."

The Arab's flashlight flicked from wall to wall as he started down the tunnel. I dropped forward on my face, half submerging in the muck in the center of the tunnel. He was in a hurry, moving fast, the light probing the walls. As he passed me, I caught his left ankle and twisted it, pitching him forward, screaming in terror, facedown into the muck. I was on him before he could turn, knee in his back, gripping his hair, holding his face in the filthy water. His slender body writhed beneath me, sucking in the water, shuddering, going limp.

"Hassan." O'Faolin's voice echoed down the tunnel. "Hassan, damn you, answer me."

I retrieved the flashlight and found the silenced Ruger twenty-two automatic half-submerged in the stream. Behind me the Irishman's footsteps had quickened. I moved across the tunnel to the right wall, running my fingers along the irregularities in the stonework, propping the light in a niche pointing back down the tunnel. As O'Faolin came around the curve, his light sketching figures on the wall, I shot for a point about a foot above and to the left of his light beam. His Uzi coughed instantly, a stream of lead blasting the light out of its niche, ricocheting spent bullets through the tunnel as the Irishman flung his light away, smashing it against a wall.

"Ah, laddie. You're a royal pain in the arse, you are. Sure, and would you not like to be giving it up? You're outgunned, you know, with that little peashooter."

I snapped off a shot in the general direction of the sound, going down and rolling to the right through the sludge as I fired. The Uzi answered the Ruger's muzzle flash instantly with a burst, and I got off another shot at the Irishman, his face reflected in ghostly outline by the machine pistol's flickering signature.

"Paddy?"

"Here, Dieter. Watch it, laddie. He's got Hassan's gun."

"What are you waiting for? Let's take him."

"You just do that thing, Dieter, me boy. He's done in Hassan, he has, and poor Ali's nothing more than a babbling psycho crumpled up like a fetus up there. Nicked me in the arm with that fucking peashooter. Waiting on his own terrain he is. Tunnel rat he was in Vietnam, that file on him says. Going after him down here would be like a mouse hunting down a ferret in his burrow. You're welcome to try, Dieter, me boy. But Paddy O'Faolin is getting his mick arse out of here. Hear that, Yank?"

"We can't leave Hassan's body down here."

"He's dead, Dieter, me boy. A canape for the rodents, God rest his heathen soul. We've got to get our tails away. That laddie's hit team may be lurkin' nearby, you know. Cut your losses, that's Paddy's maxim. Do nothing rash. Live to kill the wily bastard another day. You hear that, do you, Thompson? I'll be killing you, and I'll be pissing on your desiccated bones when I do, you and your tight-assed Scottish ancestors that came with their Protestant drivel and took our land."

It took me half an hour to find the outlet. The sewer gave off onto the Seine under the Quai Henri IV at the Pont Morland, diminishing to a hole three feet in circumference. I kicked the rusted iron grille loose, lowered myself into the river, and swam to a set of stone steps leading up from a barge mooring onto the quai. A clochard, sleeping under a newspaper, empty wine bottle at his head, awoke and stared at me, shaking his head and sinking back into a stupor.

The troglodyte stared at me wordlessly over the early edition of *Le Monde*, passing me my key. "There's a young lady in your room."

"Thanks."

"Jesus X. Christ, what happened to you?" Jenny asked, recoiling from the stench.

"Be a doll and run me a bath." I stripped and dumped my clothes in a plastic laundry sack, heaving it out into the corridor, diving into the hot water.

chapter 13

Jenny sat on the edge of the tub sipping Duque de Alba out of a water glass. "You're bleeding," she said, running a hand into the water and finding the crease along my rib cage. "That needs treating."

"Call Mathilde. She runs this place. Ask her to bring up her sewing kit."

"You need a doctor."

I sank back in the water, feeling the heat begin to dissolve the tension in the muscles at the back of my neck. She shrugged and called the desk. Five minutes later the French woman arrived with a round wicker basket full of medical gear. She examined the rough slash, its crust of blood dissolved in the water, bleeding down my side.

"Get out. Here, help me dry him off. It's not too bad. Bounced off the rib, it looks like. Small caliber, no? In the old days it would have been a forty-five, and you would not be walking around, chérie. Something to be said for progress, hein? You want a little novocaine?"

"No."

"Give him a brandy, my dear. A stiff one."

She worked quickly, painting the wound with a colorless jelly, pinching the ends together and sewing it up with quick rough strokes, slapping a thin bandage over it.

"In a week you won't even know it happened. I'll take the stitches out in three days." She looked me over. "You want some help? I still have contacts with Jules's friends. For a consideration they would supply you with a bodyguard."

"Thanks, Mathilde."

She shrugged. "If you change your mind, let me know."

I got dressed in all I had left, a seersucker jacket, charcoal-gray pants, and a pair of loafers I'd had made at Peal's in London with the remnants of the Berlin payoff.

"You're too weak to go out."

"'Life is short and death is forever,' as the poet said. Let's go live it up a little at the expense of the Purvis Oil Company."

"Are you going to tell me what happened?"

I described the incident at the health club as we walked down the Quai de Montebello onto the Quai de la Tournelle, stopping at the discreetly sumptuous building housing the Tour d'Argent.

"You're kidding," she said, staring at the entrance and beginning to laugh. "They won't let us in here. You've got to reserve a week in advance. Or be a famous movie star."

The minion in a dinner jacket guarding the elevator bowed slightly, dark beard already beginning to show through a new shave. "You have a reservation, sir?"

I unfolded the hundred-dollar bill and laid it on the reservations book. "I'd like something overlooking the Ile St. Louis."

"Certainly, sir." He picked up the house telephone and murmured into it, opening the elevator as he did so. The maître met us on the third floor.

"Monsieur Thompson? This way, sir." He led us to a table for two overlooking the river and Notre Dame, its flying buttresses lit from below, golden stone shimmering in the darkness.

"Crude but effective," Jenny said. "What would you have done if he'd snubbed you?"

"Taken you to a bistro around the corner."

"You're typically American, you know."

"How so?"

"You think money will buy everything."

"I think it's genetic."

"Genetic?"

"Yeah. You know what my father would have said if he had known what an academic makes?"

"What?"

"'Son, I could make more money looking for pocketbooks.'"

"They're going to kill you."

"Yeah. You might be right. They gave it a good shot. Which is why we're here."

"You come here often?"

"I used to walk by it a lot when I was on a post-doctoral grant here. Sniff the vapors."

"I thought you specialized in Germany."

"I got sick of the krauts and wangled a grant to do a comparative study on French and German fascism."

"And?"

"Wound up writing a book called *Céline and Nietzsche: Visions of the Apocalypse*."

"You should have called it *Two Mad Doctors*. How did it do?"

"It got great reviews and sold three hundred copies."

"Sounds like masturbation."

"Fun, but it doesn't get you anywhere?"

"Something like that. Is that why you agree to do insane things like hunting down these terrorists? For kicks?"

"No." The headwaiter bounced into view, a plump little man with an unctuous smile hiding a commanding presence. We ordered coquilles St. Jacques and the house specialty, duck pressed in a tin device designed to squeeze out all the juices into a sauce of supposedly supernal richness.

The sommelier, a blond youth in his mid-twenties, appeared lugging a leather-bound wine list the size of an unabridged *Webster's Second Edition* and opened it in front of me.

"What do you recommend?"

"For the coquilles a half-bottle of Pouilly-Fuissé. With the duck, sir, we suggest a Burgundy or one of the lighter Bordeaux, a Pommerol perhaps," he said.

We discussed the various Pommerols and moved on to the Burgundies. I finally closed the book and leaned back in the chair. His accent had finally registered.

"Salzburg?"

"Duernstein."

"In the Wachau?" I had lapsed into German.

"Yes."

"How'd you wind up here?"

"My father owns a vineyard. I'm a graduate of the hotel school in Austria. We do internships at major restaurants and hotels around Europe."

"And they made you sommelier?"

"I grew up with wine, sir." His voice had stiffened. "I am an assistant. If you wish, I can call the head sommelier."

"Just give it your best shot."

He glanced over his shoulder, locating the *maître d'hôtel* across the room. "The duck is very heavy. I would suggest a Gewurztraminer. It will clean your palate after each bite and allow you to enjoy the taste of the sauce over and over again." He smiled. "Also it is not so expensive. And, of course, you would not need the Fuissé."

I ordered it.

"He's sabotaging, recommending inexpensive wines."

"Yeah. Probably hates the French."

"He's pretty."

"Yeah. But jerries run to fat when they age."

"He's Austrian."

"Worst kind of jerries. Ever hear of Hitler?"

"If you dislike them so much, why spend your life studying them?"

"I'm not studying them. I'm studying power. What it is, how you get it, how you use it, how you keep it. And how you lose it. The Germans are the purest recent demonstration of it. Distilled hubris. That's what history is all about. The rest is bullshit. And anyway I don't dislike the Germans. I admire them. They're intelligent, tenacious, disciplined, hardworking, and they sing good."

"So the terrorists are part of your research?"

"Lenin recommended the strategic use of power to obtain clearly defined goals. He disapproved of indiscriminate killing. People like Wohlgemuth are nihilists."

"They're idealistic revolutionaires seeking a more just society."

"That's their conscious rationale. In fact, they're aging adolescents who have gotten stuck like a record player needle in the 'rebellion' groove."

"You don't see any logic in what they're doing?"

"Fifteen years ago Beirut was the most prosperous city in the Middle East. Lebanon was a garden spot. Literally a little Switzerland. The Christians and Moslems shared power, the Druzes and Armenians, and the rest of the other human detritus deposited there over six thousand years, all living together in peace and prosperity. Now the place is an inferno of death and destruction. You call that logic?"

"You're against revolution of any kind?"

A young Algerian waiter brought the coquilles, carefully arranging the plates so that the crest of the restaurant was at the top. Another waiter poured the wine from a long, slender green bottle into a crystal wineglass and stood back, one arm behind his back. I passed the glass to Jenny.

"It's superb," she said. "You didn't answer me."

"You know who Jefferson was?"

"Don't be patronizing."

"He said a nation ought to let a little blood every twenty

years. Meaning that you have to renew the elite classes periodically. In some cases killing off the old one is probably the only way you can do it, much as the ancient Greeks ritually slaughtered their kings after set periods of time. But this creates problems. You lose the institutional memory of the state if you do too good a job, and you also run the risk of getting a new bunch in who will wind up being more dynamic and efficient and, therefore, more repressive than the last villains. The Soviet Union is a good example. The czars were relatively passive and incompetent toward the end. Russia wasn't such a bad place to live until the First World War and the Bolsheviks screwed everything up."

"What a bizarre concept."

"Yeah. Well, the czars sent a few people like Dostoyevsky to Siberia, but they didn't let ten million Ukrainian peasants starve to death or send another ten million to die in the Gulags. I hate to think what shape we'd be in today if there had been no revolution."

"Run that one by me again."

"In 1912 Russian industrial capacity was growing at about ten percent a year. Europe was loaning them money hand over fist. If it hadn't been for the revolution it would probably have developed into an industrial and military giant without parallel. As it is, the crowd running it has made just about every mistake known to economics."

"Why did you really take on Wohlgemuth and his gang? Out of some macho itch to get back into the action?"

"No. I took the job to put a roof on my chateau near Langres, and so I could afford to invite lucious young limey morsels to places like this, plying them with strong liquors so I can work my evil designs on them."

The duck turned out to be overdone, the sauce a heavy chocolate-flavored syrup, but the waiter was right about the wine. Its tart, slightly herbal flavor made the meal bearable.

"The food's pretty bad."

"Yeah. But the view is magnificent." A barge made its way along the river, a 2 CV Citroën perched behind the wheelhouse like a large insect, and tied up near the modern sculpture garden winding along the left bank.

The restaurant had filled around us, a mixture of Americans and Germans leavened by a smattering of provincial French, prosperous burghers determined to mine Paris of all its glories. At a neighboring table a young man in a checked sport jacket, bow tie, and crew cut out of the fifties was making painful conversation with a homely young woman in a light tweed suit, sensible shoes, and no makeup. They spoke an exquisite aristocratic French and were in the midst of an arcane exploration of a treatise of Descartes.

Jenny leaned across the table. "Who do you think they are?"

"The duke of Angoulême, scion of an ancient but penurious noble clan, sent to Paris to rescue the family fortunes by marrying his rich cousin, Emilie de Rochefoucauld, heiress to vast truffle orchards in the Dordogne."

"Truffles don't grow on trees."

"*C'est un détail.*"

"And is he succeeding?"

"*Hélas,* Emilie is enamored of Fabian von der Strumpfbandguertel, a collateral descendant of Boris the Bold, once lord and master of Krakow and Zakonpane."

"So what happens?"

"Fabian has eyes only for a third secretary in the Albanian embassy, Ali bin Ali Raschid, descendant of a Turkish Janissary, presently a triple agent for the Chinese, Russians, and Yugoslavs, being blackmailed by British MI6 because of an unnatural lust for sheep."

Jenny's green eyes stopped laughing for an instant, flattening like glass. "You have a fertile and disgusting imagination, Dr. Thompson. Maybe you should be writing spy thrillers instead of history."

"You can't make up anything as strange as reality."

We strolled back along the deserted Quai de Montebello, locked metal booksellers' stalls lining the balustrades, cafés and restaurants across the narrow street waiting to close as the last customers lingered over coffee and cognac. The Square Viviani had begun to wind down by now, a covey of American students gathered at the feet of their bearded professor as he lined out the next day's tour, young Algerians circling the blond, slightly overweight girls like dark sharks, waiting for the meeting to break up.

The troglodyte greeted us at the door of the Esmeralda. "You are sought, *mon ami,*" he said, moving back behind the miniature reception desk and handing me a slip of paper. We walked up three flights, and Jenny disappeared into the bathroom as I dialed Clemens's number.

"Lothar?"

"Yes. I have located the woman, Alec."

"Skorzeny?"

"Yes."

"Where?"

"The Frenchwoman, Eliane de la Margerie, met her at a hairdresser's in the sixteenth this afternoon. I almost missed it. The Skorzeny woman came out with her hair dyed red, but there was no mistaking her."

"You followed her?"

"To an apartment in the Rue Vaneau."

"That's where O'Faolin's hotel is."

"Was. He checked out in a hurry earlier this evening."

"Thanks, Lothar."

"Alec."

"Yes."

"She will be killed."

"Yes."

"Do you feel nothing?"

"It's what they hired me to do."

Jenny slipped her arms around my neck and began to unbutton my shirt. "All work and no play makes Jack a dull boy."

I winced as she brushed against the gash in my chest.

"Don't worry. I'll be gentle."

chapter 14

I ran in the chilly spring air, avoiding the cobblestones, the immense bulk of Notre Dame soaring on my left across the narrow river, beyond it the oblong of the Ile St. Louis. Ahead, the barge, with its funny little car perched on deck, cast off and headed out into the stream. A black-bearded apparition, asleep on a bench, lifted himself on an elbow and stared at me in disbelief from behind a barricade of empty wine bottles, face breaking into a snaggle-toothed grin through a jungle of matted beard.

"*Quelles jolies jambes,*" he rasped as I moved past.

The sculpture garden began beyond the bridge and extended to the Jardin des Plantes a couple of miles farther along. A gravel path wound between geometric wrought-iron monsters staring through the pale morning light at crouching stone creatures full of holes, artists' neurotic nightmares exorcised in metal and granite. Ahead, pounding toward me with the tireless, flatfooted stride of the marathoner, a balding figure appeared, gunslinger's mustache drooping with sweat, slender legs reduced to tendons and ligaments. His tattered T-shirt proclaimed "CCNY: Class of 1962."

He glanced at me as he swept past and waved vaguely, disappearing down the quai. I ran more easily now, filling my lungs with the morning air, legs loosening, feeling the tension in my shoulders seep away. I made the turn two miles out and stepped up the pace coming back. The city was beginning to awaken as I moved past the Bâteaux Mouches dock and climbed the stone stairs to the Square Viviani.

"You are a fool, Alec. You will pull loose the stitches," Mathilde said as I came in.

"How about some coffee?"

"At six A.M.? Impossible!! Also, mon cher, you rented the room under false pretenses. Your bill will go up to include the young lady as of today."

Jenny lay crossways on the bed, sheet and blanket mummifying her. "You know something?"

"What?"

"I like your smell."

"Stale sweat and dried pheromones."

"God, men are gross, crude beasts. You've been running."

"Yeah."

"All Americans are bonkers."

I slipped my hand under her head and lifted her up, running my lips along her jawline.

"You scratch. No, idiot, don't stop." She leapt out of bed and disappeared, returning with one of the Esmeralda's scruffy towels. "Undress. Be still." She sponged off the sweat, pushing me facedown on the bed, straddling my back and rubbing me down in long, rhythmic strokes, throwing the towel away and stretching out full-length on my back, running her lips along my neck.

"Aren't we being a little impractical?"

"If you're unhappy, exert your male dominance."

I moved to the right, caught her left wrist, and pulled it under me, rolling left as I did so, pinning her, holding her wrists, ignoring the searing pain as the stitches stretched. She giggled, writhing beneath me. "Big strong tough man.

Beating up on poor little girl." I let her go and her small, muscular hands were suddenly all over me, running up my chest, entwining themselves in the hair, down over my stomach.

"Well, well, well. Now, fancy that," she said.

"You're late," De Crecy said as I slid onto the maroon plastic bank across from him in the café.

"You're lucky I showed up. I'm not being paid to play nursemaid. Why me anyway? You've got a whole regiment out in Neuilly."

"You speak French. You know the city. You are unobtrusive. Your clothes and manner are more European than American. Halloran's goons are useless to me in an operation like this."

"What's the drill?"

"Eric is watching her doorway." De Crecy touched the flesh-colored button in his ear attached to a wire disappearing under his coat collar. It looked like a hearing aid. He handed me a similar device. The wire was attached to a flat box the size of a cigarette package. I slipped it in my ear and Malhe's voice came over in a muted mutter.

"Nothing yet."

"What's the effective distance of this thing?"

"Three hundred yards. We don't need more. Eric will let us know when she comes out. He is parked in front of her building. In the gray Peugeot 204 across from the Vietnamese restaurant." I turned and spotted the car. The Pole was reading a newspaper. A husband waiting for his wife.

"She has a choice of metro stops," he said, opening a city map. "St.-François-Xavier on the Boulevard des Invalides, Duroc on the Rue de Sèvres, Sèvres-Babylone, or Varenne."

"What if she calls a taxi?"

"I talked to your man, Clemens. He says they all use the metro. Less of a trail that way. If she does take a taxi we'll join Eric, and he will try to keep her in sight."

"How will you do it?"

"When she comes out, I will move past her, a hundred feet in front. You will follow a similar distance behind. Use this thing. Keep me informed where she turns in case I guess wrong. There are a limited number of options. I expect her to take Babylone."

"She knows me. They must use standard techniques to pick up tails."

"The streets are packed at this time of day. But if she spots you, nothing is lost. It will distract her. What did your famous boxer say? 'She can run but she can't hide?' "

"Where will you do it?"

"Before she gets to the subway, if possible. If not, inside. Malhe will remain in contact. When the hit is made, he will pick me up. You will disappear. If there is trouble, I expect you to back me up."

I drank the bitter French breakfast coffee and watched as De Crecy took a crocodile case from his breast pocket and opened it on his lap, selecting one of three triangular blades in dull carbon steel, inserting it in the wood and steel handle formed to fit his hand.

"Ingenious device. Note the spring button here on the handle. I slide it forward once the hit is made and the blade is punched forward by a spring and released. It remains in the wound, sealing it so there's no blood. Makes it look as if the target fainted. They only discover the blade during an autopsy." He wiped the weapon carefully, put on a pair of flesh-colored silk gloves, and slipped it up his left sleeve into a leather holster. As he did, the hearing aid coughed to life.

"She's leaving."

We moved out quickly, De Crecy first, me a few steps back. Gudrun Skorzeny had stopped on the doorstep as she left the building, examining the street with cool professionalism before turning right toward Rue de Varennes, cutting her metro options to the Varenne station or Babylone. De Crecy walked slightly faster than the woman, on the opposite side of the street, head down, looking like a man late for work. He passed her a few paces before the Rue de Varenne crossed

Vaneau. Left was the Varenne station. Right would take her to Babylone. De Crecy turned right and she followed. I turned into a doorway, anticipating her quick backward glance as she rounded the corner. Standard operating procedure for spotting a tail.

A couple of hundred yards down the Rue de Varenne is the entrance to the Hotel Matignon, residence and office of the French prime minister. Two police sentries armed with submachine guns strolled the sidewalk in front of the eighteenth-century palace. De Crecy had crossed over to the left sidewalk as Skorzeny strode along at a fast clip, sensible walking shoes hitting the pavement in an almost military rhythm.

The hearing aid activated. "There's a crowd in front of the Bon Marché," De Crecy said. "They must be having a sale of some kind. Be careful not to lose her, Eric. Bring the car up opposite the Bon Marché entrance in three minutes."

Gudrun Skorzeny hesitated on the edges of the mass of French women gathered in front of a huge white banner proclaiming "Soldes d'Eté," rising on tiptoe to see what was being offered. Half a dozen women shifted positions, enclosing her, surging forward as the doors to the department store opened.

De Crecy had turned back and slipped into the crowd, slender frame engulfed in the crush. It was over in an instant. He slipped back through the struggling women, leaving Gudrun Skorzeny still standing, held upright by the dense mass, her face turned back in a reflex action, mouth open in a soundless scream, eyes clouding over as she slumped out of sight.

Malhe brought the car to a halt at the curb and De Crecy was gone ten seconds after the hit was made. I moved off toward the Babylone subway, dropping a five-franc piece into the hat of a saxophonist playing "Straighten Up and Fly Right" off-key.

I changed at Concorde and took the Vincennes line to St. Paul in the Marais. Clemens and Halloran were waiting for me in a café at the corner of the Rue Birague and the Place des Vosges, that monument to the Protestant apostate Henry the Fourth.

"Well?" Halloran asked.

I handed him the ear plug and case. "You're right. He's good."

"Two down and two to go. We're halfway to a vacation, slick."

"What have you found out, Lothar?"

"Nothing more. Le Grenedahl bank is definitely their target. On the corner of St. Germaine and St. Michel. They receive very large collections from money changers throughout the quarter just before closing every day. Several hundred thousand dollars in a half-dozen currencies will be on hand."

"So the brigade is breaking its unofficial deal with the French government not to cause trouble in France."

"Yes," Clemens said. "The arrest of the two Action Directe leaders, Jean-Marc Rouillan and Nathalie Menigon, plus the conviction of the Lebanese Georges Ibrahim Abdallah, has enraged them. There will be a day of terror all over the city. The bank robbery will be lost in the general chaos."

"When?"

Clemens shrugged. "Nobody is sure. The police informers are working full-time. Perhaps by tomorrow I will know."

"We need the date, Thompson. Now. This de la Margerie broad is our best bet. She knows. And she's an amateur. She'll crack fast."

"You'll warn them off if you take her. She's our only link to the rest of them," Clemens protested.

"Look. We haven't got much time. People are dying right and left. The French cops aren't dummies. They're going to start putting it all together, especially when they realize that a hit has been made on Gudrun Skorzeny. Once they identify her body the manure will hit the fan. We've got to move. Fast."

"What are you planning?"

"We'll take her when she leaves the lycée this afternoon."

"I will not permit her to be tortured." Clemens's normally pale face was white.

"What?" Halloran looked from the German to me. "What the fuck does that mean? You work for us, Jack. You don't permit anything."

"What's the matter, Lothar? You knew what you were getting into."

"Yes. But to kill terrorists is one thing. To torture confused intellectuals such as this poor woman. No. This, I will not permit."

Halloran stood up. "He's your problem, Alec. Just make sure he doesn't get underfoot." I watched Halloran move off, bodyguard falling in behind him like a clumsy shadow, and turned to the aging German.

"Okay. Let's hear it."

"She is pathetic, Alec. I have followed her now for days. She spends most of her free time at meetings to save the whales, save the children, save Nicaragua, stop nuclear energy, eradicate AIDS. She is not an evil woman. It is clear that she was brought into this by the Irishman. He has been her lover off and on since she was a fifteen-year-old child in that convent. She joined the Communist Party for idealistic reasons. The terrorists are for her, how do the English say, Robin Hoods. Glamorous fighters for the downtrodden. She has never harmed anyone. Never spilt blood. I will not permit her to be tortured." He stood up, bowed slightly, and held out his hand. "I am severing our contract, Alec. I can no longer work with you."

"I thought you wanted to destroy terrorism, Lothar."

"I do. But the means you are willing to employ are as bad as what you seek to destroy."

I watched him disappear into the crowd, erect, walking

with the slightly stiff-legged gait of a man on the verge of old age. Halloran was right. It was beginning to unravel. Too many people were getting hurt. We had to finish it quickly or it was going sour. I caught a taxi to Chez Maurice, the salon of the couturier Jenny was photographing. She had asked me to pick her up there.

It was in a building just off the Champs-Elysées on the Rue de Berri. His boutique was on the ground floor. It looked like a Fred Astaire movie set circa 1935, all glass and chrome with about four dresses draped over stylized metal figures with aluminum masks for faces. Nothing seemed to be for sale.

One of Maurice's minions glanced at my invitation and directed me to a staircase leading up to the second floor. Maurice was having a preview of his summer collection for fashion critics, magazine editors, and ready-to-wear buyers of his popular designs. The real opening was scheduled for that evening. Rumor had it that Princess Diana was going to show up, along with Elizabeth Taylor and a cluster of the European and Latin American super-rich who were the backbone of the trade.

Jenny, in ancient Levis and a blue cotton sweater, sleeves pushed back above the elbow, was lighting the stage and positioning half a dozen still cameras at strategic angles around the room. The models would come onstage from the right, cross it once, then climb two steps up to a long ramp and move above the audience on the narrow runway, turn at the end, stand for a split second, then saunter back.

"I thought you weren't going to make it. I practically had to break Maurice's arm to get you the invitation. This is the biggest Paris opening since Christian Dior showed off the New Look in 1947. You're participating in a historic event."

Chatter in the room hushed as a tall, slender man in a double-breasted blazer, creamy white trousers, and black-and-white wingtips bounded onto the stage. He looked cadaverous, his emaciated face emphasizing high cheekbones, flashing blue eyes, and a mop of artfully unruly black hair.

"Ladies and gentlemen. Maurice welcomes you to this, his tenth collection. A historic day in Paris fashion annals. Something totally new. A breakthrough from the years in the desert of denial through which you have all suffered. One of my competitors said that fashion follows the world. Well, my dears, perhaps his fashion does. But the world is a dreary place, full of tension and crisis. What we all need is a return to gaiety, a recapturing of illusion. So today, in this salon, we are going to attempt to make the world follow fashion. We are going to create for you—what else?—happiness, joie de vivre, and banish ugly dissonance, harsh imagery, and garishness. We are going to make you beautiful."

I stood at the back of the room as the spectacle unfolded. The audience, ninety percent women dressed in surprisingly muted styles and colors, sat poised with sketchbooks at the ready. The first model, a tall mulatto with a cap of close-cropped hair and the classic features of a Fulani warrior, came out in a body-hugging purple silk dress cut so low in the back that the beginning cleavage of her buttocks appeared at the V. It hung on her bony shoulders by tiny black straps, barely covering small, uptilted breasts. She moved like a cat, dress clinging to her body like a second skin, long legs gliding down the platform, whirling at the end, freezing for a moment, returning.

"Interesting, huh? He's the only designer around who makes women look like something you'd like to get into bed with."

Xerxes stood at my elbow, Gauloise hanging from the corner of his mouth.

"Why all the hocus-pocus? You could have called me, and I would have met you at the embassy."

"Maybe. You might also have disappeared. Anyway, the French are looking for you. They're watching the embassy. Maurice is ours. He's under deep cover. The SDECE has never made him. A brilliant agent. He's slept with the wives of half the politicians in France. And walked away with their husband's secrets."

"What's up?"

He motioned me to follow him as a willowy Vietnamese in a yellow silk pants suit cut to the navel replaced the black girl on the runway. Xerxes led me to the left behind the stage, weaving his way into a mass of models, dressers, makeup artists, and seamstresses moving frantically among racks of clothing. The black girl had stripped off the purple dress and stood nude smoking a cigarette in a long black holder as a dresser fumbled among half a dozen suits before coming up with a frilly white concoction, all lace and fluff.

"That's the silliest-looking fucking dress I've ever seen," the model said.

The couturier appeared at her side, grinning. "We're into virgins, Almah. It'll take you back to when you were ten." He had a heavy Brooklyn accent.

The girl shrugged and slipped the dress over her head as the hairdresser and makeup artist moved in to strip her face and rebuild it.

"Back here," Xerxes said, pushing behind a curtain and into a long, deserted room full of sewing machines, rolls of material, artists' drawing boards, and dressmaker's dummies. Maurice's office overlooked the work area via a wall-sized one-way mirror. It was a hymn to avant-garde kitsch. Warhols dominated the walls, and life-size plaster of Paris castings of Edith Piaf, Cary Grant, John Wayne, and Sophia Loren, illustrating some of the more arcane suggestions of the *Joy of Sex,* decorated the corners. Behind a glass-topped desk piled high with sketches hung a crude black-and-white poster of an erect penis, veins distended, under it the legend: The House God.

"I doubt if Congress would approve of your choice of agents."

"He's one of the best. We bought him twenty years ago. Paid for his first collection. We've owned him ever since. A nice little Jewish boy from Brooklyn who made good through deceit, betrayal, and talent." He motioned me to a chair and offered me a crumpled package of Gauloises.

"No, thanks."

"Yeah. None of the minor vices." He sucked in the smoke and coughed, leaning back in the black leather Wassily chair. "We got problems, Thompson."

"We?"

"Yeah. We. You and that freak Halloran are about as subtle as trucks. You've been stomping around Europe for a week like a rhinoceros at a tea party. First you go around advertising you're going to knock off the Brigade of the Fifteenth of January. Then you set up a hit team in Paris and blow away Assad. No small boy, incidentally. He was one of Abu Nidal's top guns. On loan to Wohlgemuth. So they try to take you out, and you leave a trail of bodies behind you." He sucked in another lungful of the vile black smoke. "The French are understandably annoyed."

"The French? They love to sit back and watch their criminals knock each other off. What's wrong with wasting a few terrorists?"

"Image. You know it. I know it. If these clowns begin to look vulnerable, it might occur to a lot of people to fight back instead of rolling over and putting their feet in the air. Terrorists live on fear. People quit being afraid of them, and they've got trouble. They're threatening the French with some major Paris hits now, right at the beginning of the tourist season. It will be a combined operation by Action Directe, the Brigade, the PLO, Basques, and the Provos. Remember last year? They killed a couple of dozen people in a week. Disrupted a city of seven million people. Cost the French economy hundreds of millions of tourist dollars."

"Yeah. So we should get a medal for knocking off a few of them."

Xerxes grinned, teeth gleaming against his dark skin. "If life were fair, Thompson, I'd give you one. But like the man said, it ain't." He shook his head. "You're through. The

Skorzeny hit was the last straw. The French want it stopped. Now. You get hold of Halloran and call it off."

"I work for old man Purvis."

"He's in and out of a coma. It's terminal. He's got three, maybe four days to live. Junior has taken over the business. And we're going to make damn sure he calls it off. We're seeing to that."

"The old man hired me. As long as he's still alive, he calls the shots."

"You could wind up spending forty years in a French slammer. Makes an American jail look like a boy scout camp."

I stood up. "Jenny works for you?"

"For the Brits. They liked the idea of wasting a few hijackers. Especially if somebody else did the dirty work. But they wanted you in sight in case it got hairy. So did I. She volunteered."

"So the business with Myles was a setup? You used him to glue her onto me."

"Yeah. We set the whole thing up, and you fell for it." Xerxes smiled. "You think she was in love with you? You must be getting soft, Thompson."

On the way out I paused to watch a tall blonde in a classic white evening gown slit up the side like an Ao Dai, revealing a black garter with a small red rose as she moved.

"Pissed at me?" Jenny stood beside me, camera hanging from one hand, a film of sweat on her face.

"No. How about dinner? I'll pick you up at the Ritz at eight."

"Sure." She ran a hand behind my neck, pulled my head down, and kissed me, turning quickly and moving toward the runway, Nikon clicking rhythmically. On the street I turned right toward the George V metro stop. It wasn't hard to spot them. A slim male about thirty in a French sport jacket and thirty-dollar layered haircut. What he couldn't hide was the American walk. The woman took a little longer to make. She was almost middle-aged, in a sensible skirt and sweater. I stopped at one of the sidewalk cafés where you hardly hear French and had an espresso. When I got up they were both back in place. Knowing they'd been spotted. Less careful now. Pulling in tight.

I went down into the metro, taking the Vincennes direction, moving down to the end of the platform. She followed, leaving about a hundred feet between us. The man dropped into a seat opposite the first-class cars. The lights of the Neuilly train appeared up the tunnel, slowing as it entered the station, sighing to a stop across the way. I counted thirty seconds after the doors opened and dropped down onto the tracks, leaping the third rail in the middle, and vaulted onto the opposite platform, slipping through the doors as they closed. Across the way, the man had started to climb down on the track when the woman stopped him. I got off at Argentine and caught a cab to within a few blocks of the hit team's house.

Halloran and Malhe met me at the door. "Hello, sport. What brings you here?"

"We've got to talk."

"Sure. Eric. Give him a rubdown."

"What's this all about?"

"Let's just say we're not real sure whose team you're on anymore, slick. No offense."

Malhe started to search me when Halloran shook his head. "Use the gizmo. Ol' Thompson here is real smart. He might have some spook gadget stashed away somewhere." Malhe ran the electronic search mechanism over me.

"He's clean."

"Okay." Halloran said. "Why are you here?"

"Clemens."

"The old kraut? What about him?"

"Leave him alone."

Halloran grinned. "Sure, hoss. We'll leave him alone. Don't need him anymore. Malhe here and a couple of the boys have already picked up the broad. She's going to be real cooperative."

I told him about my meeting with Xerxes. "You know the deal. If we don't get Wohlgemuth, we don't get paid."

"Yeah," Halloran said. "Looks like we better get off the dime. You want to join the party?"

chapter 15

Eliane de la Margerie sat in an immense leather chair reading *Le Monde,* looking up with a confident insolence as we entered.

"My colleague, Dr. Thompson," Halloran said, speaking serviceable French with a heavy American accent.

"I hope he is not as big a fool as you are. Are you bringing me something to eat? I've missed my lunch."

"What have we got, Luke?" Halloran asked the guard.

"Some cheese and bread. Wine."

"Bring the lady a tray. And some glasses for us. We may be here for a while." He turned back to the woman. "Now. We might as well get something straight, madame. We need information, and we need it quickly. You give it to us, and we'll let you go fairly soon."

"And if I don't?"

"Then we'll break your legs," Halloran said, smiling.

The woman threw her head back and laughed. She wasn't conventionally pretty, but her pointed face reflected vitality and a lively intelligence. The laugh was from the gut, a sensual release. She was enjoying herself, excited by the drama and tension.

"You are simple-minded, like all Americans. My mother was tortured by German experts during the war. She revealed nothing. I will maintain the family honor. Do your worst."

"Your father was a collaborator."

She turned to me, infuriated. "My father was a sincere misguided man who spent seven years in Soviet prison camps for his beliefs."

"He was a member of the Charlemagne Division, the French contribution to the SS. He fought in Berlin up to the end trying to defend Hitler's bunker."

"Yes. He joined because he thought the Nazis would purify the corrupt and degenerate French capitalist state. His only error was in choosing the wrong road. He was an idealist, a French patriot, a naval officer who was enraged when the British sank our fleet at Toulon."

"To keep it out of German hands."

"*Merde*. To reduce France to the status of a second-rate power once the war was over, leaving her colonies easy pickings for the British vultures. The same grubby instincts which drive American policy today. My father devoted his life to sabotaging the Anglo-Saxon conspiracy against France."

Halloran looked at me. "She's nuts."

"More like bewildered."

Halloran's man came back with an ornate silver tray bearing a sliced baguette, Camembert and Roquefort cheeses, and a bottle of St. Estephe. I opened the bottle and poured three glasses.

"My friend here is a rather primitive fellow. He's also in a great hurry," I said sipping the wine, a superb Bordeaux, tannin muted by time but the strength still there, like an aging weight lifter.

"You mean he will beat me if I don't answer?" she asked, grinning at me as she sliced off a hunk of Roquefort, sandwiched it between two chunks of bread, and washed it down with a generous slug of wine. "What else could one expect from a culture as corrupt as yours? Misfits. The dregs of Europe, collected by press gangs to man your factories. Debtors. Criminals. Halfwits. Religious fanatics. People incapable of succeeding in their own societies, swept up by the police of Europe and sold to your nineteenth-century recruiters of industrial slaves. Obviously your country is without a coherent center, genetically flawed, capable of the most profound horrors. Why do you think I fight you with such fanatcism?"

"Where's Paddy O'Faolin?"

"Paddy?" Her face softened. "My Irish leprechaun? I have no idea. You don't think they tell me where they live?" She looked at Halloran pityingly. "That's the most elementary of security measures. Isolation. We communicate through public phone booths. Nobody knows more than he needs to." She ate, drank, and chattered on, proud of her expertise.

"But Paddy is your lover. When you want to screw, you must know where to find him."

She stared at Halloran, aristocratic face tight with contempt. "That is the level of your awareness, clearly. Screwing. Paddy O'Faolin is one of the most sensitive, intelligent, cultivated, idealistic men I've ever known."

"Yeah. He's also an apostate priest and murderous enforcer for the Provos."

"Apostate priest?" She breathed the phrase. "On the contrary. He is a true Christian. A believer in God's need to free mankind from corruption and exploitation. He is one of the great experts on St. Thomas Aquinas."

"Makes him right at home with Marxism."

"What?"

"St. Thomas taught that revelation was the source of truth with reason as its lackey. Marxists believe the same thing."

She sipped the wine, staring at me over the rim of the glass. "Typical half-educated American sophistry. What more could one expect of a nation obsessed with vulgar egalitarianism whose tastes are personified by hamburgers and that vile concoction Coca-Cola? Simone de Beauvoir really summed it all up in her book *The Mandarins*."

Halloran looked at me. "Is that the one where she describes screwing Nelson Algren?"

"Yeah."

He started to laugh. "Guy gets his ashes hauled by some aging broad, and she writes about it as if the world were coming to an end. For two hundred pages. Longest piece of ass in literature."

The French woman stood up and threw the half-filled wine glass in his face. Her hand was still extended when he caught her with an open-handed slap, not hard, but enough to spin her back into the chair. I motioned to him to follow me into the hall.

"She'll break."

"Easy."

"She'll also lie."

"Yeah."

"Beat it out of her, and you'll never be able to separate out the truth."

"Yeah."

"You've got time."

He looked at me, pale blue eyes suddenly weary. "Shit. It'll take hours to con it out of her. Also, she's probably a pain in the ass in bed. Fucking intelligent women bore the shit out of me. Why don't you do it?"

"She likes primitives."

Halloran stared at me and started to laugh. "Okay, hoss. You win. I'll take a crack at it. Kind of funny, huh?"

"What?"

"How, when you get older, you realize it all comes down to the crotch."

"I knew it when I was twelve."

I walked up to the Avenue de Neuilly and caught a cab to Clemens's pension. The receptionist hadn't seen him since breakfast. "You are Monsieur Thompson?"

"Yes."

"A friend of Monsieur Clemens left a message for you."

Alexander Fourier. The number was a subsection of the ministry of the interior. After going through three layers of flunkeys he came on the line.

"Thompson?"

"Yes."

"Where are you calling from?"

"A phone booth."

"Things have gone very bad." He sounded like a man having trouble breathing. "Very bad."

"Lothar?"

"He is dead."

"How?"

"Hit by a car. This morning. Witnesses say he was evidently attempting to stop a kidnapping. The car deliberately ran him down. Does he have any family?"

"He has a son in Hamburg."

"I will handle the details. But you, Thompson, you must leave Paris at once. The SDECE is looking for you. If they trace you to me"—he coughed into the phone, gasping for breath. "You understand my problem? If they discover I have been passing you information, I am finished. My pension. Everything. Gone. Perhaps even prison."

I hung up as he babbled on and walked out into the pale sunshine, moving with the crowd through the narrow streets of the ancient quarter, remembering the pale old man, his light blue intelligent eyes edged with pain and memory. Paris in the late spring is life itself. Young lovers stroll arm in arm through the streets, stopping to embrace, moving on. People stand on corners, faces raised to the sun like flowers. The gray stones of the ancient buildings reflect the golden light, taking on new youth beneath the grime. Winter is the time to die. Not in Paris in the spring. I walked for four hours, working off the rage, before stopping at a café to call the Ritz.

Jenny answered on the first ring. "Alec."

"Yes."

"What's wrong?"

"I'd like a raincheck on tonight."

"You're pissed."

"No. Something's come up."

"What?"

"Clemens."

"I know. They killed him. Alec, don't be a fool. Halloran knows what you'll do when you find out. You go out there now, and they'll slaughter you. Are you at the hotel? I'm coming over." I hung up and caught a taxi to the Esmeralda. Mathilde met me at the door.

"The police are looking for you."

"They know I'm here?"

She shook her head. "They put out a circular. We didn't register you. Ivo thought it would be better. But you can't escape for long. Is it bad?"

"No. I'll be gone tomorrow morning. Thanks, Mathilde."

She grinned. "We charge double for not registering you. Take care, Alec."

I extracted Sindona's little plastic automatic from a running sock and ejected the magazine, counting seven cartridges, reinserting them, slipping one into the breach and setting the safety. I was finishing up a primitive holster fashioned from a cardboard shirt stiffener when the phone rang.

"Alec?"

"Yes."

"An Englishman is on his way up. A sinister type. He said he was a friend." I slipped the little gun in my belt in the small of my back and let De Crecy in.

"What's up?"

He sauntered over to the window and stared out at the cathedral outlined against the dying spring sun. "I was born a Catholic, Thompson. Remarkable how the sight of a great church can still move me even though I've known for thirty years it was all claptrap."

"Drink?"

"Please."

I poured us slugs of Duque de Alba in water glasses. He raised his in a toast. "Here's to a cure for AIDS." He sipped the dark brandy, leaning back in the wicker chair. "I told him it was a mistake, old boy. He's not always rational, you know. I think the German must have offended him in some way. Most unprofessional."

"Yeah."

"Halloran's quite effective, you know. Remarkably sensitive for such a brute. I assume you will kill him when this is over."

"What happened?"

"It was all very clever. We put her in a bedroom upstairs. Isolated her. Somebody watching through a peephole, of course. She paced the floor for an hour or so. Checked the place out like a cat, looking for an escape hole. Then Mike went to work on her. Took dinner up. Ate like a trooper, she did, talking the whole time. I must say our madman can be charming. Definitely some tendencies I hadn't suspected there, if you know what I mean. Most sensitive to her moods. Played her like a trout. Listened, mostly, drawing her out, pouring wine down her. I mean, women are not all that difficult, don't you know. Not nearly as clever as boys. All you have to do is listen, look sympathetic, and bleed maleness and they're really like putty. Oh, she knew what he was doing. Too clever by half, she was. That's the trouble with intelligent women. They have nothing but contempt for the stupid male."

"How did he do it?"

"He raped her. Really quite brutally. Just at the moment when she was eager to let herself be seduced. You know, get him in bed and he'd do whatever she wanted? He slapped her twice, very hard, and took her. Most impressive."

"And?"

"She was shattered, of course. That marvelous upper-class confidence completely wrecked. He slapped her a few more times, called her a stupid tramp, and she coughed it all up. It's the Bank of Lyons, all right. Tomorrow morning. She doesn't know the exact time or details of the plan, but she gave us enough."

"How do you know she's not lying?"

"Succinylcholine, old boy. I gave her a shot of it when Halloran was finished with her. Very effective, you know, when you've already got details. Not so good when you have to start from scratch. Nasty stuff of course. She suffered some rather serious convulsions."

"I'd like to check the story out with her."

De Crecy stared at his impeccable manicure. "Afraid it can't be done, old boy. Very dramatic lady. Would you believe it? She had a cyanide capsule in a little signet ring which her mother carried in the Resistance. Took it when she realized what she'd done. Felt remorse. Silly melodramatic bitch."

"Won't they miss her?"

"Apparently not. She's not an active member of the gang, you know. More like a groupie. She would not have participated in the robbery. No reason for them to realize we took her."

"So what does Halloran want?"

"We're a bit short-handed. He wonders if you'd like to take a hand. Given the money that's involved, I mean."

"How have you got it set up?"

"The bank is here," De Crecy said, unfolding a crude map of the crossing of the Boulevard St. Michel and the Boulevard St. Germain. "The lady confirmed Clemens's information. It's a collection point for money changing centers. Stuff is brought in the previous evening, counted, and ready to be transported to a government clearing house the next morning. Awfully convenient. Neatly bagged and counted, don't you know? Wohlgemuth plans to lift the lot.

As I say, she didn't have details, but there will be six of them. Four inside the bank and two on the street."

"Two cars going in opposite directions?"

"So it would seem, although, as I say, she didn't have exact details of the plan."

"Makes sense. Divides pursuit."

"Precisely. I expect they will ditch the cars very quickly in any case."

"What's Mike got in mind?"

"Very simple, really. We're only interested in the Irishman and Wohlgemuth, of course. Two of Mike's thugs will be in the bank pretending to change money. There are long lines at this time of year. We'll keep running them through in alternate pairs until the terrorists show up."

"Where'll you be?"

"I've just finished scouting the area. There are some garçonnières on the fifth floor of the building across the way. Former maids' quarters up under the roof. One is vacant. I've managed to get in with the help of Eric's invaluable skills as a lock pick."

"What's the scenario?"

"Best case is that Mike's men can take them out as they start the robbery. After all, they won't be expecting two people in the money-changing line to haul out Uzis and blast them."

"Sounds messy."

"I agree. But I can't guarantee to hit two of them on a crowded street as they come out."

"At that range? You could hit a cat in the eye."

"True, but I might not have a clear shot. In any event, we'll assume they will need two minutes to collect the loot and exit the bank. At one hundred seconds I will explode the windshields of the getaway cars and, hopefully, take out the drivers. And, of course, hit anyone coming through the door."

"Halloran?"

"Sitting in a café across the street directing the action with a radio. Malhe will be backing me. Halloran's other two men will be loitering by the entrance in case they're needed."

"The getaway?"

"On foot, old boy. We'll junk the arsenal and fade into the crowds. Much more efficient than cars in that rush-hour traffic. We should be on our way out of town within an hour heading for Cherbourg."

"What does he want me to do?"

He handed me a gym bag. "There's an Uzi and four clips. He wants you about ten paces from the bank entrance down the boulevard. Purely precautionary measure. In case any of our team gets wounded, you're to take them out. Can't have people blabbing, you know. French are very good at getting criminals to talk." He stood up and extended a thin, muscular hand. "Good working with you, old boy. Not often one finds a true professional. Tomorrow at nine."

I hadn't broken down an Uzi in years. It took a while to find the glitch. The firing pin had been shortened and misaligned a hair, just enough to miss hitting the cartridge. It snapped on an empty chamber with a satisfying solidity, but in action nothing would have happened.

"Alec?" Jenny's voice came through the door. "Still pissed?" she asked.

"No."

"They asked me to keep you under surveillance, not sleep with you. That was my idea."

"And now?"

"That Brit I passed on the stairs. He's the hit man, isn't he?"

I moved over to the window and watched De Crecy cross the Square Viviani. Two figures drifted after him. "Yours?"

"Xerxes. Stopping Halloran is top priority right now. Frank is really in trouble with the French. The CIA has several important operations going with them which could turn sour if this thing gets out of hand. He doesn't have any choice."

"De Crecy will slip the tail."

"Of course."

"Why doesn't he just turn me over to the French?"

"You're the bait for Halloran and the rest of the team. He expects you to lead him to them."

"And you're supposed to keep me in sight?"

"There's no law against combining business with pleasure, is there?" she asked, coming over and dropping on my lap, unbuttoning my shirt, running a hand across my chest. "Even spies are human."

She was right.

I woke with the first light, slipping out of bed without awakening her. The table by the window was littered with the remains of an omelette and salad Mathilde had sent up. Two empty bottles of Beaujolais Villages sat precariously on the windowsill. I dressed quickly in jeans and running shoes, taping the little automatic in the makeshift holster to my ankle, slinging the bag with the crippled Uzi over my shoulder.

Down in the square two of Xerxes' men sat on separate benches, reading newspapers. I slipped out of the room, careful not to awaken the girl, and went down one flight, opening a window onto the air shaft and jumping the six feet to the roof of the adjoining building. I crossed the red tiles, circled around an open courtyard, and slipped down a drain into an alley off the Rue du Petit Pont.

The café at the corner of St. Michel and St. Germain was full of the usual early-morning crowd. A couple of policemen going off duty. A table of late-night whores having breakfast and coming down before going home to bed. A taxi driver. An intern from the clinic around the corner, his white coat flecked with blood, stethoscope in his side pocket, talking animatedly to a pretty, bored young nurse. Over the next hour and a half, the clientele changed with the deepening morning light. Students on their way to the Lycée Louis le Grand stopping for an espresso. Secretaries wolfing down croissants and looking at their watches. Businessmen from the quarter gathering at the same tables to trade gossip.

Finally, as the sun began to beat down, the tourists. A sea of eager, anxious faces bent over guides and maps trying their French on the bored waiters.

I took a seat in the front row of tables. The corner is the navel of the city, heart of its intellectual quarter, ancient university a few steps away, ruins of the monastery of Cluny looming over it.

At eight De Crecy strolled past, ignoring me, carrying a large briefcase with the broken-down sniper rifle. Malhe trailed him. They disappeared into the entrance of the building behind me. Across the way, four members of the hit team strolled past the bank entrance, ambled a hundred yards down, and drifted back.

Halloran, unobtrusive in an open-necked shirt, gray trousers, and sandals, dropped into a chair at the table next to mine. I shoved the bag with the defective Uzi toward him with my foot. He grinned.

"It was worth a try, hoss. After all, you've been out of it for a while. Might be getting rusty."

"So rusty I wouldn't check out a piece?"

"Yeah. Well, let's just say it was a message."

"You already sent me one."

"He's dead, hoss. He got in the way. You heard me warn him. Old man was stubborn. Forget him. Just hold the thought of all that scratch." His eyes suddenly focused on the bank across the way.

Two of his men were waiting among a small crowd. As they surged for the door with the usual French disregard for priority, Wohlgemuth slipped out of the passing stream and joined them. Three young Arabs had also mingled with the group behind Halloran's men.

I turned to look up at the facade of the building behind me, searching for and finding the open window in the low-ceilinged maid's room on the fifth floor. The sun glinted off the silencer of De Crecy's sniper rifle, weaving small circles as it sought a target.

I stood up and walked toward the corner as Halloran murmured orders into the fake hearing aid. Traffic was completely stymied now, nothing moving as a gridlock paralyzed the two main arteries and defied whistle-blowing police. Inside the bank, the sudden high-pitched chatter of the Uzis was answered by the coughing of heavier-caliber Soviet grease guns.

One of the young Arabs staggered out of the bank clutching his right arm, weapon dangling from a strap around his neck. A motorcycle roared to life and climbed onto the sidewalk, scattering pedestrians leaping for shelter behind the cars. The cyclist careened up to the wounded man who threw himself onto the oblong seat. As the machine revved up, the helmet of the rider was suddenly spun in a half circle and his body flung violently to the right as the machine, still running, collapsed on the sidewalk. Wohlgemuth moved out from the doorway of the bank, then stepped back as the sniper rifle barked again, slug chipping marble off the bank facade.

The German elevated his grease gun and sprayed the open window with a prolonged burst, moving out onto the sidewalk and beginning to run to his right as he fired. The second motorcycle, ridden by Paddy O'Faolin, scattered the sidewalk crowd and slowed, allowing Wohlgemuth to leap on the seat.

Halloran's two remaining men moved to block the motorcycle's path, dodging back into the crowd as Wohlgemuth opened fire under the Irishman's arm. Weaving wildly among the cars, O'Faolin turned the corner, De Crecy's sniper rifle spattering shots in his wake. I turned in time to see Halloran rise from the café chair and fade into the crowd.

Jenny was on the phone when I got back to the hotel. "Yes. Okay. He just walked in. I'll tell him." She put the receiver down. "Five bombs just went off all over town. One in front of the Bon Marché department store. Ten people are dead. It's an action in solidarity with the Brigade of the

Fifteenth of January. The French are seriously annoyed. Xerxes just gave you to them. They'll be here in five minutes. Christ, why wouldn't you tell us? We could have stopped it."

"Caved in to the terrorists, you mean. Let them win another one. Crumple up in a little ball every time they make a threat."

She stood up and came over to face me. "Ten innocent people are dead because of you. Plus three more in that bank who were killed in the crossfire. Where is Halloran? If you can give him to us, you might get out of this without being guillotined."

The distinctive sirens of the French police drifted up from the Square Viviani below. Ahn-ree, Ahn-ree, Ahn-ree.

"I've got an appointment with Halloran," I said, turning toward the door. She held a little twenty-five-caliber Colt automatic in a professional two-handed grip aimed at my right leg.

"Don't force me to use it, Alec. Knees are a bitch to put right."

chapter 16

The Service de Documentation Extérieure et de Contre Espionage (SDECE) is a shadowy organization somewhere between the CIA and the FBI in the French scheme of things. Its primary role is hunting down foreign spies, but in the seventies it also took over the pursuit and elimination of terrorists. Hamstrung by politicians unwilling to offend either important trading partners in the Arab world or the intellectuals who sympathized with the goals of the leftist guerrillas, its leaders had negotiated a series of truces with the various organizations, effectively putting France off limits to terrorist actions. The peace was periodically violated but, until recently, had managed to spare France and its capital from the worst outrages.

Xerxes' men delivered me to an eighteenth-century palace tucked away in the Rue Barbet de Jouy, which served as SDECE headquarters. The brass plaque at the street entrance identified the building as the headquarters of a nonexistent international agricultural organization. Xerxes, flanked by a slim, expensively tailored young Frenchman, met me at the massive glass doors of the building. "This is Bernard Pivot,

Thompson. He represents the Quai d'Orsay." Nobody offered to shake hands. The Frenchman led us into an ornate main hall hung with Jacques Louis David paintings of Napoleon's victories and a few priceless Gobelins, up a marble staircase and into an imposing, high-ceilinged room dominated by an immense Bonnard nude over the fireplace.

José Maria Sindona y Suarez, Wilbur Purvis, Jr., and Jenny Blanton sat with another elegant Frenchman around a delicate Louis XV conference table inlaid with ivory and semi-precious stones, a Sèvres coffee service in the center.

"Hello, Frank," the Frenchman said in perfect public school English. "Good of you to come." He rose, bowed slightly to me, and introduced himself. "Dr. Thompson. Jean Louis Aujard. Please be seated. Coffee?" He looked like an ad for Savile Row in an impeccably tailored navy blue suit with an almost invisible stripe, polka-dotted tie repeated in a breast-pocket handkerchief. He dropped into a chair at the head of the table and took command, lighting a cigarette and leaning forward on the table. "I think we all know why we're here, gentlemen. Seventeen people are dead in bomb attacks in Paris this morning, ten of them at the Bon Marché. Another three innocent Frenchmen were killed in that assault on the bank and the attempt by your group to eliminate them. Needless to say, my political leaders are outraged. They attribute this slaughter to the mindless attempt at vengeance set in motion by Mr. Purvis, tacitly abetted by you, Frank, and implemented by Dr. Thompson."

"I wouldn't call it mindless," Purvis said. "Kill a few of the bastards and they might think twice about murdering and hijacking. All you gutless Europeans and our gutless spooks want to do is cave in to them."

"Mr. Purvis, I will thank you to keep your opinions of my country's courage to yourself. I do not find it useful to conduct international relations on the same basis as you do in some Texas cow town. The fact is that you have caused the tragic deaths of a large number of my countrymen. The carnage must be stopped. You had an opportunity to head off the events of this morning and you did not avail yourself of it. Now I must insist. Your team must be called off immediately. There must be no further action against the Brigade of the Fifteenth of January on French soil."

"So you're groveling to the bastards," Purvis said. "Why don't you just cut off your balls and serve them up on one of these silver platters?" He gestured toward the table. "We're not stopping anything. Two of the assholes are already dead. Halloran tells me he can deliver the other two in a day or so. Just sit tight, and we'll clean things up for you."

The young Frenchman from the foreign office intervened. "Mr. Purvis, your company has investments in France of some five hundred million dollars. There are, how do you say, some irregularities that have been discovered in your repatriation of profits. Serious irregularities. We are prepared to negotiate a sensible solution to the problem provided you prove yourself reasonable in this matter. If not"—he shrugged—"you may well find your assets impounded and possibly confiscated."

"Why, you little pissant. Who do you think you're dealing with? Some penny-ante wildcatter? You try it, and we'll litigate your skinny little ass off in the U.S. courts. Shit, sonny, Purvis Oil owns four senators outright and rents another six. You want trouble, you just pull some shit like that. We'll go in the alley with you and your second-rate country, and see who comes out."

Aujard held up his hands. "Gentlemen. Gentlemen. I understand your concern, Mr. Purvis. You wish satisfaction for the death of your niece. But you cannot expect us to sacrifice the lives of our citizens for it."

"He's right, Junior," Sindona said.

"What the fuck does that mean? She was your daughter."

"It means you've got to quit thinking with your gonads. Dolores is dead. Killing these maniacs won't bring her back. They are total fanatics. And they have a web of connections with the other terrorist groups who support them."

Aujard nodded. "That's what's happening here. We have information that not only the PLO and the Irish Provos but the Basques and Red Brigades and an Armenian organization all participated in these bombings."

"Why?" I asked, knowing the answer, wanting to see if he did.

"They cannot afford to see one of these bands wiped out. It would be disastrous for the morale of the others if we were able to eliminate one of them. Also, their cooperation is much closer now than previously. There is even an organization, the Revolutionary Coordinating Junta, set up in Cuba some years back, which acts as a clearing house for their actions. These bombings are a highly sophisticated, orchestrated joint reply to your attempt to destroy the Brigade of the Fifteenth of January."

"And you plan to let them get away with it?"

"We have no choice. There is no way we can track them all down. Paris is full of foreigners. We cannot control the environment they swim in. The only practical thing is to make a deal. This we have done. And you have broken it. We must insist that this operation be terminated immediately."

"He's right, Junior. We don't have any choice," Sindona said.

"I thought you were going to stake this Wohlgemuth out on an anthill and let them eat his eyes, José. What's going on? Why the fuck are you changing your mind?"

Xerxes intervened. "They've threatened the Mexican oil fields, Mr. Purvis. There is a plan to blow up the oil pipelines to the coast, set the storage tanks on fire, disrupt production. Mexico is broke. It can't pay the interest on its debts. Without the oil, it will go under economically. Mr. Sindona is simply being sensible."

"She was your daughter, José," Purvis said.

"Yes. My daughter. And now she is dead, and life continues. I cannot sacrifice my country's interests to my personal desire for vengeance. The old man is in a coma. You are in charge, Junior. Call off the team. It was an old-fashioned piece of romanticism in any case. Personal revenge has no place in the world today."

I interrupted. "Keep giving in to terrorist groups and they will eventually spread chaos and anarchy to such an extent that the only answer will be extreme repressive measures. Which is exactly what they want. To drive legitimate governments into acts of counter-terrorism to maintain public order, assuring popular discontent. That's the beginning of the end." I sounded like a broken record. That was the danger with being right. It began to bore people, and they tuned you out.

The Frenchman shook his head. "You are a scholar, Dr. Thompson. Your analysis has a certain intellectual appeal. But one must govern with pragmatism. Right now we have no means of combating terrorism supported by Soviet assets. If we can persuade our adversaries in the East to stop helping these groups, we can move against them. Under present conditions, this is hopeless. Their revolutionary élan is still too high. The belief in the inevitable victory of Marxist-Leninism too powerful. We must temporize until they can be persuaded it is in their self-interest to suppress these people.

He turned to Purvis. "I repeat. You will order the team to stop all its activities on French soil as of today. I hold you personally responsible for any further actions. And you, Dr. Thompson. I want their location."

I looked at Xerxes. "Your men followed De Crecy last night when he left my hotel."

"They lost him."

"I don't know where they hole up. Halloran is psychotic. He trusts nobody."

"How do you contact him?"

"I don't. He gets in touch with me."

"Mr. Purvis. Where are they?"

The oil man stood up. "You can go fuck yourself, Aujard. Even if I knew where Halloran is, and I don't, I wouldn't tell you. As far as I'm concerned the operation is still on." The big man started toward the door.

"You have more than thirty tankers at sea, Mr. Purvis," the Frenchman said.

"So what?" Purvis had stopped in his tracks.

"Do you have any idea how easily they can be wired to explode?"

"The Arabs would be fools to start something like that. It would cost them a fortune." He didn't sound convinced.

"We're not necessarily talking about the Arabs," the young Frenchman said, his voice silky with menace.

Purvis slammed the door behind him as he left.

"Perhaps we should have him arrested," the young Frenchman from the Foreign Office said.

Aujard shook his head. "He has dined with the president. The treasury minister was entertained at his ranch last fall. If we move against him overtly the American ambassador will create an uproar. We have him under the closest possible surveillance. Perhaps he will lead us to this man Halloran." He turned to me. "What are the"—he glanced at his notes, eyebrows raised in amusement—"Heracles Commando's plans?"

"I don't know."

"Will they contact you?"

"Probably."

Aujard penciled in a number and pushed his card across the table. "You are to inform me immediately of any contact. Failure to do so, Dr. Thompson, could lead to very serious consequences for you."

"Yeah. I haven't had dinner with the president."

"Precisely. We are agreed then, gentlemen? We'll do our utmost to cancel the hit team? One way or another."

Xerxes and Jenny stayed behind with Aujard as Sindona and I were led out into the cobblestoned street by a uniformed flunky. The Mexican turned to me. "You're pulling something, Thompson. What?"

"You ever read Sun Tzu? The Chinese military writer?"

"No."

"He advises those besieged by many enemies to turn them against each other."

Sindona held out his hand. "Good luck. I commend to you an old Mexican tale."

"Which is?"

"A rich man saw death in the marketplace in Mexico City and immediately mounted his horse to ride like the wind to Guadalajara. There, as he dismounted at an inn, death was waiting."

"But I just left you in Mexico City," the rich man said.

"Yes." Death replied. "I was surprised. For I had an appointment with you in Guadalajara."

It wasn't hard to spot Aujard's men. There were four. Two in a small Peugeot and two on foot, boxing me in, making no effort at concealment. I shook two by taking the metro at the Rue de Varenne, changing at Concorde for Port de Clignancourt. At Clignancourt you emerge from the metro into a gelid mass of tourists surging toward the Marche aux Puces, the immense flea market whose stalls sell everything from diamonds to second-hand shoes. It sprawls over six untidy acres. I strolled into the furniture section, a warren of jerry-built shacks housing the residue of centuries, selecting an ancient Gypsy guarding a collection of copper pots and antique sewing machines.

"Monsieur desires?" Vivid black eyes stared at me out of a mask of age.

"There are two men following me. It would be desirable if I lost them."

She glanced over the crowd and spotted Aujard's men.

"Flics."

I nodded.

"What is it you wish?"

"Your shop has a back door?"

"Yes. And my pockets have holes."

"Then you are in need of something to fill the holes."

"Five thousand francs."

"Two."

"Three," she said, standing to point toward the rear of the shop at a large and battered chest of drawers, leading me toward it. I counted out the money and stuffed it into her hand. She extracted a key and, talking and gesticulating toward the piece of furniture, opened the door into a narrow alley, pushed me through, and locked it behind me.

I turned left, running for the open street at the end. Behind me, a high-pitched screech cut off abruptly as the door to the alley smashed outward. They were a little too slow. I had already melted into the crowds by the time they reached the street.

I hailed a taxi at the Boulevard Ney and got him to drop me at the nearest post office. It took me five minutes to get through the French phone system to the health club in the Marais. I recognized the voice of the handsome receptionist.

"I'd like to talk to Karl." She put him on.

"Yes?"

"This is Thompson."

"Thompson?"

"I paid your place a visit the other night. Left via the sewer."

"What do you want?"

"I want to leave a number for Herr Wohlgemuth."

"I do not know such a name."

"Give it to him anyway. Tell him to call me back at this number."

I occupied the booth for ten minutes before the call came through.

"Thompson?"

"Yeah."

"What do you want?"

"To make a deal."

"What kind of a deal?"

"We've knocked off two of your group. You and O'Faolin got away mostly by luck this morning. Next time, we'll close you out."

"What is your deal?"

"I can deliver Halloran."

There was a long silence at the other end of the line.

"Why?"

"Do you know the name Lothar Clemens?"

"The old German policeman who was following Eliane?"

"Yes. He worked for me. Halloran killed him."

Wohlgemuth was silent again, folding it into his computer.

"You are hardly a sentimentalist, Thompson. There must be another reason."

"The money."

"The money?"

"Yeah. On your head. The French are demanding that the operation be called off."

"I know."

"Since we've managed to knock off only two of your group, we get half of what we were originally promised," I lied. "Split among the survivors."

Wohlgemuth started to laugh. "So you want me to kill Halloran to raise your share?"

"Halloran. And the Brit who left the blade in Gudrun."

The German was silent. "It is tempting. How do I know it is not a trap?"

"You don't. Life has its little risks."

"As few as possible, Thompson. However, this one may be worth it. We have to meet. You will walk down the Boulevard Raspail in the direction of Montparnasse. Start at the Rue Grenelle in half an hour. If you are followed, we will kill you." He couldn't resist making threats.

Boulevard Raspail was built when Paris exploded in the nineteenth century. A canyon of imposing mansions fallen on evil times, luxury apartments above the ground floor, jewelry shops, boutiques, offices, restaurants, and grocery stores at ground level.

I threaded my way through the plunging crowds until, just short of the junction with Montparnasse, Paddy O'Faolin pulled up to the curb on his 750cc BMW.

"Hop on, mate. Show you a bit of excitement."

He did.

We ended up somewhere near the Gare de l'Est in a working-class slum. A dark youth standing guard opened a big double door leading to a fetid inner courtyard. Two others fell in on either side of me as I dismounted. We went up two flights redolent of garlic, couscous, humus, and tabouli. Small, dark children peered around banisters and vanished. Women in veils opened doors a crack as we passed.

Wohlgemuth sat on a spavined divan with David Mifsud and a slim young Frenchman. The Maltese stood up and came around to shake me down, grinning up at me as he found the little plastic automatic taped to my ankle. He examined it with interest.

"Look at this, Dieter. There's not enough metal in it to activate a magnet."

"We have an order in for a dozen," the German said. "Well, Thompson? Why did you come? What makes you so sure we won't simply kill you?"

"You will. Or you'll try. But not right now."

"Yes. You are right. Because I want the rest of the hit team. Very well. Talk."

"They're in Neuilly." I gave him the address.

"House or apartment?"

"House. You can't possibly take it by assault. He's got too many people. Professionals."

"And you think we're amateurs?"

"Not at killing unarmed women and children. But these are seasoned soldiers. They'll hang your asses out to dry if you go after them head-on."

"So?"

"There is a way."

"Describe it."

"They order food from the local market. It's delivered by an Algerian in a little blue 2 CV Citroën van."

O'Faolin grinned. "So we put a few pounds of plastique in among the groceries, and boom."

Wohlgemuth frowned. "You Irish love bombs. If we use explosives, the French will be furious. They've just agreed to reinstate the truce. We can't risk killing any more innocent Frenchmen."

"Sure, and we won't need a big one, Dieter," the Irishman said. "Just a wee bit of a bomb to shake them up. Then we'll go in and finish them with shillelaghs."

"It might work."

"We would need somebody on the inside." Wohlgemuth picked up the little plastic gun. "Can you get in with this? Take out one or two of them when the bomb goes off and give us a chance to get in?"

"Sure."

The German thought it over. "We can do it," he said, voice rising with excitement.

"What about the plane?" O'Faolin asked.

Wohlgemuth turned to the Maltese. "What about it, David? Are all the arrangements made?"

"Yes. One of the mechanics is an Algerian. He will smuggle the equipment on board."

"You're positive it's the right one?"

"Yes. There is no doubt. Several people were bumped to make room for him and his group. There is no doubt." The Maltese grinned. "The airline is a CIA front, you know."

"Excellent. Then we have plenty of time to do both," the German said, pounding his palm with a fist. "Let's get going."

It was late afternoon before they had everything in place. Two of the Palestinians had followed the grocery van, sapping the young delivery man and leaving him trussed up in an alley. The Irishman had concocted the bomb. "The explosive force will go straight up," he said. "Nothing to worry about. A lot of noise and smoke. Just enough to create confusion. We'll time it so that it goes off one minute after it's delivered. Ali will punch the timer just before he hands over the sack at the front door. You should be able to knock off a couple of them with your little toy in the confusion after it goes up. We'll come in and handle the rest."

O'Faolin dropped me a couple of blocks from the house. Malhe opened the door and held a stubby Heckler Koch submachine gun on me as I came in. "Hands behind the head, Alec," the Pole said. "Face the wall." One of the mercenaries ran the little electronic metal detector over me.

"He's clean."

"Inside," Malhe said. De Crecy and Halloran were looking over a road map as we came in.

"What the fuck are you doing here?" Halloran asked. "You search him?"

Malhe nodded.

De Crecy moved away from Halloran, positioning himself at an oblique angle. He was frowning. It was a large rectangular room with big French windows overlooking a sliver of lawn in front and doors opening onto a terrace in the back. A big concert grand occupied one corner.

"Why the road map?"

"Didn't Purvis tell you? He's decided to call it off."

"Why?"

"Afraid for his fucking tankers. The French are threatening to blow a couple up if we don't ease off. Like they did that anti-whale hunting boat. The *Greenpeace*."

"And you agreed?"

"He's paying us the full contract price. We're hauling ass for Cherbourg in about ten minutes. One of the Purvis tankers will take us aboard. If you want to come along, you're welcome."

"And wind up with a bullet in the back of the head and some chain wrapped around my legs before I go over the side?"

"He's come to kill you, Mike," De Crecy said. "How disappointing. I thought you a professional, Thompson, but you're really nothing but a sentimental romantic. Revenging a dreary old man's death like some stupid Don Quixote."

"Why'd you kill him, Mike?"

"He got in the way when we picked up the de la Margerie woman. Tried to stop us. Strong old bugger. Put an armlock on Madden. Goddamn near dislocated his shoulder and shook the girl loose."

"So you ran him down like a rabbit." I dropped into a chair, back to the front windows, cocking my right leg on the left knee.

"He got in the way, hoss. Just like you now." The doorbell rang, and De Crecy's hand moved toward his shoulder holster.

Malhe appeared at the door. "Groceries."

"Pay him off," Halloran said impatiently. "Get everybody ready to go. Except you, amigo. You're going to have to stay." De Crecy slipped an automatic out of its holster and began screwing a thick silencer onto the barrel, never taking his eyes off me as I counted the seconds. With three to go I yanked the little plastic pistol loose and shot Halloran in the throat, backflipping out of the chair as I did, hearing De Crecy's bullet hit the soft stuff of the chair behind me. I went through the window in a ball, smashing the glass with my back, landing in a hedge as the building behind me lifted on its foundations when O'Faolin's bomb went off, imploding into a pile of rubble.

I was in a tunnel. The walls had caved in, smothering my mouth. I was suffocating, clawing my way toward a dim light. "Easy does it, old boy," De Crecy said. He was holding his hand over my mouth, stifling a scream, bright ceiling light behind his bandaged head. As he saw the fog clear in my eyes he eased his hand off my mouth.

"Awake, are we? Didn't want you calling out, bringing the nurse."

"Where are we?" I had a tube in my left arm and something was wrong with my shoulder.

"Hospital in Neuilly. Looks as if everybody else is dead. Rather clever of you, old boy, I must say. Bit risky though. If you'd been a second or so later you'd be buried with the rest of them."

"How'd you get out?"

"Went under the piano when I heard it start to go. Took a bit of a knock but nothing seems to be broken. Firemen dug me out. They don't appear to have found out who we are as yet. But it won't be long before the place is crawling with flics." He got up and began to dress. "Hope you don't mind, old boy, but I'll be taking your clothes. Mine are really too much of a mess to be seen in. I must be going. Won't do at all to be found here."

I tried to get out of bed, but whatever they were dripping in my veins took over. Then I was back in the tunnel, trying to breathe, feeling the walls close in around me. This time there was no light. I crawled out of the hole a couple of hours later, Jenny shaking me, ignoring the protests of a young intern at her elbow. He left in a huff, threatening to speak to the director of the hospital.

"Get up."

"What's going on?" I was groggy as she threw De Crecy's ripped and filthy clothes on the bed.

"Hurry. If the French find out you were involved in that explosion, you'll wind up in one of their slammers for the next couple of dozen semesters."

"How'd you find me?"

"Purvis told Xerxes where Halloran was. He had some second thoughts about losing tankers to the terrorists. Or having the French mine a few of them."

"How did you know I'd be with Halloran?"

"Do hurry, Alec," she said, helping me into De Crecy's torn pants. I grabbed her wrist. Forced her to look at me.

"You looked like some sort of primitive savage when you left Aujard's, darling. The veneer of civilization was stripped away. Frank said it was the Indian coming out.

Anyway, it was clear you were going after Halloran. Frank decided to let you try."

"Why?"

She yanked the tube out of my arm, and pulled me to my feet. "Look, Alec. The French are out for blood. That house looks like the Second World War. We have to get out of here. Aujard is sure to put it all together once they figure out who the dead in the safe house really are."

I was feeling my way out of the fog. "Why did Xerxes want me to take out Halloran? Why not just turn him over to the French?"

"I think Aujard pissed him off. He was pretty brutal after you left the meeting. Threatened to protest to Washington. Anyway, Frank's a Greek. He understands vengeance. Also, you might all kill each other, which would have wrapped the whole thing up neatly and gotten him off the hook."

"So he sent you to pick up the pieces."

"Don't act like a shit, darling. Otherwise I might just leave you here."

"Where are we going?"

"To the airport. I've got your clothes and passport in my car. And two tickets, thanks to Xerxes. On one of the spook-subsidized airlines."

"Two?"

"Yeah. I've got an assignment in New York in a couple of days. A legitimate one this time. My talents are being recognized. I thought I'd go with you." She drove with her usual ferocity through the early-evening traffic. I cleaned up and changed from De Crecy's ripped suit into my ancient blazer and chinos.

"There is one problem."

"What's that?"

"Junior Purvis is on the same plane. Xerxes arranged that, too. He wanted him out of town quick. The French are really pissed at the whole thing."

Something important kept trying to push its way through

the drugs and the pain into my consciousness, but I couldn't focus long enough to retrieve it.

"Get rid of De Crecy's clothes," Jenny said, swerving onto the shoulder and slowing.

I wadded up the bloodstained mass and was about to throw them out when in the inside pocket of his tweed jacket I felt a bulge and slipped out the leather case with De Crecy's killing tool. I opened it up. The mahogany handle and two blades nestled in the felt. I put it in my jacket pocket and made a bundle of the torn clothes, flipping them out the window.

chapter 17

We were on New World Express, one of the oddball new airlines risen like a Phoenix from the wreckage of mergers and bankruptcies. The flight was headed for Baltimore in an aging recycled 747 with the name of its original owner still showing through the new paint. Almost three hundred people were crammed into tourist class. We had aisle seats up near the first-class compartment, shut off by a curtain.

Young, pretty stewardesses, replacements for the unionized old dragons who had lost their jobs during a strike that had destroyed the original airline, raced around in officious confusion. Fourteen seats had been sold twice, and we were an hour late before the foul-up was resolved. I had lapsed into a drugged sleep when the plane lifted off and headed out over the Atlantic.

"It's a spook front," Jenny explained. "Ninety percent of its flights are legitimate charters. The other ten percent are CIA-sponsored clandestine operations helping the guerrillas in Angola, Afghanistan, and Nicaragua. The planes are configured so they can be altered to transports in a couple of hours."

"So Xerxes bumped some paying customers to get us on?" Again, something at the edge of consciousness kept trying to fight its way through the envelope of drugs around my brain.

Jenny shrugged. "Whoever said life was fair? Try to get some sleep. You look like death warmed over."

An hour into the flight, Jenny shook me awake. "Alec."

"Yeah?"

"Something's wrong."

One of the stewardesses, a fragile-looking blonde whose face had turned the color of porcelain, stood rigidly by the little kitchen aft of the first-class curtain. Behind her a young Arab murmured into her ear.

She picked up the microphone. "Ladies and gentlemen. Could I have your attention please? This aircraft has been taken over by the Brigade of the Fifteenth of January. I repeat, this aircraft has been taken over by the Brigade of the Fifteenth of January. A charge of plastic explosive has been emplaced in such a way as to destroy the aircraft if you offer any resistance. The lives of three hundred people are at stake. Please remain in your seats, follow orders, and stay calm." The microphone went dead.

A few seconds later a male voice came on. "This is your captain speaking. I have been ordered by the leader of the Brigade of the Fifteenth of January to pass along the following instructions. Any resistance will result in the instant destruction of the aircraft. I repeat, any resistance will result in the destruction of the aircraft. All passengers must lean forward with their heads on their knees and their hands behind their heads. No one is to leave his seat. Talking is not permitted. Further instructions will be issued later."

As he stopped speaking the plane banked sharply to the left. "We're heading back," Jenny said.

"Yeah. Probably toward Libya or Yemen."

"What are you going to do? They'll kill you, Alec."

I slipped De Crecy's weapons case out of my inner pocket and inserted one of the triangular blades into the handle, snapping it into place and slipping it up my sleeve, bending forward. The Arab had picked up the microphone and begun to talk.

"All men seated on the aisles will change places with women. No men are to be seated on the aisles." He started down the narrow corridor, stopping to slam his 9mm Browning into the side of the head of an aging man who raised his head, raging at him.

"You don't hear? You don't hear?"

The man answered in German, blood spurting out of his temple. The stewardess quickly intervened, telling him what to do. The Arab turned on her, lashing out with the gun, its forward sight tearing a gash in her cheek.

"Speak only when I tell you to."

He turned to face the passengers, pulling a grenade out of his belt, ripping the pin loose, holding it high. "You all die if you don't follow orders." He swaggered down the aisle and stopped beside me.

"On your feet," he said, the black eye of the automatic about an inch from my forehead. "Quickly," he snapped, prodding me with the gun.

At my side Jenny suddenly screamed, a piercing yell of terror. The gun turned toward her for an instant and I slipped the dagger free, driving it upward under his rib cage, feeling it smash into the denser mass of the heart muscle. As he fell I caught the grenade, depressing the lever, handing it to Jenny.

"It's probably a phony, but keep the lever down someway. Tape it or tie it." I picked up the Arab's gun, ejected the magazine, and examined the ammunition. It was a special antipersonnel bullet, designed to shatter on impact with metal. I freed and cleaned De Crecy's weapon and inserted it up my left sleeve, punching it through my jacket to hold it in place. Around me people were beginning to chatter hysterically.

"What are you doing? My God, you are going to get us killed," an elegant woman with an upper-class British accent said. "Didn't you hear him say the plane has a bomb on board? You horrid man, you'll get everyone slaughtered. They're only interested in the Americans and the Jews. It's nothing to do with the rest of us. Put that gun down and stop being a silly fool."

"Yeah, buddy. What are you doing?" a fat man across the aisle asked. "Playing hero? You use that gun, this thing will go up like a roman candle. You gotta go along with them."

"Where are the others?" I asked the stewardess.

"One is in the cockpit with the crew. Another is in first class. There is a passenger there they seem to dislike. They have taped his hands and feet and beaten him. Two more are somewhere in the back of the plane."

"What do they look like?"

"What?" She looked confused.

"Arabs? Europeans?"

"The one with the pilot has a lot of black hair. And the one in first class is German. The others"—she shrugged. "Arabs, perhaps. What are you going to do?"

"A little hunting. Try to keep the passengers quiet."

I moved down the aisle toward the next section, past row on row of passengers leaning forward with their heads on their knees who had not noticed the scene up front. I dropped to my belly at the midships rest-room area. A steward and stewardess sat on johns with hands, feet, and mouths taped. A sudden scream in the compartment beyond was cut off by a blow and a stream of Arabic. I moved to the edge of the rest-room area and dropped to the floor again.

A young Arab was stalking up and down the aisle, posturing, occasionally lashing out with his automatic, pulling men to their feet and forcing them to shift seats with women on the inside. His face was glistening with sweat. He walked to the end of the seats about a yard from where I lay concealed and turned his back toward me, holding the gun up in a two-handed shooting stance, shouting at the passengers. I came up behind him, locking an arm around his throat, clamping a hand over the hammer of the automatic and ripping it from his hand. He writhed within my grasp, a slim, almost feminine, figure, until I tightened the choke hold and felt his larynx go. He lay at my feet, gasping for air, turning blue, looking up in despair. Then he died.

Three women screamed. A man across the center of the plane in the other aisle stood up and pointed wordlessly toward the back of the aircraft. He died with his hand outstretched as David Mifsud shot him in the head. The light load in the special bullets made a funny popping sound.

"Drop your gun," the Maltese said, holding a grenade over his head. "Drop your gun or everybody dies."

I tossed the Arab's Browning into the aisle and watched Mifsud leap up on the center seats and walk across the legs of the four people. He jammed the gun against my nose, pushing my head back, screaming at me. "Fool. Stupid, ignorant fool. You wish to die? To kill everybody on the plane?" Behind him a balding man in a three-piece suit picked up the Browning by the muzzle and calmly brought it down on the back of Mifsud's skull.

I dove for the grenade as it rolled along the aisle, bouncing from side to side. An aging man in a Sikh headdress reached down and picked it up, tucking it into his stomach and bending forward, enveloping the metal sphere with his body. The explosion lifted him out of the seat and dropped him back, a crumpled mass of blood and intestines. Next to him a small, dark child began to sob.

Pandemonium broke loose among the passengers as they scrambled to move away from the body. A stewardess appeared, eyes wide with hysteria.

"Get a blanket. Cover him up. Tell everybody to sit down." An older woman moved down the aisle, leaned across the crumpled body, and lifted the boy out of his seat, enfolding him in her arms.

The balding man in the three-piece suit had expertly removed the magazine from the automatic and ejected the spent cartridge in the chamber, examining the pistol and reloading it.

"You want help?"

"No. Try to keep the passengers quiet and in their seats." I took the gun and retraced my steps.

In the front compartment Jenny and the stewardess were dragging the body of the dead gunman toward the little kitchen, trailing a smear of blood on the passageway. He had emptied his bowels as he died, and the stench permeated the cabin.

The public address system suddenly came on, overloud. "Ali. Haddad. Report to first class. Report to first class immediately."

"Where's the grenade?"

Jenny took it out of a pocket of her oversize Lorenz suit jacket and handed it to me, lever held in place by a bent hairpin, almost invisible against the dark metal of the grenade.

"Wish me luck."

Wohlgemuth stood over Purvis, pistol at his ear, when I pushed through the curtain. I showed him the grenade. "It's got about four seconds left on the clock."

"Don't be a fool, Thompson," Purvis said, sweat dripping from his face, eyes wide with fear. "Put that fucking grenade pin back in. All he wants is money. Five million. I've agreed to give it to him. You work for me, you son-of-a-bitch. Put the pin in and give him the fucking grenade. Hear? I don't want any goddamn heroics."

"Your father won't agree to it."

"Listen, asshole. The old bastard is in a coma. He's dying. I'm running things now. And I'm not gonna let some stupid cowboy blow me off the face of the earth just when I get everything in my hands. Five million is a tip for Purvis Oil, mister. You do what you're told. Give him the grenade."

Wohlgemuth grinned. "Heroics are out of style, Thompson. The grenade, please?" He held out his hand. I tossed it across the five-foot space separating us. His eyes flicked wide as he grabbed for it left-handed, almost missing, turning in fury as he realized the lever was secure. His shot was high as

I went for him in a crouch, De Crecy's triangular icepick taking him in the throat, driving upward into his brain.

"Oh, shit," Purvis said as the German's body draped across him. "You dumb son-of-a-bitch. There's still one up in the cockpit with the pilot. He'll blow us all up, you fuckin' maniac." I cut him loose.

"Yeah. I know. He's the last installment on the hundred thousand."

The oil man stared at me, rubbing his wrists. "Jesus H. Christ, Thompson. I'll pay you the fucking hundred thousand. Just make a deal with the bastard. Hear? That's an order, Thompson. Just don't get us all killed."

I climbed the little circular staircase to the flight deck and knocked on the pilot's compartment.

Paddy O'Faolin's brogue came through the door. "Yes?"

"Thompson. Open up."

I looked into the barrel of another of the ubiquitous Browning 9mm automatic about three inches from my nose. "Sure and if it isn't himself returned from the dead. I thought for sure Cerberus was gnawing on your bones by now, laddie."

"Your boys are all dead. You're the last one left, Paddy. Time to call it a day." I held out my hand for the gun.

"Sure, and is that a fact, now? All dead, are they?" He turned, and the copilot, rising to jump him, sat back down. "Let's take it easy, lads. One shot from this nasty little thing and that windshield will explode in ten thousand pieces and we'll all be in Davy Jones. And now you're proposing that I surrender, are you? Not an attractive prospect, Dr. Thompson, you'll forgive me for saying. A lifetime in a French jail would severely curtail my love life. I think I'll pass. Captain, you'll be doing me the favor of redirecting this bird a bit more to the left. You'll find that will take you across the southern tip of Ireland."

"What are you planning?"

"Laddie, Edward Patrick O'Faolin has not lived these forty years without gathering unto him some smarts. I had an inkling that this project was not going to be as easy as it looked. So I brought along a little memento of my days in the British Army paratroop battalions.'' He reached down into a knapsack at his feet and extracted a small emergency parachute, the one kept in reserve by military jumpers in case the main chute failed to open.

''Stand clear, laddie, while I don this thing.'' He turned to the pilot. ''Now, Captain, if you'll slow this bugger to just above stalling speed and drop down to about five thousand feet, I'd be most grateful to you. You might lift the wing a trifle as I leave the aircraft. Wouldn't want me smeared across the tail assembly, now, would we? Add to your cleaning bill, it would. Dr. Thompson will be kind enough to let you know just as I exit, won't you, me boy? Sure and there's the Emerald Isle itself, pretty as a picture it is, too. Never would you suspect the pain and torture inflicted on it by the evil English.'' He had slipped a simple harness over his shoulders and attached the small chute to his chest.

He waved the gun at me. ''We'll go down to the exit just aft of the engines.'' Somebody had broken out the champagne in first class, and the room was crammed with passengers well on their way to getting loaded. Purvis held court by the galley.

''I sent my man up there to make a deal with the last one. Offered him five million. All we have to do is settle details of payment and where we drop him off.''

''Five million? You're kidding.'' A gray-haired man in a pinstriped suit stared at him and gulped down a glass of champagne.

''Ah, Mr. Purvis,'' O'Faolin said. '' 'Tis a lucky man you are, laddie, meeting me like this. It means your worries and cares are over.'' The bullet caught the oil man just under the left eye and flung him back up against the galley in a crumpled heap. I had begun to move, but the Irishman was quick as a cat, the gun muzzle unwinking in my face.

''Careful, laddie. Not your turn just yet.''

"You just blew away five million dollars," the man in the pinstriped suit said.

"Ah, sure, and it's only money. We Irish are more spiritually oriented, you know. There's no poetry in money. Dirty, filthy stuff." He stared down at Purvis and made the sign of the cross with the Browning.

"Sure, darlin'," he said to a stewardess, frozen in a catatonic trance looking at Purvis's body, "if you and your friend there will be kind enough to open the door, I'll be takin' my leave.

The stewardess stared at him in panic. "We can't. We'll all be sucked out of the plane."

"Well, darlin', you have a really unpalatable choice. Either you open the door, or I shoot you. Now, move your lovely little ass. Quickly. Ireland is about to disappear beneath us."

The steward came forward and pushed the girl back down the aisle and into an empty seat, clamped both hands on the door lever, and lifted. The sudden blare of the emergency siren tore through the cabin as the door opened and slid to the left. A blast of air swept through the plane which had slowed to just above stall speed. O'Faolin had wrapped an arm through a handhold. "Now, Dr. Thompson, if you'll tell the skipper to lift the wing a bit, there's a good lad."

I picked up the phone and passed along the message. O'Faolin shifted the gun to his left hand, wrapped around the handhold, and extended his right toward me. "It's been a pleasure knowing you, Professor."

He started to laugh as I automatically extended my hand. "Sure and we'll have a nice talk on the way down, lad," he said, big paw enveloping my hand, letting go the stanchion.

Jenny shot him then, the big automatic kicking upward in her hand. O'Faolin turned in surprise as the hole appeared in the parachute on his chest, loosening his grip on my hand and flipping backward through the open door as the big plane lifted its left wing in a gentle arc. The Irishman's body just cleared the tail assembly, tumbling like a rag doll in the wind. I snared the handhold as the suction of the wind grabbed me, jamming a leg against the metal door rim, feeling myself being sucked out as the steward put his shoulder to the door and pushed it slowly to. Jenny was slumped against the seats, big automatic dangling from one hand.

"Where'd you get the gun?"

"Wohlgemuth," she said, gesturing toward the German's body sprawled in the first-class cabin. "Jesus, Alec. I killed him," she said, coming into my arms.

chapter 18

The helicopter circled once and drifted in, settling gently on the landing pad on the roof of the Etta Mae Purvis Memorial Hospital. The medical director met me just outside the range of the rotors and escorted me into the silence of the building.

"How is he?"

"Weak. He's dying, of course. The cancer has metastasized throughout his body. Amazing old man. Anybody else would have been dead a year ago. He's fought it with the kind of ferocity he's fought everything else during his life."

"Is he lucid?"

"He was this morning. He goes in and out. Fades away in the middle of a sentence. However, he very much wants to see you. I'm sure once he realizes who you are, his willpower will take over."

He was wired to a variety of tubes, old man's body shrunken to bones and ligaments, big, once muscled arms lying like sticks on top of the sheet, thick veins showing through the translucent skin. Sindona stood by the window smoking a slender cheroot.

"Hello, Thompson." The old man extended a big hand, grip still firm. "José tells me you pulled it off."

"Yeah."

"I want to hear. In detail. Each one."

I told him how each of the terrorists had died. The fierce old hawk's eyes never left my face as I talked. "The Irishman?" Purvis asked. "They didn't find his body. There were reports of a parachute opening in the area. He might have gotten away."

"He had a nine-millimeter slug in his gut. His body probably drifted out to sea."

"So I suppose you want your money, Thompson?" the old man asked. "Even though you got my son killed."

"He wasn't part of the deal."

Purvis started to laugh, frail body dissolving into a series of racking coughs that brought a nurse on the run. He waved her away. "Goddamn, Thompson. You're a man after my own heart. Wasn't part of the deal. Hear that, José?"

The Mexican smiled.

The old man struggled to a sitting position and motioned the nurse to open the drawer by his bed. She handed him a checkbook and pen. He filled out the sliver of paper laboriously and handed it over. "Better collect it real quick, Thompson. Once I buy the farm, they'll stop payment on it. Now get out. It's time for me to cash in my chips."

Sindona followed me out into the corridor. Two orderlies moved a bed down the corridor, an inert figure visible under a sheet covering it from head to foot. "This is the dying floor," Sindona said, crossing himself automatically. "I want to thank you, Thompson."

I shrugged, folding the check and slipping it in my pocket.

"It's possible that I might be able to use your rather special talents in the future. If you are available," the Mexican said, offering me his hand.

I thought of the central heating system at the chateau. Its radiators had frozen the previous winter and turned into grenades, spitting chunks of iron at the walls during a heavy freeze when the caretaker had neglected to fire the ancient furnace.

"I'm available."

The party was in an apartment overlooking the park, Metropolitan Museum across the way. The living room took up three levels, a circular stair winding upward toward a dining room on the second floor and a library on the third. The walls were covered with fashion posters from the turn of the century and original cover paintings of women's magazines from the twenties. One end wall was taken up by a massive black-and-white photograph of a nude youth in a contorted yoga position, face invisible under a mop of hair. Opposite him, framing the room, a portrait, identical in size, showed a slender blond woman wearing a miniskirt, ancient predator's face encased in a mask of makeup, smoking a cigarette in a long ivory holder.

The apartment was done in chrome, glass, and black leather. So were a lot of the people.

It took me a while to spot Jenny. I saw her back first. She was wearing a skintight pale green dress cut high in front, dipping in the back to just above her taut behind.

"You might as well be nude."

She turned and threw her arms around my neck. "I am, lover," she said in my ear. "Meet your host, Seymour Simon, better known as Mr. Mongoose." I shook hands with the designer, a tall, graying man with a classic profile, deep tan, and eyes the color of slate. His symbol was a tiny mongoose embroidered on his line of sport shirts and shorts for men and women. He had a diamond in his left ear and another in his nose. At his elbow the woman in the portrait chattered like an aging bird.

"My dear, who is this divine man? The one who saved you from a fate worse than death on that horrid airplane? I hate airplanes. Uncivilized way to travel. We always go on ships, don't we, dear?" she said to the Mongoose, who bent over her solicitously.

"Yes, Mother."

"The last bastion of true luxury, my dear. Servility has disappeared everywhere else." She wandered off still talking, and the host moved purposefully across the room in the direction of the boy who had posed for the portrait.

"He hangs his latest conquest like a dead pheasant," Jenny said. "It usually lasts about as long as the birds do."

"He must have quite a collection."

"Willy La Coeur is coming out with a book on them."

"What are they going to call it? *Les Culs Inconnus?* Can we get out of here?"

"Where do you want to go?"

"I have to put a roof on the chateau. You'll love northern France in June."

epilogue

The banker spread his hands, palms up. "I'm afraid I can be of no help, Herr Clemens. The bank draft arrived from the Delta National Bank of Louisiana yesterday. It instructed us to pay"—he glanced down at the papers on his desk—"$27,775 into the account of Herr Ludwig Clemens."

"And that is the equivalent of fifty thousand German marks?"

"To the pfennig, Herr Clemens, at today's rate of exchange."

"But who sent it? And why?"

"We have been unable to find out. The sender paid cash for a draft and refused to give his name. Perhaps it had something to do with the unfortunate death of your father."

"Perhaps."

The shop was on the outskirts of Stroud deep in the Cotswolds, a winding lane of thatched-roof, stone cottages. The pale, slender man in a houndstooth jacket and gray trousers wearing a regimental striped tie set off a jangling bell as he entered. Classic hunting prints decorated the walls, and an assortment of knives were laid out under a glass counter. An aging man with thick glasses and a fringe of gray hair emerged from the back.

"Good afternoon, Baron. Good to see you again."

"Have you finished my order?"

"Indeed I have, sir." The old man unlocked a drawer behind him and laid a crocodile case on the counter. The pale man unzipped it and extracted an aged oak handle edged in stainless steel with identations for his fingers. He inserted one of three triangular carbon steel blades and held the instrument in his hand, palm up.

"Balance in order, sir?"

"Perfect, as always."

"That'll be a hundred and fifty pounds, sir. Will you pay cash, as usual?"

Forty Japanese tourists trooped into the ancient pub and seated themselves expectantly, staring at the scraped and fly-specked mirror running the length of the long mahogany bar with its brass rail and spitoons at either end. Above the bar a copy of Goya's famous nude courtesan reclining on a divan, darkened by a century of cigar smoke, stared down at them. The leader of the group chattered away as the waitresses served glass after glass of warm dark Guinness to the absorbed, disciplined Orientals.

"Clancy, what the fuck is going on?" the tall man with a mop of black hair, the profile of an aging hawk, and searing blue eyes asked, staring at the scene over a lager.

"Sure, Patrick, they're professors of literature, they are. Specialists in James Joyce."

"James Joyce? Sure, and would you mind telling me what Clancy's pub has to do with James Joyce?" The speaker winced and rubbed his chest as he reached for the large beer.

The bartender leaned across, wiping the gleaming mahogany in an automatic gesture. "Sure and did ye not know, Paddy, me boy, that it was here that Leopold Bloom, Blazes Boylan's cuckold, stepped into the doorway when the Lord Lieutenant's coach passed by?"

"Clancy, you are a wicked prevaricator and distorter of the sacred texts. You know well it was not here."

"Aye, Paddy, that I do. But the poor slant eyes would be verra unhappy if they knew that the true shrine was torn down and converted into a greengrocer's in 1937. So the professors, druids, literary bicycle-seat sniffers, and other keepers of Jamie's myth are all agreed that it was Clancy's place where Poldy halted in his little odyssey."

"Sure, and it's a fact, Clancy. You can't trust anybody anymore."